D.L. CROWSON

ISBN-10: 0692105123
ISBN-13: 978-0692105122

DEDICATED

To my children Alexandra, Nathaniel and Kara for making me write a story with them in it.

ACKNOWLEDGMENTS

To my wife, thank you for everything you did to help me accomplish this.

Jason Tasi, thanks for listening to me ramble.

Laura Isbell, thanks for correcting my historical and pop culture references.

To Google and Wikipedia, thank you for all the mythological verifications.

To my Coworkers, Yeah Man…

The Truth

Magic is real, monsters, vampires, witches and all the Gods; old and new. In the past, a really long time ago Gods and monsters walked amongst mankind, they shared their knowledge of magic. Magic is used to manipulate environmental energy in order to effect change. Magic is universal no matter what Realm you live in or Deity you worship.

In every religion there is the Tree Myth. The Norse, Yggdrasil the World Tree is the closest. Celtics called it, The Crann Bethadh, the tree of life. The Egyptian, Iusaaset, the Grandmother tree. Christianity in the Garden of Eden, Adam was forbidden to eat from the tree. Let me explain. Magic comes from the spark that is inside all living matter, your soul. Magic gathers and runs through what most call ley lines, magical super highways if you will, roots. Roots which wrap around the entire planet. They flow and verge into a magical trunk of a great tree. At the North Pole the trunk is formed of concentrated magical forces that flows into outer space. You can see the magic within the northern lights. The magic extends out, branching off...out into the multiverse itself. The Galactic Tree literally pushes out into the solar system, creating a forest with other Galactic Tree across all the universes of existences.

With that knowledge mankind decided they were better than all the other supernatural creatures. Millions were massacred and a million more were enslaved. So, a Council was formed and all magic was hidden forever from the Mundane. They took a single idea, this one book, and went around the globe with it. This single story eradicated all beliefs of magic until it was forgotten from the minds of men, known as the Dark Ages...

To keep magic secret, the Council put in place The Keepers of the Hidden. These chosen are a highly specialized police unit that enforces all of the Council's rulings. They keep extensive records on all magical related phenomenon to ensure that magic and myths stay hidden, a WetWorks Men in Black if you will.

Angus, Minotaur of Minoa

Chapter 1

Looking up at the Dragon Con banner hanging from the light post, the Atlanta skyline looming over us as I wait.

"Dano, you… ready?" Tasi asks me.

YANK

The relief was instant as he pulled my eight-foot black feather wings off my back. *Man, I love Dragon Con*, my inner voice rang out in my head, my whole pack gathering around Honey Bear, my solid white full sized 3500 Chevy Passenger Van, yes I named my van after a car in one of my favorite books. All of us compared notes on today's events.

We always meet in the same parking lot at Dragon Con every year. So, all of us had our cars parked pretty much right next to each other.

Tasi's holding the wings up like nothing. He's only an inch shorter than me but his huge Samoan frame gives him Hulk size proportions. With one hand he holds the wings off the ground with the other opens the back of the van. As soon as he opens the door you can hear Imagine Dragons' Thunder coming from the Van's speakers. My best friend for 22 years is a little overweight now. Still stronger than an

Ox, he put the massive wings in the back of Honey Bear but leaving the doors open. Tasi's 5'10" solid 280 lbs. of pure Samoan teddy bear covered in more tattoos than me. He even has the Samoan tribal designs tattooed on his face, not all over his face. Just over his left eye, across his forehead and up over his skull. He's been doing tattoos even before we met in college. We really don't look like the typical Comic Book Geeks but believe me we are, hell I even made my own hidden "Batcave" in my Office.

Cindy, my super-hot Thai wife hands me PJ pants then takes them back. She's not really into the cosplay stuff, or superheroes for that matter so she's just in jeans and *I slept with Green Arrow* V-neck t-shirt. I smile at her shirt knowing she put it on just for me. I always dress up as Green Arrow, my own version of Old Man Ollie. Cosplaying has been my thing for a very long time. It's the look on my kids' faces that I really enjoy, when they see their hero standing in front of them and those little eyes are overflowing with joy and full of amazement. I actually have a really long goatee it flows down about to my sternum. I pretty much have had some version of a goatee on my chin since right after getting out of the Navy, and my mustache could rival Wyatt Earp's. So, I have been dressing up as Oliver Queen from before he showed up on Smallville.

"I kind of like," her voice gets deeper, "the... this is SPARTA," her voice going back to normal and finished with, "thing you have going on." But hands the black active wear PJs, with the words *Han Shot First* written down the left leg below a logo of Han Solo's blaster, to me.

"Cause you like Daddy's six-pack," my son Nathan, dressed as Damian Wayne's Robin, says as he climbed into the side door of the van.

"What's with you… and not wearing pants," Liz, my little sister, just turning 30, asks as she pokes her bright blue hair up from behind her Hamster car.

Alex my oldest daughter, at the age 13, looks like her Mom but takes after her Auntie Liz with her pink and purple pixie haircut, starts a recap of the cool stuff and the celebrities we saw that day, changing the subject from not wearing pants.

“So, what's the coolest thing about today?” she asked nobody in general.

“Everything!” Kara, my youngest at 5, flying in circles in the empty parking space between Honey Bear and Liz's car. Her red cape extended behind by one hand the other hand straight out in a little fist yells out.

“Dad, when's the next time you're going to Uncle Tasi's shop?” Nathan, who is 11 and is the spitting image of his mother ...but with my coordination, asks as he falls out the side of the van while taking off his cape.

“Did you hurt the concrete?” I ask him, just as my dad did to me when I was his age. He shakes his head no as he jumps up like nothing happened, and no one saw anything, and climbs back in the van without waiting for my answer to his question.

I’m covered in ink, but I started getting tattoos at 31, fairly late in life. Between the Military time and other military contracts I took on after I became a civilian, tattoos were discouraged because they got you caught or killed. But that first tattoo felt like magic, and after Tasi gave me that first tattoo I haven't slowed down. Now at 42, I have a lot of ink. Tasi my Samoan Chewbacca has done every one of my tattoos. When people ask me how many tattoos I have, I shrug and tell them more than one. Both my arms are sleeved, both my pecs, my entire back, both sides of my ribcage the list goes on, but always room for more.

Putting my Spartan helmet and shield down in the back of the van, I grab my tactical boots and sit on the bumper sliding them on my blisters. Cosplay can be hard on you.

Bonk uuff

Looking to my left Kara is brushing her Supergirl costume off. She looks up smiling with her long light brown, almost blonde, braided hair that hung down to her butt.

“Mommy said to give you this,” handing me a hair tie. Bouncing on her feet she says “Up, up and away!” With those famous words starts flying in circles once again.

I grabbed the very top of my head, running my hand across my own blonde hair. My braids run from my forehead along the top of my skull to my bald spot on the back of my head. Pulling the loose braided tails into one bunch and popping the hair tie around it. My head is completely shaved on the sides and back. The four tails of my braids fall just past my shoulder blades. Everyone compares me to the History channel's TV show The Vikings, some dude name Ragnar. I just smile, not telling them my hair was like this way before the TV show made Vikings cool again. I don't watch the show because I actually know the real myths of the Aesìr. They are part of the four pantheon's I share my faith with. I also worship the Tuatha De` Danann, The Olympians and the AllSpark, what you interrupt as God, his Old Lady Mary and their son Jesus. The nuclear reaction to the collision of Art History, Martial Arts, and the Military opened my eyes to the possibility of the impossible. Pulling my Spartan inspired gauntlet off my right arm I toss it with the Red Hood gear also piled in the back of Honey Bear.

"Get in the Van," Auntie Liz says as she rounds up the kids, "Alex, help Kara with her car seat."

Finally finished getting my cosplay outfit off, I close Honey Bear's backdoors.

Tasi's grabbing my left forearm looking at the fresh tattoo he did last month. My youngest had signed her banner below her brother's and sister's names with a sharpie marker directly on my skin and T inked it exactly like she signed it. Turning my arm from side to side.

"Healing nicely," he said.

"Yeah man!" giving him the traditional Samoan hello and goodbye we grasp our right forearms. Bowing our heads to touch at the crest of our forehead… inhaling through our noses we breathe in each other's Mana.

"You know where the shop is?" he smiles as he gets in his little Batman decorated car.

"Yeah man," I nod, both of us knowing that anytime I wanted ink he'd take care of me.

“Hey!” Liz calls out. “I’ll be at your house later. I'm going to go and see Patrick.” she tells me for the millionth time, hell it's the reason why she drove her car instead of riding with me. She lives in Milledgeville and is almost done with her doctorate in Archaeology and Ancient History. Her husband is a flatbed truck driver and has an overnight in Ellenwood.

“Hate you!” I call after her, while smiling, when she is pulling out of the parking lot. My little sister and I never say, love you to each other.

I watched Tasi pull out of the parking lot as I climbed into the Van. The kids finally finished with their seatbelt and I put the Van in reverse.

Kara pointing at a nightclub sign with a young lady dancing asking if she can dance there, she liked dancing.

A tidal wave of memories about working in the nightclub industry for years as I put myself through college. To get a Master’s degree in art history, yeah art history. Do you know how much you can learn from past cultures life just by looking at their arts? Sorry where was I? Oh yes, I did security. Bouncer, problem solver, I pretty much hurt people and got paid really well doing it. The memories flooded in all at one time, washing over me. I have a photographic memory with a house cat’s disorder, if you ever had an evil cat you would know exactly what I am talking about. My brain absorbs every fucking thing. It's on permanent download; what I watch, what I read, what I hear, what I smell, what I even taste. It’s all jamming itself into a High school locker not in any particular order. Then hacks it out like a hairball to wetly hit me in my frontal lobe. I shake it off physically because with the memories comes all the raw emotion with it. I try to get the tangled mess of memories back into the closet. The older I have become the more shit is slammed back in the same size locker. Unlike the geniuses on the TV show Scorpion, I have emotions and didn't grow up in a lab, classroom or behind a calculator. I grew up tearing down the Ferris wheel. I actually didn't even start going to school till after my Mom met my Dad (no I don't call him my Step-Dad) and I started the 6th grade, while my brother started 5th grade in Lancaster, CA. My Mom had my sister and my baby bro back to back. Then we all moved to Georgia.

Cindy answers because she knew my reason for a lack of an answer... giving Kara her cellphone to distract her, while putting her hand on my arm.

"You can smoke when we get home," she says as she hands me nicotine instead. Merging onto I-75, I-85 south I light my cigarette driving on autopilot.

With my brain working at warp speed, starfields screaming by its hard to concentrate on one star at a time. To slow down and focus on that one star, I smoke weed. It's like putting a governor on the engine of a car, that way it only goes 65 MPH no matter how hard you push down the gas.

"Yeah Momma..."

It was 12 years of experience of violence that I excelled at it and enjoyed. Pushing the emotional landslide back is the hardest and takes longer to lock away.

Waiting on traffic on the onramp for East I-20 looking east, dark purple pink storm clouds crest the far horizon.

My Mom noticed my disorder early and recognized that it wasn't violence that I excelled at. That violence just seemed to follow me like a rain cloud follows Eeyore. So, I spent a lot of time in one type of Dojo or another. Growing up on the road, going from State to State, I studied at quite a few places. I grew up a Carnie, no I'm not a military brat. So, over the years I have studied almost every different form of fighting technique, and it kept me out of jail mostly. I don't have photographic reflexes so I had to practice. My brain could remember everything my instructor, at the time, would show me but my muscles took hard work.

Grumble Rumble CRACK

Storm clouds forming halfway between Atlanta and home on I-20 turned day to night, black lighting danced between the glowing purple cotton ball shaped clouds. From a very tiring day, the youngest asleep with her mother's phone clutched in her hand. Alex was also passed out, her head against the armrest opposite of Kara's car seat.

Nathan was spread out across the backseat of the van going through his collectables which he had gotten that day.

Crash ZZZNAP CRAAAACK! RUMBLE KaBOOM shake...shake... shake

Reverse lighting snapped right over Honey Bear rocking us back and forth. We had just passed under an overpass when the sky split with a huge bolt of lightning and the sky boiled over.

WOOSH Wish Ruuuummmmble Swirl WWWOOOOSSHH

Purple clouds barreled and then a twister appears in my rearview mirror ripping the very asphalt from the freeway. The steering wheel trembled in my hand due to the vibrations of the tornado like a freight train.

"DAD LOOOOOOOKK…..!" Nathan screams out.

I turned my eyes from the mirror to see another tornado, as Johnny Cash *God's Gonna Cut You Down* starts to play, spitting out an eighteen-wheeler right in front of the van. I could not believe my eyes, and I jerked the steering wheel hard.

RK! RK! RK! RK! VAROOOM SCRUNTCH!!! RK! RK! RK! RK! WHURL WHOOSH

Slamming on the brakes at the same time. The van veered to the left heading towards the medium, and I stomped the accelerator to the floor and cranked the van right as fast as I could turn the wheel. The eighteen-wheeler hit right next to the passenger side of the van, the trailer still in the air as we drive under the airborne back tires. The two tornadoes slammed together twisting around one another morphing into one massive storm. In the rearview mirror the big rig disappears back into the funnel. I forced the van to straighten out while dodging traffic, which is not easy in a huge cargo van.

"Hold on!" I yelled out, as I start to cut to the shoulder, three lanes over, intending to get to the next underpass when the van is hit by an unseen object.

SHATTER sprinkle tinkle shattering YAAIIII….

Glass shattering and the screams of my children rang in my ears. When shit gets real, time seems to slow down for me, I see everything and all the possible outcomes are outlined.

BLAM Swipe YANK

The side of the van crushed in, I reached out and behind me grabbing Alex's leg while pulling her in, just enough to miss the metal shrapnel and forcing her seat belt to lock. In doing so some of her body leans back over her baby sister.

SMASH FLIP WHOOSH FLIP CRASH FLIP SMASH FLIP CRUNCH

We hit the medium with the driver's side rolling us over and over. The van coming to a stop on its roof on the opposite shoulder. All of us hanging upside down, the front window is nothing but spider webs. The only sound is the breeze blowing through the shattered side windows.

"Roll call," I turned my head to look behind me at the same time I asked.

Click...Smack

Nathan unfastens his seatbelt and thuds against the roof of the van while calling out, "Yeah man…"

Alex somehow as a death grip on her baby sister's car seat. Letting go she uncovers her sister, "Present," now hanging by her seatbelt her blue and purple hair waved back and forth.

Kara yells, "I'm downside up, Daddy!"

Me and my wife locked eyes and start to laugh. I painfully undo my seatbelt crashing to the roof. I blink trying to focus my eyes. My fingers search my face to reassure my brain that, nope no glasses, "dammit" I muttered. I kicked open my door to check where the super tornado was and I feel the pressure around me change and I sprang back covering as much of the windshield as I could.

ZZZZT CRACK

The flash was so bright when the lightning struck the windshield that my eyes could not adjust fast enough.

BBZZTTTT ZAP SNAP BBZZTTTT CAAARRAACK BBZZTTTT BBZZTTTT ZAP SNAP BBZZTTTT ZAP

Then, intense heat hits the center of my back. With no shirt on my skin sizzled, burning. I could smell ozone and my own charred flesh. I felt, more then saw, the energy pass through my left arm and out the passenger window sending discharges of energy into my wife's eyes. I absorbed most of the impact but two separate bolts, one huge charge leapt from my chest leaving burnt flesh in its wake. Alex is hit by the discharge then it jumped to Kara and the cellphone in her hands erupted into sparks. A second bolt of energy erupts out from my hip bone arching off the roof of the van hitting Nathan hard.

ZAP BBZZTTTT KABOOM Shake rattle-rattle

The back doors of the van explode open with Nathan's impact. He hits it hard enough that one of the doors hinges gives way, sending one of the doors into the road while the other crumbles.

Nathan jumps up, "I'm good…" at that moment the world goes fuzzy and turns gray. I shake my head as I come to and try to push myself up.

"Daddy, Dad, DAD!" Alex called snapping me back to action. "I can't get Kara's car seat undone" she finishes.

I looked towards the passenger seat, Cindy's seat was empty, and I crawled towards Kara's seat and ask Alex, "Your mother?"

"With Nathan," she replied.

I unfastened Kara's belt and like a little monkey she locked onto my arm and all three of us crawled out the non-existent windshield. The storm rages all around us. Rain the size of water balloons assault us while crawling from the wreckage. Looking up I see Nathan holding his Mom's arm.

"She can't see, Dad ...the lightning." Nathan says while choking back his tears.

"Alex take your sister," she did with no hesitation while I stand. I took Cindy in my arms, "Hey babe... does it hurt?"

"No," she says, surprising the hell out of me.

WHURL WHOOSH CRASH RRRUUUMMMMMBLE SSHHHUUUUCRACK

"SPIN-A-ROONIE!" I yell. Cindy in front of me, I grab for Alex with my left and I reach around my back with my right and grab Nathan's jacket. I snap my hips and lock my knee around my wife's knee.

SWISHHH TWURL WWOOOOOSSSHHH SK! SK! SK!

Twisting my body counter clockwise. All of them tucked into my spin, Cindy matching my movement. I pivot causing us to launch at almost a right angle from the ground, a Honda Civic corkscrews over us, and I see this very old black man just staring back at me from the driver seat. We break apart, Cindy still with her eyes sealed shut spins to a stop while Alex slides to a stop with Kara still in her arms.

"Again! Again!" Kara yells.

FLIP SMASH Thud SCREECH..CRUNCH

When I grabbed Nathan to pull him around to me I added more momentum to his spin so when I came to a stop I had launched him up in the air. I hit the pavement on one knee, knuckles smashed into road.

"And he sticks the landing!" Nathan lands on his feet next to me proclaiming. "Your superhero landing was good too, Dad. But your execution needs some work." he says, with a smug little smile on his face.

CRACKLE BOOM WOOSH SWOOSH

I stand as the lightning flashes overhead as the storm rages. The Honda Civic smashed into the pine trees that lined I-20, shredding the blue sedan. The thunder hides the sounds as the car falls to the ground. Not even looking at the car I pulled my family to me and pointed.

"Over there... we are getting under that bridge before that," I pointed to the tornado, "gets here. Now MOVE." Running towards the bridge I did the stupidest thing ever, I look at the mangled car…

"Fuckin' shit…" I give Kara back to Alex. "Nathan make sure your Momma..." he looks at me like *I got this*. I nod at him and he pulls his mom towards the bridge.

"Be good at it," Cindy calls over her shoulder, I smile as I ran towards the Honda.

SMACK WHOOSH BLAM FLOP

Something hits me. Like a fuckin' bus. I am sent flying sideways, crashing into my own van. It's not like the movies, you don't just stand up. I moved my arm first rubbing the concrete with my knuckles. Kneeling, I look up to the woods, the tree line had a perfect part. I stood on shaking legs, and walked to the back of the van. My flak jacket, from the same cosplay my tactical boots are from, is in the back. I put it on, feeling the burns from the lightning as I do so, and then I grab my bronze Spartan helmet and put it on as well.

PING PING

I knocked on the helmet twice, and ran towards the Honda, rain beading down my helmet, but I can still see so much better with the rain out of my eyes. *I am so glad I found a real Spartan helmet*. I can pat myself on the back later. The wind has picked up greatly, the storm is thrashing about growing in intensity and girth. Pushing into the wind I plowed my way towards the old man. The Honda Civic sits about 7ft above the ground, the engine impaled by a broken pine tree. I climbed up the back of the car and opened, I should say pried open, his door. The airbag had deployed, but was flat now. The driver seat had shifted counter clockwise to a ten o'clock position, making it impossible for the old black man to undo his seatbelt.

"Hi, I'm Dano," laying on my stomach and waving at him upside-down.

"La Hidden est cassé," the old man lifted one gray and very bushy eyebrow and spoke in the deepest voice I have ever heard, more like felt.

"Cassé?" I pointed at myself and waved, "No, not broken yet."

I pointed at his seatbelt. He shook his head in the negative.

"What's your name?" I ask.

"Louisé, la tempête est magique," the old man's thick Cajun accent drummed over the storm, while I reached around him trying to get between him and the seat belt. *Almost got it,* I cram my arm in a little further.

Click

I looked up at him. "Nice ta mee..."

I was interrupted when a huge wind rips the pine tree from the ground, that's the pine tree we are currently attached to. The car pitches sending me sliding off the roof and the old man, with unbelievable force, grabs my forearm, with hands bigger than Tasi. Ham sized meat hooks. The tree-car and we are sent spinning around the tornado.

WWWWOOOOOSSSHHHH Whirl Woosh Whirl Woosh

Faith is Magic

Magic is a supernatural force that can alter the fabric of reality at fundamental levels. The ability to use magic is a matter of faith and knowledge, traits passed down from a Being's ancestors. With this knowledge and faith, practitioners can use magic in millions of ways and combinations. Magic can be accessed by spells, charms, runes, rituals and countless other ways to cause or control events, to govern certain natural or supernatural forces. There is no Dark Magic, Dark Arts or Evil Magic. Magic manifests in the eye of its wielder. Magic is accessible to any being with a spark, a soul. As per the Accords of the Hidden, magic must constantly be hidden. Thus, most of the Mundane are completely unaware that magic even exists…

Angus, Minotaur of Minoa

Chapter 2

Tryin' ta get Louisé, this old Cajun man, out his wrecked car probably wasn't my best rescue attempt. We had been picked up by the tornado, Lou holding on to my left arm while we are thrashed about by the Gail force winds. The car does an arch in the air, testing Lou's grip.

WWWOOOOSSHH ZZAAP… KKaaaBBBOOOOOMMMMM Smack

Sailing in the air, polarized negative lightning bolts streak the sky all around me. Imagine you looked at the negative of a picture and a thunderstorm, the lightning is reversed, no color, but has a halo effect. More and more bolts of reverse lighting thunder across the storm. Then from every angle lightning hits me, making every one of my muscles tighten. I screamed but no sound can be heard. My body hovers for what seems a lifetime, the wind flowing around me and blowing the smoke from my burnt skin and clothes up my nose. Me and the ground get reacquainted with a wet smack.

TTTIIIIZZZZ TTTIIIIZZZZ TTTIIIIZZZZ TTTIIIIZZZZ

On my hands and knees the reverse lightning arcs across my skin. It's black electrical energy skipping from tattoo to tattoo in arcs, making my muscles seize in pain.

ZZAAPP BZZZZZZZZTT..CRACK

The lightning's energy blasted out from me. Released in all directions, the wave of energy pulsed out covering everything. Something smashes into me. No- *snatched* me across the pavement, as the Honda's trunk slams to the ground like a huge hammer. Exactly where I had been. Looking up at the car, running up the trunk of the tree with my eyes. I see a huge blue hand gripping the trunk tree.

The improvised war club was being lifted up again. I turned to see who had yanked me out of the way and catch Lou's eyes. Lou, whose bushy gray eyebrows, water dripping down them from the pouring rain, are frowning. I look past Lou, to the newcomer. Down his face the water flowed over his Ogre face. His mouth had huge tusks jetting up from his lower jaw, his massive lips silently chanting or maybe praying when the Honda comes straight down on top of us.

"LOU!" I screamed as I bounced my legs into position and pushed with my hands, then my legs turning and twisting my body, as I did propelling me straight up.

CCRRUUUSSHHH

The Honda's full weight crashed down on us. But I had jumped through the back window. Now in the backseat the car and trapped inside the head of the hammer. The car hammered the pavement over and over again. My insides vibrating as the back and front seat forcefully try to become the same seat. The car crushes in all around me.

SPLATTER SCREEEE SPLATTER SCREEEE

The back of the car smashes in around me with every strike to the ground. Blood and meat invade the car's interior, with one final blow Lou literally explodes sending bone shrapnel into the backseat of the car. Lou is pulverized into nothing. I can't move, crushed into the back seat, my body bruised and riddled with bone fragments. *Damn, Louisé...* I think to myself as the car is lifted high into the air.

Rattle Rattle Rattle

My brain is shaken hard. My leg comes free but in doing so I see a huge piece of Lou's bone sticking out from my shin... I moved my leg *it facken hurt... oh hell...* I touched it, running my fingertips along the bone.

SSSKKKKRRREEEE RRRRRRIIP

The car's roof screams while the metal is torn away. Huge blue, like the clearest ocean blue, fingers wrapped themselves around the roof and peeled it away. I pulled the bone from my leg and stuck it into the meat of the giant blue hand.

"AAARRGGGG!" the huge ice-hand cried out and yanked back more in surprise then pain, pulling me free of the car. Holding onto Lou's femur as tight as I could I pulled my feet under me. The giant lifted me towards it's' face to take a closer look at what pained it. I waited until the last minute to yank the bone out the back of it's' hand and lunged myself at its' face, Van Zan style. *Hopefully it doesn't just eat me.*

"RRROOOAAARRRR!" my anger boiling over to rage. The foot-long bone drives right into its eye. I just hung stuck to a wall of Jell-O, no more than an annoying eyelash.

The monster reflexively goes to rub his eyes with the back of his hand. Grabbing Lou's femur bone with both hands swinging my legs back in a donkey kick.

KerPOP AAAAAAHHHHHHHHHHHHHH

He drives me and the bone deeper into his eye. Have you ever watched "Bizarre Foods" on the Travel Channel when Andrew Zimmerman talks about eyeballs and how it's just liquid? He is right, the eye is just a big ass water balloon and it popped glowing blue blood everywhere. But it was ice cold, in fact freezing.

The Frost Giant bellowed cover his now empty eye socket. He moved his hand down to check his hand for blood and I rode his hand out of his empty eye socket. With only seconds to judge if I could survive the distance to the pavement, I jumped.

Swish Swoosh SPLAT

The Frost Giant must have caught movement with its other eye and swung out with both hands wildly. Trying to catch me on the way down. I hit the ground running, who am I kidding the ground hit me, I bounced skipping across the pavement. I rolled to a stop and braced myself to get stomped on. Looking at the white stripe line painted on I-20… when the oldest pair of boots I have ever seen took up my view of the pavement.

"You just going to lay there?" The boots spoke in a heavy Scandinavian accent.

Lifting myself up off the ground, took all my will and strength, it took even more not to puke as I did so. The pain was intensely increasing with the smallest of movements. He said nothing just stood there, never even looked down. I finally stood up and promptly fell backwards. It took a minute to right myself again. He just stood there watching the tornados dance a perfect circle around us. He reminded me of Gandalf the Gray if they casted Arnold Schwarzenegger to play the wandering wizard.

CRUSH SWORLING WOOSH

The tornados dug a channel around us locking us inside the storm, the clouds of debris made visibility after the circle near impossible. But a shadow was coming out the vortexes of chaos.

"Move old man!" Holy facken shite...the alarms in my head screams as my mouth yelled. I didn't know if I was talking to him or me.

But boy did I move, running right towards the first Frost Giant emerging from the circle that the tornados created. I had Lou's bone in my hand it looked and felt more like a crude knife. I could have sworn I dropped it.

Smash SWOOP Whoosh creek

A Dodge pickup truck landed in front of me, I leaped into the bed while it lurched back and forth as it left the ground. I surfed the bed like facken Teen Wolf and waited till the right time. I sprinted and used the cab of the truck to launch myself at the Frost Giant's groin.

Thunk SSSSLLLLLIIICCCE

Lou sunk into the Frost Giant's huge cock and I pulled down with gravity and my body weight ripping that huge dick in two. Me and the Giant hit the ground on our knees.

AAARRRRRRRHHHHH

He held his mangled junk. Lou in my hand the bone edge gleaming blue with the Giants blood. I swept Lou across the Frost Giant's neck. A line appeared shortly later and then a fountain of blue ice cold blood erupts. I look back in the same place like facken Wyatt Earp. The old homeless man stood with a spear, a gleaming golden spear in his hand.

Woosh Wirl Woosh Wirl

The minivan twirled in the air, its headlight lit up his face. His long silver hair tangled whipping around his face. His beard was long and full, gray with a sprinkle of silver and hadn't seen a hairbrush in a long time. The man's one eye squinting from the blinding light. His arm pulls back.

SSSSSSWISSSH KARRACK

His huge muscles launched the spear as it flew and created a comet's tail. My eyes following it over my head and it struck the next Frost Giant in its chest exploding out the other side. The spear turned in midair towards the one eye warrior's outstretched hand. I saw the blur of movement first.

TaWhip TaWhip TaWhip TaWhip TaWhip TaWhip TaWhip TaWhip

Then arrows appeared jetting out of Mr. One Eye's back and outstretched arm. The force of the impact made him stumble forward, his arm dropping to the side. He turned his head towards the source.

PING Ting Ping.. TiiinnNgGgGGggg

The golden spear dropped from the sky not 12 feet in front of me pinging off the concrete. In a full run, with the rain and wind beating me like Mike Tyson, I plowed my way towards the fallen weapon and tucked Lou in the back of my waist band. Mr. One Eye turns towards his unseen adversary.

Snap Snap Snap Snap…

Raking his left arm down his right, braking the arrow shafts that are protruding. We stared at a Native American, straight from another age, with the biggest damn Mohawk I have ever seen. The Native American partially appears out of the debris cloud.

A wooden recurve long bow pulled back.

"Not this time!" I snatched the spear off the ground. Extra energy from the lightning bolts, coursing through me, jumped from my fingertips to the spear.

I caught it over my shoulder and with all my will I flexed my muscles. The spear leaves my hand with a snap of thunder. The Indian's features morph, his sunken eyes glow like a cat, and he moves his head just enough. The spear misses his cat like ear then falls to the ground.

Moving to Mr. One Eye side I grab him under his arm before he fell. More arrows are in his chest.

"Shit, shit, shit!" While trying to hold him up I realize how big my new friend was. Even with him slumped over he towered above me.

"He changed forms just enough," he said softly.

"He must know Atticus, the Iron Druid," I said as I chuckled a little from my own geekdom.

Stumbling with his weight I reached out with my left arm to get my balance and a staff made of a bone hit the pavement. In my left hand Lou supports both of us. My head turned side to side looking for the Indian. He was gone, but I could hear him in the wind.

He starts to chant. The storm reverberating the notes of the song making it stronger. Four Frost Giants from the North, South, East and West of us walk from the tornados circle.

The Indian walked, I should say struts down the center of I-20 towards us. The wind and rain slashes across me as two crows, the size of giant condors, swoop down out of the storm towards the Native American.

Mr. One Eye looks down to me, "He is after them, not me."

I looked at the two crows, "Huginn and Muninn."

As I shuffled us to the center medium I leaned Mr. One Eye against it, so he can prop himself up. I looked back at the bridge where my family took shelter. Pulling my helmet off, I dropped it with a thud. Then looked him in his one eye and tipped my head to him.

I pivoted towards the Indian and at the top of my lungs screamed, "FOR ODIN…!"

Running towards the Indian I didn't notice Lou had become a broadsword, the size of one those ridiculous Manga Anime weapons. The bone sword was perfectly balanced. I took a two-handed grip on the hilt and brought the sword up to a ready position. I have studied martial arts since I was a preteen.

That's a lot of muscle memory and I let loose.

WHOOSH Splish.. Splash SLASH SPLLLOOOOSSSHHHH

In a few movements I was inside the huge Indian's defenses, while the bird scratches at his face and is distracted wrestling with Muninn. I hit one knee and pushed my left foot out, like sliding into second base and with a pivot of my hips I slashed out. Lou sank deep into his thigh. The slick pavement carried me farther than I expected sending me sliding past him. I shifted and turned my body towards him as I stood opposite of him, bringing Lou back in a ready position.

"**CAAAAWWWWWWW**!" Huginn, the condor size bird, landed with a bellowed cry to Muninn.

The Indian had the crow by its wings trying to rip Muninn in half. The wounds in his leg oozed out black blood.

"He bleeds," I said to myself.

The Indian danced around in circles, his knees kicking up in the air. Muninn thrashing desperately to get free. He chanted and swung himself around holding the bird outstretched.

I knew that dance, he's Diné, a Navajo Indian. The Diné warrior continued to dance, feathers falling from Muninn.

“CAW!” Huginn crowed in protest with my lack of action.

I whispered, “Hold.”

The Diné arched his back and with the bird held high above his head.

“NOW!” I called to Huginn.

Hopefully the bird was on the same page as me and we were. Huginn grabbed Muninn and flaps his wings as hard as he could and let me tell you I felt the wind from it as I came underneath the Diné.

A helicopter rotor blasted wind and hit me.

Swishhh Slash Slice FLAP FLAP WOOSH FLAP FLAP FLAP

Lou at ready position with one clean movement. The upstroke took the Indian across the stomach flipping Lou around and I kneeled slashing with the down stroke cutting another clean line. This time something fell from his belt. The Diné jerked in surprise and that's all Huginn needed, with one last flap of his mighty wings he tore Muninn free then he flew away with Muninn safely clutched in his talons.

“AAAAAAHHHHHHHHHHHHHH!” The Native American screamed grasping at what I had cut from his belt. He searched the ground frantically and then looked at me. For the first time I really saw all of him and he was pissed.

“Cowboy,” the tone in his voice carried years of hate in it.

The Navajo Indian stood to his full height of 7’. In my amazement I watched the black ooze he had for blood suck itself back into his wounds and closed not healed, just closed. Then the very earth under my feet shook with the Indian’s rage.

SONIC BOOM WHOOSH

At a young age my Mom met my Dad, shortly after, we moved from Minnesota to the desert in California an hour and some change from Los Angeles where the Air Force constantly goes supersonic breaking the sound barrier. Sonic booms scare the living shit out of most people. They can't help but to flinch.

WHISSSHH WHISSST WHISSSSP WHISSSHH WHISSST WHISSSSP

The sudden crack of the sound barrier being torn then the rush of air that follows the shockwave is really intense. In that brief second, I swooped Lou across the ground snagging what looked like a medicine pouch, a black horn with blue spirals and three black feathers all bounded together. In a wide arch I slung the items off Lou's blade and sent it sailing towards whatever had caused the distraction.

To my amazement a rainbow had busted through the black storm clouds streaking and arcing across the sky in kaleidoscope of colors. I watched as the horn and feathers with the little leather bag disappear inside the rainbow.

SNATCH BLAM WOOSH SMACK THUD

The massive Indian grabs me so fast spinning me over his shoulder and down to hard road. I bounced like a deflated basketball and with two hands he grabbed me up again. With no effort he tossed me 30 feet across I-20 rolling to a painful stop.

"Cowboy," he says to me as he drills ice daggers into me with his evil glare. He slowly reached behind him drawing a tomahawk in each hand.

I watched him walk slowly to me. Rain poured down his bare chest, his red war paint never washing off his pale bluish white skin. He was extraordinarily ripped with the physique of Hercules. He flipped one of the tomahawks up into the air catching it by the handle repeatedly and unconsciously. He only wore an early loincloth and leather fur lined moccasins tied up to his knees. Multiple leather belts and fur straps crisscross his body forming his belt and shoulder bandoliers. Hung from odd places around him are skulls, claws, teeth and other trophies. He was getting so close I can see his chest, right thigh and left arm are riddled with over a dozen of gunshot scars that bubble off his white skin like braille.

From behind the 7' tall Super Indian a thunder began to rumble from inside the rainbow. With a roar a huge voice carried by the storm itself declared.

"FFFFOOORRR OOODDIIIINNNNNNNNN."

Thor

Thor was the most widely worshipped and beloved deity amongst the ancient Pagan tribes of the North. He was viewed as the protector of the common man. This was a natural extension of his role as protector of Midgard, as the majority of the Asér were average working-class people. Thor is a man of considerable size and musculature with a long mane of fiery red hair with a thick beard and mustache. However, the god of thunder has sometimes been envisioned with blonde hair and clean shaven or with a little bit of stubble an image popularized today by his depiction in Marvel Comics.

Thor didn't actually use Mjolnir to propel him through the air as his comic book counterpart often does, but rather utilized a chariot made of lightning pulled through the heavens by two large male goats named Tanngrisnir and Tanngnjóstr. These two goats also could be killed and eaten when other sustenance was unavailable and subsequently resurrected the following morning via magical spell work. With one stipulation, Thor had to have all of their bones and they had to be left intact.

Thor also carries a belt of strength that, feeds off his own magic, would triple his already prodigious level of strength. He also sometimes carries a pair of metallic gloves that he requires to handle the full magical energies of Mjolnir.

He is married to the beautiful golden-haired goddess of agriculture, Lady Sif. Together they have a daughter Thrud.

Angus, Minotaur of Minoa

Chapter 3

From inside the rainbow a shadow moves at least 8 feet tall. The side of the rainbow explodes sending rainbow sparks in all directions by a rectangular shaped object. It strikes the Indian in a shower of lightning. Blasting the Indian into the air to go crashing through the circling tornados.

A hammer, the size of my head, hits the ground at the same moment my face also hits the concrete. For the second time I am lying face down on the road looking up at a pair of boots that I don't recognize. I see that they are wrapped in leather with a fur lining. Looking past the boots, up the tree trunk sized leg as the man stepped over me and then stops.

So, with this huge man with legs covered in leather and a kilt of fur he whispered, "Mjolnir."

I tried to get to my knees and throw up. He stepped forward and a huge hammer suddenly appears in his hand.

Without looking down at me, "You intend to fight?" In the tone of his voice it was not a question.

He knew my intentions as I stood, my head spinning, and lost a lot of blood I thought to myself. I leaned starting to fall, Lou appears in my hand becoming a staff and saving me from falling.

“It's been a long time,” he reached behind his back pulling of a WWE sized championship belt, “put it on,” now holding the belt in my direction.

Four Frost Giants held their ground, North, South, East and West. The storm raging around us, rain gathering, freezing into iceberg size weapons. I didn't take it and took my fighting stance, he put the belt back on and stood his full height. I'm 5’11” no not 6’ and have met some big men while doing security for the Riviera. Hell, I put Kevin Nash in an arm bar when he wrestled for WCW, a story for another time and this dude made him look tiny. 7’ 10” tall his chest was the size of a small bus and covered in glowing white and blue tattoos that ran down his shoulder to his bicep. We both fell into a step circling back to back, never staying in one place. With no words spoken we made a defensive circle around Odin. The one eye God leaned on one knee making a good impression of a porcupine.

The wind blows his red beard sideways when he bends, a bow, “All Father.”

At that moment a Frost Giant made his move so did I. I mentioned before that I see things differently, my brain is wired wrong, and it processes information differently. Lou morphed from staff to spear while I ran towards the giant. In one step, it cleared the distance between us. It paid me no mind to me knowing the real threat wasn't me. I took complete advantage of the opportunity. Its foot landed, so I did a running leap, landing on the giant’s foot sinking Lou into the top of the Frost Giant's foot pinning it to the concrete.

With a blinding blue flash, lightning rings my bell, still holding onto Lou pinned the foot to the ground I looked up to see that the Frost giant was missing his upper half, the legs finally started to fall to the ground. I pulled Lou out running up the leg as it fell towards the next nearest Giant.

"For the ones I cherish, I will do Great and," I yelled and with the next step I leaped swinging Lou who had changed to a great big long sword.

"TERRIBLE THINGS," I said landing in a roll as the second Frost Giant's arm came off at his elbow. I growled as I turned towards Thor.

Thor tilted his head and turned bringing his wooden shield up.

SHATTER KABOOM ZZZZ..CRACK

Ice shattered when the Frost giant's weapon struck. Thor brushed the snow from his fur and held up his war hammer. Lighting cut the sky and I noticed the color of the lighting from the storm and Thor's was different. Thor brought his hammer down, literally, slamming it into the ground an explosion of concrete, he called the thunder. The lighting struck the rest of our enemies, they fell and my world went fuzzy, I puked again and joined the Frost Giants falling to the ground.

"Wake up now!" I heard Kara's voice first. "I have to potty!" with her fingers spreading my eyelids open she informs me.

When you have children you know that sound, I sat up in pain and started to answer her.

"Trick you..," She cuts me off, "you not want to wake up, sorry Daddy."

I smiled. Cindy bent to me and kissed my forehead, they must have taken off my helmet when I was passed out. Looking around I see Nathan and Alex right next to us. Cindy scooped up Kara in her arms.

"Your eyes?" I asked her.

Nathan reached his arms out to help me up to my feet. Alex took her sash off her waist and tied it around the still bleeding hole in my thigh, my head went back in pain. Thor reached down to help his father to his feet and Odin batted Thor's hand away but could not stand on his own. Thor just stepped to one side of Odin and watched over him. I leaned on Nathan and started towards Odin, my Robin, matching my steps. My three ladies followed us. With only a few steps to go I let Nathan go and I tried to stand. I wobbled, Nathan went to help me again and I shook my head and he didn't move. I slowly made my way to the old man, I grabbed him up under his arm, and he let me.

“Time to go,” groaning I heaved pulling him up draping his arm over me.

Odin just looked at the ground. He held me up more than the other way around with his one eye locked on mine. Odin turned to Thor, and Thor looked at me then at my family.

“Gather them,” Odin pulled me with him as he walked towards the Rainbow Bridge and called back to his son.

“The Keepers will not be pleased, “the huge man rumbled and crossed his massive arms over his chest as his braided beard resting over them.

“Uppie…,” Kara wiggles from her mother's arms and stands in front of Thor. He reached down and gently cradles her in his massive arm. When he walks by Nathan he grabbed him up and sits him on his one shoulder.

Nathan looking smug says to me, “Dado, if you're going to ride,” pats Thor's shoulder, “ride in style.”

“Yeah man,” I smiled at him knowing he was so happy because he got to use my favorite quote from the transformer movie.

WHISSSHH WHISSST WHISSSSP WHISSSHH WHISSST WHISSSSP

I stopped in front of the rainbow bridge and waited. Odin must have felt it cause he stopped at the same time I did. Thor didn't even break stride, passing into the rainbow bridge. I watched as if the rainbow was a waterfall. It cascaded over them like water.

Cindy walking up to the rainbow bridge with an uncertain look on her face. I reached out putting my hand into the rainbow waterfall. It felt like putting your hand in the bottom of a cooler trying to find the last Mt. Dew in a sea of Cokes. When I pulled my hand out instead of it being wet it was completely dry.

"Just facken cold babe," I said and winked.

Alex took her mother's hand and without a sound Alex pulled her mom gently, they stepped in it together. In the screams from the rushing winds of the storm I heard drums. The old man let go of me as he stepped into the rainbow waterfall disappearing in a shower of colors.

DRUM DRUM drum...drumDrum....

The drums grew louder and I not only heard it, I felt it.

"COWBOY!" the Indian screams.

I managed not to shit my pants.

"Yay!" Points for me as I back pedaled straight into the rainbow bridge. I mentioned that it was cold, it was very cold as the rainbow flowed over me as I shivered.

Okay you know in the middle of summer when it's 97 degrees outside and you step into Walmart, it feels something like that. I stepped out of the cascading rainbow into a pass through, a hallway of sorts.

"Holy shit!" I said out loud, "I'm standing in the middle of the rainbow bridge to Asgard."

I paused to reflect on where I was standing and felt the air pressure change as my ears popped. The crashing sound of waterfall combined with the sounds of reverse glass shattering echoes in my ears.

WHISSSHH WHISSST WHISSSSP WHISSSHH WHISSST WHISSSSP

Nine Realms

The 9 Realms of Asgardian legend are actually Pocket Dimensions, the size of a small Moons that hang from the great branches of the tree Yggdrasil like Christmas tree ornaments. Pocket Realm are literally its own planet.

Asgard, the realm inhabited by the great majority of the Norse deities and it's the original home of the war-loving Aesir tribe. Asgard is described as an amazing and majestic realm of towering spires and palaces of gold and silver situated within a remarkable city. It is surrounded by miles and miles of enchanted woodlands, rivers, and seas, which are populated by a large number of life forms, just like Midgar creatures, such as dogs, cats, and horses, and others. It is also home to Mythical Creatures unlike anything natural to the biological kingdoms of Midgard including dragons, griffins, dire wolves and various other types of unknown creatures.

Vanaheim, home of the Vanir, a tribe of peaceful but powerful fertility deities. Vanir went to war with the Aesir of Asgard and eventually achieved peace with them. Vanaheim, like Asgard, is a spectacular realm that is dotted with vast, unspoiled forests and bodies of water, all of which are inhabited by nature spirits and equivalents of Earth animals.

Alfheim, the realm of the Light Elves. The light elves are the enchanted shape-shifting beings of great magical power who were known to the Celtic people as the faerie folk, or Faye ruled by Tuatha De` Danann. Alfheim is simply another word for the twilight realm. It is also known in Ireland and Scotland as Underhill the land of the Faé.

Svartalfheim the home of the Dark Elves, an offshoot species of the inhabitants of Alfheim, who have been known to people in the western world as goblins, bogarts, and many other names.

Jotunheim, the realm of the Jötunn or Giants. A third tribe of humanoid beings of great magical power to rival the Aesir and Vanir. The Jotun never made peace with either of these other two tribes and are considered their sworn enemies. This realm is distinguished by an extremely cold, snow-capped tundra and huge mountain ranges.

Nidavellir, rocky realm characterized by miles of caves the lower levels are inhabited by the diminutive and elusive race of humanoid beings. Known as the Dwarves, where they maintain their forges that they sometimes use in the service of the deities and occasionally for a few select mortals.

Helheim and Niflheim are the same realm divided but ruled by the same Goddess. Helheim, this is the twilight realm of the common dead, the souls of those mortals and deities living under the purview of the Norse cosmology who were neither truly heroic nor truly evil and are ruled by the death goddess Hela, where her great palace resides. Helheim (not to be confused with the Hell of Biblical legend) is described as having a gray, barren, and bleak landscape.

Niflheim is a frozen landscape of endless snowcapped mountains. The relatively small number of mortal souls of those people who were truly and remorselessly malicious or murderous while alive. It's described in the legends as being an extremely cold, frozen landscape of endless night. The souls confined to that realm are subject to frequent hardships and tortures, and also fall under the rulership of the death goddess Hela. Niflheim is also the same dimensional plane as the afterlife realm sometimes referred to as Winterland, where a small number of Wiccans fear that the most malign amongst their number may dwell at least temporarily following their mortal demise.

Muspelheim--this is the realm of unending fire, possibly a manifestation of pure magical energies. The only Realm not attached to the tree Yggdrasil or any other Galactic Tree. It is inhabited by a little-known race of dangerous warrior beings with wings of fire. Most people in antiquity knew them as the Anunnaki. They were described as angels in Judeo-Christian lore. The Anunnaki are ruled by Surtur the ancient and incredibly powerful giant fire heart where Tolkien got his inspiration for the great eye of Saruman in Lord of the rings.

Midgard, meaning Middle Realm or Middle Earth for it sits in the center of the roots of Yggdrasil, is the Asgardian name for the Earth. Midgar is the only realm that magic is forbidden and operates under a set of physical laws recognized by science.

Angus, Minotaur of Minoa

Chapter 4

WHISSSHH WHISSST WHISSSSP… WHISSSHH WHISSST WHISSSSP

Standing inside the mythical bridge to Asgard …. The facken rainbow bridge to facken Asgard, Thor… Odin, the Old Man…is the All Father from Norse mythology.

My head swam as I closed my eyes walking out the rainbow. The air was cool and fresh, moist against my skin, mountain air. The grass was shin high damp with dew and I opened my eyes.
A truly gorgeous view lay before me. Then I was slammed to the ground…

"CAW, CAW…!" Huginn said as he stood on top of me.

"Huginn!" I called out.

He flapped his wings, shaking his head side to side. I put my hand on his head rubbing it like a dog, the huge bird purred.

"How's Muninn." I asked him.

He jumped up and down, bobbing his head.

"All right but you have to get off me first," I told him.

Have you seen *The Sound of Music*, the scene of her spinning around in the middle of picturesque panoramic view, it was like that. I looked around and blacked out... my injuries catching up to me.

I woke up in a fireman's carry, being bounced around, thrown over Thor's back.

“I'm awake now. You can put me down,” I grumbled.

Thor just kept walking. I tried to get my bearing then noticed Nathan still sitting on Thor's other shoulder. I wondered if Thor was still carrying Kara. So, doing the only sure thing I knew to get put down I dry heaved, making that almost vomiting sound.

Thor dropped me with a quickness. Hitting the ground, I actually did vomit, mostly blood. Damn that isn't good. I wiped my mouth getting ready to stand as Alex took my arm and tired helping me up.

Alex asked, “Where the hell are we?”

Answering her, “Asgard and language young lady.” She rolled her eyes at the language comment.

We walked down a wide well-worn path through the fields of grass making our way to a modest Long House, the center chimney smoked with fluffy white clouds. Not realizing till that moment Odin was missing.

“Muninn!” I called stopping in my tracks.

“CAW!” The crow landed in the nearest lone tree in answer.

“Odin?” I asked him He cocked his head to train one eye at me and I saw images and emotions in my head. I saw and felt Odin asleep in a great fur lined bed.

“Dad your nose is bleeding!” Nathan tells me.

“Hurt bad kiddo,” I mumbled. Tunnel vision started and my eyes didn't want to focus and I heard my son's voice lined with concern.

"Dad…" I collapsed to the ground pulling them with me. The last thing I heard was my face hitting solid ground.

THUR PLUNK

"A Battle on Midgar with Frost Giants?" I heard a strange woman's voice first. I tried to open my eyes and could not. She asked someone and the pain hit and lights out again.

My body shuddered and lurched, shit, going to puke. My body without my permission sat up and throw up. I fell off the bed and was not pleased to land in my own blood laced vomit. Pain, dizziness and darkness washed over me.

Pain rocked me, my leg was on fire, my nerve endings screamed for me to do something. This time I did leaping out of the bed my feet hit the cold floor and so did my face. I didn't pass out immediately, 2 points for me.

The same lady's voice, "You are either the bravest or the stupidest mundane I have ever" and my eyes closed once more, my last thoughts were of my family while the darkness enveloped me.

Someone wiped my face, I know that touch, "Babe," it came out garbled whisper.

My eyes focused on my wife's face, her almond shaped eyes red from tears. I sat up scaring her, "What's wrong are the kids ok?"

She crossed her arms and gave me that look, all you married men know that look. The look that says you are a dumbass and you have no idea what you just did. She pushed me back down to lay on the bed flat.

"You lost a lot of blood. You are still really hurt, keep still. Thor needs to ask you something," she put her hand on my chest. *Oh hell, this can't be good* I thought to myself. "Just tell him yes whatever he asks, he thinks it's the only way you will survive." Tears welled up in her eyes.

I put my hand on hers, "I've already walked on water."

She pinched me, "That was one time," she replied.

"From what I recall Jesus only did once." That earned me a smack I laughed which started a coughing fit, blood sprayed from my mouth and nose.

Cindy yelled, "Thor!"

I felt the huge man footsteps shake the room has he ran in.

His huge hand held me up, "Do not close your eyes1" Of course, I did as he asked, barely. "You of your own free will and of your own accord must make the journey to healing pools," he bent over me and removed the fur that covered me.

Of course, I was naked, but I sleep naked all the time so it did not bother me. I looked at my leg where Lou had been sticking out my leg, the wound was nasty and a tear rolled down my face. Sorry Lou and put my hand on top of the hole in my right leg. With one move Thor had me on my feet. Bent over hands on my knees.

"So where am I going?" I asked standing up slowly. *Don't puke, don't puke* my inner me called out. But in reality not even facken crickets dared make a sound so I did, "Do I at least get pants or boots," wiggling my now very cold toes.

Everyone took a step back like I had the plague, Cindy head down, never stop looking at the floor. I took a steadying breath and tested my resolve. Rolling my shoulders back, hearing the familiar snapping and popping of my joints, I mentally prepared for a fight. I took my first step, well my brain sent the message to my legs, but said message must have taken a wrong turn. So, when my legs didn't get the message and stayed in one place, Physics 101… Lou now a walking cane carved and ornate held me aloft. With all my willpower I moved my left leg. I took a step, the slowest and most painful step of my life. I held Lou up for the first time. The bone was carved all along the shaft but I really can't see shit without my glasses, but I could make out a car in a storm, Frost Giant's missing eye. It was a story and I stumbled and Lou extended to a staff, smacking the ground hard with a thud.

Thor's booming laughter and the accompanying smack on the back in prays, made me grab Lou with both hands, "Name?"

“Lou, well, Louisé, was the White haired old Ogre’s name,” I answered without hesitation.

“Lou”, he repeats, “Humph, you go now. Find the pools.” like he was reading my mind answering my questions before I could form them. “Your family is under my protection.”

With that I made my way out the Long House naked and bleeding to snow. When did it facken snow, my balls crawled so far up my arse it should be physically impossible as soon as my foot touched the cold frozen ground. I scanned the snow-covered valley, even the lake had a thin sheet of ice on it. My body shivering, I walked towards the nearest tree line into the cold forest. The snow had just fallen there had been no time for even animal tracks. I walked in no particular direction across the frozen meadow and into the forest passing tree after silent tree.

Muninn sprung out too, “Caw.”

I peed a little in response. After my small heart attack, I greeted her. Yeah man, Muninn is a girl. She bobbed her head, her neck feathers on display and tail lightly sweeping the ground. My spider sense tingle, working in nightclubs and doing side Military contracts, gives you this extra sense of things in your peripheral vision.

“Don’t you facken do it,” I spoke over my back.

Huginn cawed in a laugh hopping from one foot to the other his wings flapping joining his wife. His head dancing while he continues to giggle.

“Not funny, fucker. Your old lady there already made me piss myself,” I told the bird.

He lost it then he rolled over and over his laugh made scowl at him. I leaned hard on Lou, when Muninn and I joined Huginn in his laughter. A huge chunk of snow fell from a nearby tree with a thump getting all of our attention.

KerTHUMP

In a fighting stance facing the threat, Lou a short scimitar held tight ready to strike. I scanned the sky. Huginn and Muninn just hopped to a stop looking at the fallen snow mound and back at me.

"What... it could be a Frost Giant, shit," shrugging?

Muninn turned her head just slightly, her eyes intense and focused on me.

"Muninn, you okay?" I asked her, puzzled at the strange look in her eyes.

An emotional wave hits me telepathically. First the images then the emotions that turns into thoughts downloads into my brain. I fall on my bare ass in the snow with an instant headache. I just laid back in the snow and watched two crows the size of pit bulls fly away.

I laid there, I don't know how long until my inner monologue spoke, "Get up, it's time ta make the donuts," nothing happened. I didn't move a muscle.

I closed my eyes trying to get everything to stop spinning. Millions of emotional languages that Muninn forced fed my brain danced under my eyelids. Opening my eyes to see my feet blue…

"Shite!" I called out, and I made the mistake of looking at the rest of my body. I need to get moving I told myself as I vomited blood as I rolled to my side.

CLIP CLOP CLIP CLOP NEIGH

I slowly looked up to see a brown and white palomino unicorn bobbing his massive head up and down at me.

"Yeah Man, I am definitely lost." I answered him. I slowly rolled into my stomach and got to my knees.

"Whinny Neigh CLOP CLOP Huff," He informs as he waves his single spiraling horn at me like I was an idiot.

"Yeah, I know that I am dying," I tell him as I try to get my brain to focus. The world begins to spin faster and faster.

"Would by any chance you know where the healing pools...," I asked the unicorn right before tunnel vision completely takes over and I pass out. The last thing I hear is my head hitting the ground.

THUD

Odin

All-Father Odin is the grand king of the Gods of Asgard, one of the most powerful beings in the cosmos, and certainly the mightiest of beings in all the Nine Worlds comprising the Asgardian cosmology. One of the oldest of the Aesir tribe of Asgard, Odin gained his extraordinary levels of power and wisdom through great sacrifice and struggle and he expects nothing less of those mortals who wish to gain his favor and assistance. Nothing worth having can ever come easy or it's effectively worthless in the scheme of things because no lessons were learned along with its acquisition. Only through trial and perseverance can one gain all worthwhile goals and desires. Odin will be quick to remind all who follow and revere him of this, should they ask him for aid.

According to legend, Odin acquired much of his great power through no less a tribulation than hanging from one of the branches of the cosmic world tree Yggdrasil via a rope around one of his legs for nine days and nights without food or water and it was through this trial that amongst what he earned was the secret of the runes. He sacrificed one of his eyes to the Well of Mimir in order to acquire the Wisdom of the Ages, which was not only a vast surfeit of wisdom but also a great amount of knowledge of the universe and how its physical laws are structured.

Often appearing to his reverence as an older but quite robust man of impressive height, Odin is said to oftentimes take on the role of the Wanderer. In this guise he is said to walk the common lands of Midgard (Earth) while appearing as an elderly man with a long gray beard who is attired in simple clothing and a wide-brimmed hat (which Odin often uses to cover his missing eye).

He wields the mighty spear Gungnir. It serves as a weapon that can penetrate almost anything he hurls it against, as well as benefiting from an enchantment that enables it to return to his hand immediately after it strikes its intended target. Always at his side are his two honored comrades, the great gray wolves Gerri and Frecki, and also at his beck and call 24/7 are the two legendary ravens Huginn and Muninn (Thought and Memory, respectively) who fly about the Nine Worlds gathering information that they then whisper in Odin's ear upon their return from their routine forays of data-gathering. He rides the amazing eight-legged snowy gray steed Sleipnir, who was birthed by Loki, his blood brother, while shape-shifted into the form of a mare and impregnated by a giant's incredibly powerful stallion; Sleipnir is capable of running through the skies of any of the Nine Worlds at velocities that would be considered astounding to mortal perception. This mystical horse can breach dimensional barriers separating different planes of reality with ease, thus making him the perfect mount for a deity of Odin's stature.

Angus, Minotaur of Minoa

Chapter 5

Have you ever been so tired on the way home from work, you realize 15 minutes later after you've been sitting on the couch you don't remember the drive home. Well it was like that, as I sank into the steam covered pool. The water felt like it was sanding off my skin as I stepped into the pool and sunk until I was completely under water. I came out slowly, just my face at first, until my neckline reached the surface of the water. I found a comfortable place and rested. It's never a good idea to fall asleep in a bath, and I held my middle finger up. Then leaned my head back against the stone closing my eyes.

Splish SPLOOSH

As my right arm falls into the pool my eyes opened wide. I felt fish nibbling on me but not just under the water, so in such an event you have two choices I could leap out of the pool, screaming or not move at all. I didn't move a muscle, afraid of what my new visitors may be. Dragonfly size creatures darted all around me, glowing light trails shimmering off their double beating wings.

Zip-Zitter Zip-Zitter splish splash Zip-Zitter Zip-Zitter splish splash

I just moved my eyes, carefully not to move a muscle, harder than it should sound but with the feeling of 500 spiders crawling all over me. A female hovering by my arm, right above the water line it was definitely female. If you have ever seen James Cameron's Avatar, it had a female form but not human. She had no hair on her body. The dreadlocks on her head were made of skin. Her dragonfly wings kept her hovering perfectly still in midair. No clothes covered her salamander like skin. I felt her toe pads grip to my skin her gecko like toes gripping tight. Her wings finally came to stop given me a good look at her. She was no bigger than a large dragonfly.

Her bright orange and blue skin shimmering with every slight move she made, beads of glowing sweat ran down her body. She started to crawl up my arm, I noticed her knees bent the other way. She circled a spot on my upper arm, once, twice, three times, she turned her head up and opened her mouth. Her face extends gums pushing her lips back exposing rows and rows of needle teeth. Mouth like a snake her jaw got impossibly big and made a perfect circle of teeth.

"What Da Fuck?" spilled out my lips before I could close my mouth? Without reaction to me she bit down into my arm it felt like a horse flies bite. She stayed attached to me for just a minute or so then she stood and flies up to join the rest, still flying around me. The veins in the muscle around the bite started to glow and I saw all the bites glowing. My eyes flutter with waves of dizziness.

SNNAAAPP Zip-Zitter Zip-Zitter Zip-Zitter Zip-Zitter Zzzzzzzziipppp

Something from far off in the woods spooked them and they started to swarm. Then darted off in all directions as I opened my eyes again. I stood up, the cold air felt good against my hot wet skin and found myself covered in glowing mosquito bites. I mentally wondered then checked my junk.

"Fuck," I moaned. Sure enough the little facken shits bit me everywhere.

Glancing at my thigh, noticing, my wound was just a glowing scar and completely healed. Checking again I was completely healed, wait my glasses. My vision wasn't blurred. So, I went to get out of the pool and a shimmering light on my forearm caught my eyes.

"Hey," Looking at a purple and green male still attached to me. As I poked the little guy, "Meal times over, off with you."

His dragonfly wings started to flutter, with that he let go and flew off to join the rest of the bioluminescent flying salamanders still hovering over the hot springs. Steam rushed off my body as I step out the pool. I rung out my goatee and braids and started back to my family with sounds of their Dragonfly wings. The weather had drastically changed from snow and frozen earth to springtime with the new flowers blooming.

Zip-Zitter Zip-Zitter Zip-Zitter Zip-Zitter Zip-Zitter Zip-Zitter

The last thing I remembered, before I found myself standing by the hot springs I was hallucinating a talking unicorn, and really had no idea where the fuck I was, I paused. Closing my eyes, I took a slow deep breath through my nose taken in the fresh smells of the water and the forest. When I caught the slightest whiff, there was a distinct smell of a smoke. So, I headed in that general direction. Still quite naked I tenderly made my way through the underbrush to the forest beyond.

I have been walking through the woods for hours when it goes completely silent, not an insect chirped, nor an animal rustled. Even the breeze itself stopped. I stopped dead in my tracks and crouched low scanning for the threat. I slowed my breathing focusing not with my eyes but with my ears.

SSSSlither.. SSSSlither.. SSSSlither..

Looking straight up over my head into the rainforest canopy. A bright green and gray pit viper the size of Titanoboa slowly makes his way closer and closer to the biggest eagle's nest ever. The long snake the size of a school bus extends out towards the other tree branches.

SSSSlither.. SSSSlither.. SSSSlither.. CREEEEEEK

Hanging half its body out into midair. The branch sags from the giant snake's weight. The gray patterns on the stomach of the massive snake flexed tight and in an "s" coil and froze motionless. Me and the giant snake just stared at the mansion sized bird's nest. Minutes passed by as the snake silently sat frozen in midair. The nest and snake must be 80 feet up in the treetops.

SSSStrike.. KaBlam SSSSlither.. SSSSlither.. SSSStrike.. CRASH SSSStrike.. SSSStrike.. CRASH

Before I could blink the green snake struck the nest like a SCUD missile. Huge venomous fangs fully extending from the snake's mouth as the nest exploded. Branches the size of tree trunks rain down to the forest floor. The snake crawls fully into the nest and repeatedly bites at baby birds inside the nest.

SSSStrike.. SSSStrike.. SSSStrike.. RRRUUUMMMMMBLE SSSStrike.. SSHHHUUUUCRACK KaBOOM

The nest explodes, sending wood shrapnel in all directions. Tucking myself tightly against the Giant Redwood from the falling debris. Huge clouds of dirt filled the air when the snake and what was left of the giant bird nest hits the forest floor. As the dust settles slowly I stepped away from the tree trunk, out of the corner of my eye I catch movement of a fluffy black cotton ball the size of a golden retriever dart by. I made my way around the huge broken tree limbs, some the size of a full-grown pine tree to find a big chunk of the giant bird's nest still intact. In the wreckage of the nest three Griffin chicks huddle together, shaken and frightened.

SSSSlither.. SSSSlither.. SSSSlither.. S-S-S-S-S-S-SSSSlither

Poking my head up like a prairie dog, I scanned frantically for the snake and realized that the green body of the massive snake was coiling around the circumference of what remained of the nest. His Mazda Miata sized head slowly craned over me.

H-H-H-HHHH-S-S-S-S SSSSlither.. HHHH-S-S-S-S SSSSlither.. SSSSlither.

Lou martializing in my hand morphing into a long bone battle staff ending in an Elf style curved spear point. Spinning the staff with a small movement of my wrist I began a simple warm up Kata. The pit viper tracks my body temperature as I stepped away from the baby Griffins. Like a Cobra under the snake charmer's spell his huge green head sways as my dance picks up speed. Time just kind of slowed down.

SSSStrike.. SLASH SSSSlither.. SSSStrike.. SSSStrike CUT SLASH STAB..

Timing every one of his bites, I would side step with the spinning battle staff. Lou's blade barely scratched the snake's super strong scales. Keeping as much distance from the solid black, still covered in down feathers, baby Griffins as I can and still avoid the giant snake's fangs. For just an instant a huge shadow blocks out the sun casting me in complete darkness.

WWWOOOOSSHH SNAP CRASH SSSlither..SSSlither.. FLAP FLAP FLAP SSSlither.. SSSStrike.. SSSStrike..

With hurricane force winds sending small debris and worried for the dog sized chicks, I tried to shield them as best I could. Scooping them under me I braced and waited to be crushed. Huge lazy-boy recliner sized black panther paws delicately prances over us as she protects her chicks. With her Raven beak not only did she bite the snake, she would drive her closed beak at the snake like a jackhammer. The sharp end would stab deep into the snake's flesh. Getting a good grip of the snake with her panther's claws. She snapped her beak around the base of the snake's head. The solid black panther tail of the mother Griffin swished back and forth making the tuft of black feathers at the tip, quiver.

RRRIIIIIIIP KaRACK SPLASH

The Raven Panther flexed her cat body spreading her wings fully as she pulls the snake's head off. Fountains of blood erupt from the headless body of the snake as it convulses in the Griffin's sharp claws.

CHOMP CHOMP CHEW GURGLE GURGLE SPIT! SPIT! SPIT!

Now sitting naked with twigs poking me in the ass, half of me is covered in snake guts and blood. The three baby Raven Panthers start to play like little kittens as they take turns being fed. Slinging my right hand like I had a can of Copenhagen, I flung the slimy substance off me. As the Kitts curiously gets to know me, the Momma Griffin yanks and in one piece deskins the reptile. With motherly gentleness she draped the inside out snakeskin around me.

"Thanks!" I tell her as I tilted my head to the side just a little nodding to her as well, "but what I really want is directions."

"CAAWWW CAW CAAAW SQUAKE CAAWWW CA Caw!" she glares down at me pissed.

"I have two good feet," I tell her. "And would never dishonor you in assuming that," bowing my head as I tried to let her know that I had no intentions of riding her like a common horse.

"CAAW CAW!" She tells me as she bobbed her head up and down, a very crow like gesture, towards my 7 o'clock. Turning to look in the direction she was pointing to.

"That way?" pointing with my left hand as I asked her and wondering in the back of my mind how she knew where I wanted to go.

"CAW Caaaw **CAAWWW**"

Three kinds of Faerie

Fairies are generally described as humans in appearance and having magical powers. Diminutive fairies of one kind or another have been recorded for centuries, but occur alongside the human-sized beings; these have been depicted as ranging in size from very tiny up to the size of a human child. Even with these small fairies, however, their small size maybe magically assumed rather than constant. Some fairies though normally quite small were able to dilate their figures to imitate humans. They are short in stature, dressed in various types of clothing and sometimes seen in armors. Wings, while common in artwork of fairies, all fairies flew with magic, sometimes flying on ragwort stems or the backs of birds. Nowadays, fairies are often depicted with ordinary insect wings or butterfly wings. Fairies have green and yellow eyes that reflect with magic. Some depictions of fairies either have them wearing some sort of footwear but fairies are always barefoot.

Pixies seen in folklore, are smaller than fairies. They are depicted as little people with butterfly wings. The pixies are four inches tall and have no need for clothes, their bodies are covered in a fine caterpillar like hair. The pixies always live away from the crowds or people and create their own surroundings. With the gift of plant magic, gardens spring up everywhere Pixies live, they do not make gardens for any other person but themselves only. They are very territorial; the pixies are seen to be in a constant fight with fairies. Pixies thrive on nectar and magic and are known to live for about twenty years. Pixies are quick in their motions though they are not violent, they will go an extra-long way in fighting for their territory. They are also known to defend those people who love them and whom they love. Pixies love stealing ponies and horses. They are also allergic to silver. They are great explorers familiar with the caves, the hidden sources of the streams and the recesses of the land. Pixies are winged pygmy-like creatures that do not glow.

Sprites are dazzling in color and about the size of a super large insects. Sprites have glistening membranous wings. In fact, they are often confused with exotic insects or flowers at first glance. Sprites real appearance compares to more of a salamander humanoid with dragonfly wings. Considered to be the most common type of faerie. They are known to live in every ecosystem but the desert. Some make their homes high in the branches of trees while others prefer to live near ponds and streams. They particularly love to live in the forests, inhabited by tree folk and other Faé and enjoy cool weather and a calm serene environment. If sprites are spotted, it is a sign that the area has a high concentration of faerie activity. Sprites travel in swarms and can bite if provoked. Their bites can kill instantly by draining your magic or can heal bodily injuries. They are playful and at times obnoxious. One of their favorite past-times is pestering butterflies. This is a great game for them as they are able to fly much faster than butterflies and can go greater distances before requiring rest. At night their bodies give off a brilliant bioluminescent glow that can be mistaken for fireflies along with other flying insects and spirit orbs. They wrap themselves in foliage at night or sink into silky blooms.

Water sprites will sometimes sleep on lily pads, oyster shells, or curled up on a nice pile of seaweed.

Ironniesous O'Keeffe

Chapter 6

The sun was low in the sky when I reached the forest edge. The meadow was alive with spring flowers and long soft grass. Nathan and Alex running through the tall meadow grass, two flying goats were hot on their heels. Kara on the back of the biggest goat, her hands were white knuckles as she held onto its horns. Watching the show has my two oldest do zig zags to try to avoid the dive bombing goats. The goats were only a little bit bigger than a normal goat. Long hair hung from their faces. No wings, they just galloped through the air, think of it like Santa's reindeer.

Kara saw me first and pulled on the goat's horns in my direction. “Daddy?” she proclaimed.

Both flying goats veered my direction. Standing my ground, I stared at the approaching goats. They seemed to speed up to see if I'd flinch.

“Monster,” I steadied myself dropping the huge snake skin I was dragging and was ready for impact and to catch Kara, clenched my jaw I grumbled with a smile.

The goat did a flyby so close its horns came inches from my face. Kara naturally timed it perfect leaping into me. I mentioned an impact she hit like a cannon ball, I wrapped my arms around her and pushed back absorbing as much momentum as I could. It took me three steps to gain my balance.

But I was doomed from the beginning, Alex and Nathan spears me in a hug and we all fell to the grass.

"EWW, Daddy you're naked!" all at one time my kids spoke.

Then they just scrambled away, like bugs when you turn on the light.

Which in turn made me laugh. The kids returned to their goat shenanigans and I picked up the snake skin and made my way to the longhouse. The grass was long but not enough to cover my balls fully so with my junk out anyways I made my way to a brick walking path that I didn't notice before. Pulling the skin along behind me. It was not just one longhouse but a few spread out each with gardens and people.

"CAW CAW!" Huginn warns me.

I looked up to see Huginn perched directly over my head, "Don't you even!" I side step while proclaiming this to the bird.

A huge amount of bird shit, just missing me.

Huginn starts to laugh, "CAW CAW…"

"You almost got me," I replied.

The bird flew down landing next to me, "CAW CAW CAW!" he said flapping his wings.

"OK, you warned me first," confirming that he did.

Huginn danced, "Caw caw."

"Well I'm glad you thought it was funny. Hey Huginn have you seen my wife?" I ask him.

"CAW!" and he flew towards one of the smaller longhouses.

My beautiful wife sitting outside on a handmade rocker chair with a quilt draping over her lap. The light twinkling off the intricate designs, her eyes doing the same lighting up as she notices me.

"Babe…" I did one of those one eyebrow up looks, you know the look that Dwayne "The Rock" Johnson does so famously, yeah that one.

"Even in the cold... hung like a," she had just a small evil grin on her face. She stood up with no rush. My wife at 5ft nothing was a Muay Thai champion and not in the women's league, her Dad… never mind, a tail for another time. Before she could finish I kissed her. She pulled away her eyes looking me up and down like she was going to eat me, "Let's cover you up before you make Thor jealous," she proclaimed with even more evil intentions wrapping the quilt around my waist.

"Thanks babe." I said as she sat back down in her chair and paused just looking at me. "What?" And looking myself over, "Oh," I pointed to the glowing bites, "Glowing flying salamanders if you can believe that."

She shook her head in the nope, "WHERE ARE WE?" Not a true yell but the tone was close.

"Asgard. I think," I answered quickly.

She waited for her question to sink in. But I was still clueless.

"What," I asked her?

"How in the hell are we in Asgard?" she asked.

"Rainbow bridge," as I said this I pointed back to the meadow where we had walked out the rainbow bridge.

She punches me.

"Okay, okay... I give," I smiled at her. I stroked my goatee absently thinking to myself if we are in Asgard, then how do we get home?

"Ohf!" all the air in my lungs forcefully exhales out my mouth. Thor snatching me up from behind in a huge bear hug unknowingly saving me from the wrath of my wife.

“Full of surprise you are,” he put me down slapping my back pointing to the bus long snake skin and knocking my quilt off.

“Yeah!” he laughed now pointing at my manhood. “Come, I think we can find some children's clothes…”

I looked at him and gave him my middle finger not even considering if he knew the hand gesture. He stood straight up, his 7’10” massive frame over shadowing me.

“I know this. Means fuck you,” Thor scowled.

“Yeah man,” I looked up meeting his eyes returning his scowl.

Thunder erupted from Thor, a huge barrel laugh came rolling out of the God. He puts his arm around me still laughing, “Little brother, come.”

I looked at my wife, she smiled and nodded towards the kids as I winked. Thor leads me into this smaller longhouse.

It was like the History channel before sitcoms and reality T.V. ruined it. Walking in to the central hall portion of the building. Built-in benches supported the walls. They were lined with fur pillows and animal skins provided sitting, working and sleeping platforms. A stone hearth was set in the middle corridor. Fires in the hearth lighting the room. On the other side of the great hearth rooms were set off to one side or the other of the longhouse.

“What's going on?” I asked him as we walked.

He ignored me.

“Are we in Valhalla?” I asked after a few minutes go bye.

Thor doesn’t say a word and stops suddenly in front of a barn door. He puts his huge hand on the door knob but before he opens it he looks down at me.

“Valkyries would have been there not me,” then opens the door.

A huge armory slash closet. I squeed. Forgetting that I was supposed to be holding the quilt that his around my waist in place. It hit the floor while I walked into the room with nothing on but a grin.

I lost myself for a minute as I walked. Looking at all the magical weapons that hung on the walls.

SPLISH SPLOOSH SPLASH Drip.. Drip.. Drip..

Thor dumped a huge barrel of warm water over me washing me clean. Shaking the water off me like a dog. A pair of dark gray leather skinned pants hit me in the face. I slid into the pants, maybe a couple sizes too big.

Boots hit me right in the chest so hard that I felt it in my ass. Shrugging my shoulders and shaking my head, I put the boots on. They fit perfectly. I jumped up and the pants stayed where they were, meaning around my ankles. Thor laughed again. I started to give him the bird.

But he beat me to it holding up his middle finger, laughing he said, “Come!”

Turning, he bent and opened the wooden chest. I pulled the pants up again and of course the shirt smacked me in face. “You actually waited for me to pull my pants up,” I explained while putting the sleeveless paper-thin chainmail shirt on.

Pulling the very light gray chainmail shirt down over my head, I felt the pants slip and snagged them. It only took the slightest touch from Thor's one finger and I fell on my ass.

“Could not stop,” he coughed. I rumbled at his laughter as he finished saying, “Myself.”

“Ha, Ha, ha ha!” This time I joined him in laughing.

“CAW CAW!” came from behind me.

Without looking, “Muninn, how ya doing gorgeous?” I ask her.

“CAW!” she called hopping next to me.

I stopped laughing and Thor did the same. “He wants to see me?” I asked the crow.

“CAW CAW!” came from Huginn as he flew in something clamped in one of his feet.

“CAW!” Muninn scowled him.

“CAW CAW!” Huginn bobbed his head at her.

I interrupted them, “Hey both of you can escort me.”

They stopped and looked at me.

I returned the look then, “Huginn what ya got there,” I asked him.

“CAW!” he answered excited remembering he had it then flew up dropping it in my open hand. They both flew out the door waiting in the rafters for me. Thor his arms crossed over his massive chest.

“What?” I asked him.

“You know what they say,” he returns.

“Yeah, no ... it's…” I paused trying to put in words.

Thor spoke up, “It is a feeling, an instance of emotion and images no words, yet you know?”

Puzzled I answered him, “Yeah man.”

He just said while walking by me, “Finish, the All Father waits.”

I watched him walk out. I tugged the pants up to my waist and looked at the brown leather bandolier and belt. Like a preteen girl looking at her first bra I just held it out, it reached out and wrapped around me holding my pants up. It went down one leg creating an empty sheath. Up my side it winds its way up finishing off in bandolier shoulder rig.

I looked at the sheath, “Hey Lou!” tapping my hand on his hilt.

The shirt I wore looked like it was made from tiny gray and silver reptile scales but as soft silk or cotton. Running my fingers across the green intricate needlepoint. A beautiful embroidered tree of Yggdrasil. It was directly in the center of the shirt, the roots started at the bottom seam. Running the trunk up the middle of the shirt to blossoming tree branches that spread over my chest.

Belt of Burden

Belt of burden is a magically imbued belt, quiver, holster or sheath enchanted with spatial, mass and dimensional manipulation. It can magically change size, teleport items back to itself, reload itself, and displace weight.

Ironniesous O'Keeffe

Chapter 7

Odin looks like a badass Santa Claus as he came into the room. He was wearing a dark red robe with white fur lining. His sleeves rolled up to his elbows revealing thick blue lined tattoos running up his forearms and under his robe. He sat in a modest leather chair draped by fur in front of a huge fireplace. His gray and silver beard braided in one massive single braid. Matching the single braid that pulls his silver hair back out of his face, to hang down his back.

Puff Puff Puff

He just sat there staring at the fire, smoking on a long gray tobacco pipe that he must have gotten from Gandalf.

“Sit!” Odin gestures to the chair that was opposite to him with the pipe.

I apparently stroked my long goatee as I sat in the oversized chair across from the All Father.

“I am not going to play twenty questions,” Odin began. “Every mythical legend is true.”

Puff Puff Puff Puff

“Magic is real and kept secret,” Odin tells me. “New magic has not happened or been revealed since the great accords.”

“The Great Accords,” I asked but he didn't answer me.

“Knowledge of magic is passed down. Father to son, mother to daughter, master to apprentice and always kept hidden. It's forbidden for any god or practitioner to bestow or even reveal magical abilities to a non-supernatural being or a mundane,” Odin pointed his pipe at me. “You're a Mundane of odd character,” he informs me. “You worship the four winds equally, sharing your faith to give others strength and have always believed in the unseen,” he smiled at me encouragingly.

“I know about magic now,” I started to say as his eye narrowed. “No,” correcting myself, “WE...” meaning me and my family. I stood and paused.

“Indeed,” as he puffed his pipe. He leaned forward tapping out the ash from the pipe.

“Let me guess, because of the Great Accords you're not allowed to tell me shit.”

Without repacking his pipe, he lit it, the amber of bowl glowing, “Indeed,” he blew out pink smoke and handed me his pipe.

“So, magic is facken real, Vampires, Werewolves and all the other things of folklore… real too?”

Of course, he did not answer me. I puffed on the pipe on instinct after he handed it to me. The taste was unforgettable, weed, best shit I have ever tasted. Running the stick over the bowl heating the goodness in the bowl to a perfect red.

I blew out the hit and sputtered, “And we can't ask or tell anyone about this.”

Handing him his pipe back he took it, relighting but the smoke pink again, “Indeed.”

I flopped into the oversized chair lined with thick fur, “Now what?” asking him.

He stood, his impressive 7’4” frame leaning towards me handing me his pipe.

Cough Coughing choke

“Damn it!” I blurted. Looked in the pipe blowing out the smoke. Bright green blue bud perfectly ground filling the bowl. He patted my shoulder while I finished my coughing fit. He walked back and forth contemplating, I sat smoking his pipe waiting on him.

Swishhh creek fafwoosh

I heard whispers on the wind, voices in the creak of the wood from the chair and singing from the flames of the fire.

The room went quiet Odin kept passing, he spoke but I don't think it was directed to me, “We each have Heroes, Warriors, Champions, Knights or Chosen,” he stops in mid step. “Fingers on separate hands, now we have all those fingers on one hand, a true Fist of the GODS.”

SHWISH CREEK FAFWOOSH TWANNNG TNNNNG

Odin looking at me with his one eye intensely. The wind blowing gently around me, the wood in my chair sighed with relaxation and the flames heat brushed my skin. I felt something stirring inside me. A cold heat from my center push in all directions flowing down to my fingers and toes. Looking at the pipe again.

“This weed is fantastic,” I muttered. Lighting it up hoping like hell to repeat the sensations.

Odin shook his head in the negative, yet smiled at me knowing I was displacing the truth on purpose. I exhaled out my nose, a big white puffy cloud and handed the pipe back to him.

He looked at my outstretched hand and pushed it towards me.

“A pipe that will always be full,” he said.

So I turned to lay it on the table and he stopped me.

"Take it! It has always helped me think, may it do the same for you," Odin tells me.

Going to refuse him he stops me again shaking his head. Without argument I slid the pipe in the bandolier as I stand. We went outside in the fresh afternoon air as we walked.

He talked, "You and yours must keep the secret when you arrive back on Midgar." he said something else but I stopped dead in my tracks in a fraction of a second when my big brain caught up.

"Midgard, home, when," I blurted.

He stopped a couple of steps ahead of me not turning, "Heimdall is ready when the time comes." He continues while he starts to walk again, "Dano, you must ensure that the secret is kept. Children cannot lie and you have three."

My posturing changed atomically with the mentioning of Alex, Nathan and Kara. Knuckles white with pressure as I held Lou tightly not remembering that I pulled him from the sheath.

"They could scream it to the facken world at the top of their little facken lungs," I began my rant in full protection mode.

Odin's laughter just like his son's boomed. He smacked his chest while he laughed at me.

"And I won't expect you to do no less," he said between burst of laughter. "No wonder my son has grown fond of you. Like a wolverine ready to attack no matter how big his adversary is."

"I don't look for violence, sir." Relaxing my body Lou disappearing from my hand, "it just finds me."

"Indeed." He said while he stopped laughing, "Indeed."

We both paused me regaining my composure, Odin taken in a long breath.

"The truth of magic will change you, a door that can never be shut is now open, secrets shared but never repeated will weigh heavily on both you and yours," Odin said turning his head to gaze off.

I followed his gaze to my family and his, they sat all around a huge outdoor dining table. They all chatted and cut up with one another while they ate. I looked at Alex sitting with three other young girls at the end of the table a huge smile on her face. She looked up at me, doing a little wave with her fingers and before I could wave a reply, her attention was drawn away. Nathan was leaned over the table questioning Thor who sat right across from him.

We went to join the feast in silence. Odin was greeted first by two bear size gray dire wolves, jumping up on him licking his face. He took his time with each dog in turn. I couldn't help but watch, he caught me, of course he did and looked at me like my Dad does when I should be doing something but I'm not. So, with that I made my way to a conveniently vacant seat by my youngest daughter Kara sitting on her mother's lap.

Sitting on the bench between Cindy and Nathan, “So what's good,” I asked as I sat down, “smells so good,” inhaling dramatically through my nose.

Kara clamped onto my neck with Glee, “Daddy!”

Hugging her back, “Love you too, monster.”

“Love you more,” and she went back to picking at her food.

Cindy leaned to me with a frown, I kissed her before she could form the question on her lips. She smiled at me but with an annoyed glint to her almond shaped eyes.

Starting to fill my plate I asked her, “So give me the 411... Kardashian style on Alex's new friends.” Winking at her as I said it.

“Really?” she asked befuddled knowing I loathe the show.

“Hit me,” scooping steak into my mouth.

She started as Odin patted his son Thor on the shoulder and sat down right across from me and to Thor's right, “Down at the end of the table.” She paused, scanning the opposite side of the table and looked at Alex sitting at the very end of the bench.

I was starving and my brain filtered through what my wife was saying combining it with what I knew about the Aesìr. So, as I ate and looked from one end of the long table to other feeding my mind as I filled my stomach.

The girl that sat right next to Alex was no older than my daughter. She fidgeted with the leather strap that tied her long platinum blonde hair back into a thick braid as she listened to Alex, was Thrud. The young lady had got all her mother's, Lady Sif, beauty combined with her father's, Thor, strength. She wore simple sleeveless leather tunic lined with fox fur, a wooden shield strapped to her back. A beautifully designed tattoo of Norse ruins started on her right shoulder and ran all the way down to the back of her hand. Thrud draped her left arm over Alex's shoulders as she points to the redhead's forehead that sat in front of Alex.

Across from Alex, Frevja put her hand on her forehead. Her red hair catches the light, highlighting it with oranges and yellows as she pulls it back to show my daughter the blue tattoo on her forehead. Frevja reminded me of a seventeen-year-old *Merida* from the Disney movie *Brave*, with tattoos. Frevja's father is Njord, the God of the Sea and her mother Skadi, the Goddess of Winter and the hunt.

Fulla, Frigga's servant and secret mechanical genius, sat next to Frevja and opposite to Thrud. Fulla had on a paint and oil stained sleeveless mechanic coveralls, her short dark hair was tucked under a dirty rage. She propped herself up with both her arms to get a better look at Frevja's tattoo, her arms were wrapped like *Rey* from *Star Wars: The Force Awakens.* She then wiped her face with her arm and smudged it with motor oil mimicking Frevja's tattoo and they all started to laugh. The four teenage girls varied in every way imaginable, each as unique as a snowflake. Together they had created their own little snowstorm.

I looked back at Cindy with Kara on her lap then from left to right to the Gods I had given my faith and prayers to. I had stopped eating and was trying to wrap my mind around who was sitting at the same table with me and I couldn't help myself as a shit eating grin spread across my face.

There was Tyr his dirty blonde hair and beard danced as he points over the table at Bragi with his right forearm the golden stump gleaming from the afternoon sun. His leathers and armor where brand new except for his cape which was ripped, tattered and stained red with blood.

Next to him, Njord and Skadi talks to Frigga. Njord armor looked like it was made of living crustaceans. The dreadlocks of his long hair and beard framed his face like a lion's mane of dark brown and red. The shells and beads that was woven through his dreadlocks constantly clicked when he moved. Skadi's cloak shifted on her shoulders as they talked, the solid white fur sparkled silver like fresh snow.

Frigga fights off her husband's wandering hands as she tries to listen. She finally takes Odin's hand in hers, locking it in a vice grip.

Odin looks from Frigga turning to watch his son Thor and my son Nathan getting ready to arm wrestle across the table.

"Remember this boy," Odin says to Nathan, "Strength does not always win battles."

Heimdall who'd been sitting between Nathan and the teenage girls put his hand over Thor's and Nathan's to get ready to start.

KISS Boom

As soon as Heimdall's hand twitched. Lady Sif sits in Thor's lap giving him a big kiss and Nathan pushes Thor's arm to the table with ease.

"Poetic," Bragi starts to laugh elbowing his wife Idun, playfully into Cindy, which knocked her and Kara into me.

And with that it felt like we were all family.

Heimdall

Heimdall called the shining god and whitest skinned of the Aesir gods. His dwelling is called Himinbjörg which sits at the top of Bifröst, the rainbow bridge that leads to Asgard.

He requires less sleep than a bird. His eyesight is so keen that he can see for hundreds of miles by day or by night. His hearing is so acute that he can hear grass growing on the ground and wool growing on sheep. Here he watches and listens, holding at the ready the horn Gjallarhorn, a resounding Horn, which he sounds when intruders are approaching.

During Ragnarok, the gods know that their doom is at hand when they hear the dire call of Gjallarhorn signaling the imminent arrival of the giants, who cross the rainbow bridge to storm Asgard and kill the gods.

The disloyal Loki, the particular nemesis of the unwaveringly dutiful Heimdall, is with them.

Loki and Heimdall slay each other as the world burns and they sink into the sea.

Angus, Minotaur of Minoa

Chapter 8

Heimdall set the huge keg of mead down and wipes his mouth, "You have always surprised us," he said to me off hand.

I turned to him, "What?"

He pushed off me playfully, but his 7'1" frame made me go sideways. Taking a couple of steps to get my balance I watched the light shimmer off the gold runes embroidery on his green Jedi Robes. His shoulder length bright blonde hair also shimmering with the gold beads that were braided in his locks. Then the light catches his intricately designed blue tattoos that started at his knuckles on both his arms then disappears under his royal tunic and reappears on his neck to crawl up his cheeks.

He stroked his forked blonde beard. Has he stepped into the open field I waited for something dramatic and nothing. I waited looking down at my kids and my wife. Cindy just shrugged. He bowed, I swear he broke out in a Riverdance, clapping and spinning in circles. All of our mouths hit the ground.

Heimdall stops with the most terrifying grin and started to laugh uncontrollably, pointing at us, "Your faces," grabbing for his stomach laughing deeply.

I looked at Thor and in unison we started to laugh.

Heimdall stops us, “Wait I got this.” And pulled his pants legs up his calf. He clicked his heels together three times. Again, three times...

“Fuck we're not in Asgard, this is facken OZ!” I explained to no one in particular.

“No, not that one,” Heimdall held up one finger in a great fan fair, “Opensaysme…”

And I facken lost control. The laugh hurt when it erupted from me. Heimdall crossed his arms and bobbed his head blinking his eyes hard. I started to cry when he twitched his nose.

“Facken Bewitched... stop,” I coughed out between laughter.

He stumbled over to the keg and sat on it. For a second, he just sat there, his hands on his lap and his chest moved up and down slowly. He lifted his head breathing deeply. His body relaxed bringing his head down with the exhale of his breath.

With a whoosh the air blows hard and mist fills the air. Heimdall opens his eyes slowly and the rainbow bridge descends from the sky.

He stands, his hands outstretched palms up. The mist starts to become a light rain that starts pooling in the palms of his hands. His hands fill with water until it spills out between his fingers like miniature waterfalls. In time with the descending bridge he kneels. His palms still up are filled with small lakes turning his hands over for the water to pour on the ground.

Crack BOOM WHISSSHH WHISSST WHISSSSP WHISSSHH WHISSST WHISSSSP

The rainbow bridge flows over the ground at that precise time. Heimdall standing gestures towards our way home. Nathan without a sound runs ahead and disappearing in spray of colors. Alex looking at me for permission I nod in the direction of rainbow, she takes off at a sprint. Cindy with Kara in her arms walks to the waterfall of colors Kara giggles when the cold rush of colors washes over them.

I turned to Heimdall, “It's been a pleasure” grasping his forearm.

“It has!” he replies.

Turning to Thor to say my goodbyes to the giant of a man and instead I watch his huge frame vanishing into the rainbow bridge. Looking back at Heimdall he shrugged and I returned the gesture.

WHISSSHH WHISSST WHISSSSP WHISSSHH WHISSST WHISSSSP

I walked out the rainbow bridge into my front yard. Liz stood surrounded by the kids, super excited they talked all at one time. She just grabbed them in a huge hug, kissing them each all over their faces.

Kara cried out, “Ick… Auntie Liz.”

The rainbow bridge fades away as I looked at the ground where it had been. My yard was covered in sparkling multicolored Easter eggs. All the rocks where now perfectly round gleaming in the sunshine. The rest of the grass and plants in my yard that the watercolors of the rainbow bridge flowed over didn't seem to have been affected.

Cindy went straight into the house I knew she was going to call her Mom. Thor followed Cindy into the house ducking his head as he did, I shook my head in disbelief.

To distract the verbal assault on Liz I lifted up one of the brightly colored river stones rubbing my fingers against the rock expecting the colors to come off onto my fingers. It didn't, the stone was perfectly smooth and round.

“Oi!” tossing the rather heavy rock up in the air, I called out.

Looking at all the colors of stone as it lands back in my hand. The three of them came over to find out what I was doing, Liz following after. The kids noticed the rainbow stones and started inspecting them.

Talking to Liz, to bring her up to speed with the storm and fighting Frost Giants, until I drop the rainbow stone I played with it cracking it. I picked it back up and like an outer shell flaked off, some of the rainbow colors of the stone broke away revealing…

"Holy, facken, shit Batman!" I proclaimed.

Liz took the stone, "Holy. Fucking. Shit. Batman!" repeating my words.

I looked at her, "ah..."

She was already moving, "We need baskets." calling out to my oldest, "Alex, we have a mission!"

Alex took off after her Aunt, "Mission?"

I looked at the solid gold stone in my hand and remember Thor. I found him sitting on my couch brooding. I went to riddle him with questions.

He abruptly stood, "You have already broken your oath."

Starting for the door I did the only thing you do to a 7'10" man, I throw the gold stone at the back of his head. He stopped as the sky darkened outside.

He spoke, "You dare?"

My son had just come in the house curious. I took the rainbow stone from his hand. Thor turned to me, lightning arched from his eyes and another rainbow stone shattered against his face.

"Yeah man," the gold stone rolls across the ground with my answer.

Lighting flashing and the thunder rolled, Cindy got off the couch and told her mother "bye", while hanging up her cellphone. She picked up Kara telling her, "Let's go see what is going on in the other room."

Liz chose that time to walk in with Alex, her hands full of old Easter baskets and then vanished out the garage. She came back in the kitchen and looked at Thor standing in living room, "Do you mind? Rain… hello. Come on Nathan." She tugged on him.

Thor and I just stared at each other.

"It's still raining!" Liz's voice called out from the garage...

Thor's eyes blinked and the arcs of electricity slows.

"Thanks!" Liz yells.

Thor with clenched teeth says, "You test Odin's son's wra…"

The last rainbow stone I had got from Nathan hit him in the balls. He, of course, fell to the ground clutching his manhood. Not saying a thing, I fell into my couch, grabbing the remote control for the TV on the way down. With a click the huge flat screen came to life. Thor crawled up onto the couch, still holding onto his junk. For a second I thought he was going to throw up but he held it in.

He leaned back gingerly, "You are?" and pauses, searching for the right word.

Liz poked her head in, "Asshole, the word you're looking for is ASSHOLE," and then again disappearing.

I called back, "Hate you!"

Thor closed his eyes swallowing hard, "Yes, Asshole!"

"Well you had your pussy all hurt because I told Liz," I said in response.

He sat up fast, dizziness washed over him and in regret he sat back, "I do not like this," he squirmed.

"What, part," I asked, "Getting hit in the balls or the whole magic secret thing?"

"Little bit of both I think," Thor rumbled his reply. "It is big picture," he finished.

"The TV," I said knowing that he was not referring to the television.

He shoved me in a friendly way, "No, why do you jest?"

I laughed picking myself off the floor to get back on the couch, "So you going to tell me or what…?"

"I cannot," his head hung lower as he said it.

"No matter the crime or atrocity committed, you are now part of my pack. Things that can't be spoken will not be, for you are bound by oath that you cannot repeat, I will honor your oath. For you are family and welcome to stay as long as you wish under my protection," Without reason words came spilling out my mouth.

His eyes lighting up literally, "That is truth," he said.

"Yeah, look I'm going to take a shower where I don't have to worry about flying salamanders biting me," I got to my feet.

"Sprites," Thor said.

I froze in understanding, "So if I have encountered something personally then you can tell me, that's the catch 22 of the oath," I looked back at him.

He picked up one of the gold stones, "They translated it wrong," looking at the stone, "It's not a pot of gold at the end of the rainbow, its stones of gold."

"I figured that out on my own, Thor," as I headed towards the bathroom.

"The Faé would not give up their own gold even if captured. A leprechaun was captured in an open field with no trees to escape through. He called the rainbow bridge. He wiggled free and darts into the bridge," Thor stood and places the gold stone on the coffee table, heads towards the front door.

"And the men saw the stones of gold at the end of the rainbow," I said to his back as he stepped out the front door.

SSSSHHHHHHHHHH drip..drop SSSSHHHHHHHHHH drip..drop drip..drop SSSSHHHHHHHHHH

The hot water felt amazing as it ran down my body. I couldn't think, it was so hard to focus on one thing, so many things had happened. So, I didn't, I let it all flow at once like the shower water that was running down the drain. In a blink I rewind and fast forwarded the events of the last few days. Putting mental sticky notes of coordinated facts I have knowledge of. Spinning a web of overlapping myths and facts.

BOOM

I was interrupted with a crash that vibrated through the house. Running out in my towel, sliding to the front door.

“Everyone ok?” and started to count kids,”1, 2...3 “.

BOOM

Cindy walked up next to me handing me a glass of sweet tea.

“He asked me if he could move some stuff around in the yard,” my wife tells me.

BOOM

Thor with a huge rock propped over his shoulder walks across the front yard. He places the third huge monolith of solid stone on the ground shifting it back and forth to get it standing upright. With a grunt he shoved it deep into the ground. Thor wipes his hands off in the grass and walks off into the woods. I look at the three Stonehenge size rocks pointing at each one.

“East, South, West. Next one will be over there!” I said pointing to North.

Thor sounds like a herd of elephants when he stomps into the yard from the North. Over his shoulder the biggest by far off the four stones. With a great effort he holds the stone straight up in the air for just a breath. Thunder crashed as he piledrives it into the ground. He pulled what looked like a chisel he had tucked in the back of his belt. Pressing the end of the chisel against the stone he raised his arm Milnor flying to it.

Ting, Ta...ting ting

Gently Thor tapped away, little flakes exploding from the rock face.

Liz puts a plastic lawn chair down in the center of the yard sitting, “Standing stones.”

I rebut with, “You got Standing Stones from that Scottish show you’re watching. What’s it called, Outlander? No I think he's making ward stones of some type.”

Cindy now with her own plastic lawn chair sits down. “Wards from what?” she asks me while she starts rubbing my naked leg.

I remembered I had just a towel on, “From ourselves,” I answered as I made my way back in the house the sun hanging low in the sky.

Liz yells out, “You know you have to work tomorrow!”

Of course, I reply to her, “Hate you!”

She smiled and signed “Fuck you, dinosaur!” at me.

With that I fell asleep to the rhythmic sounds of Thor's hammer and dreamed of magic.

Ting, Ta..ting ting, Ting, Ta..ting ting, Ting, Ta..ting ting, Ting, Ta..ting ting.

Ward Stones, Lodestone and Rune-stone

A ward stone is a minor artifact, a magical item of incredible power, generally beyond the ability of mortals to create. It is a spell inscribed with runes which wards against all kinds of magic. Its power must be maintained by regular prayers and rituals. The ward stones can be infused with many different types of magic to ensure its effectiveness. However, these obelisks of rocks must be continuously maintained with magics and protected from attack. The ward stones also prevent any form of teleportation magic from functioning across the borders, whether from an invading enemy or otherwise, but does not hinder such magic from functioning normally after permission has been granted.

A lodestone is a naturally magnetized piece of the mineral magnetite. They are naturally occurring magnets, which can attract iron. The property of magnetism was first discovered in antiquity. Throughout history, lodestones have helped sailors cross the oceans and blacksmiths to test if steel was tempered. Pieces of lodestone, suspended so they could turn, were the first magnetic compasses. Their importance to early navigation is indicated by the name lodestone, which in Middle English means coarse stone or leading stone. Lodestone is one of the few minerals that is found naturally magnetized. Magnetite is black or brownish-black, with a metallic luster and a black streak. A lodestone enchanted with magic can be used in a compass to navigate in a variety of ways.

A rune-stone is typically a raised stone or rock monolith with a runic inscription, but the term can also be applied to inscriptions on boulders and on bedrock. The tradition began in Asgard and spans the 9 realms. Most rune-stones are located in Asgard and Midgard, but there are also scattered rune-stones in locations that were visited by Aesir during the Viking Age. Rune-stones are marks of navigation and gives the Aesir an anchor to Midgard. They also can be used to contact or summon the Aesir. Rune-stones were usually brightly colored when erected, though this is no longer evident as the color has worn off. Rune-stones are found in present day on every corner of the 9 Realms.

Angus, Minotaur of Minoa

Chapter 9

Beep Beep Beep Beep Beep Beep

I always take a few days of vacation after Dragon Con from work to recover, this year was no exception, and I was so glad I did. At 4am my alarm went off. Liz was passed out in my office, she stayed over to help take kids to school. Down to one car, I have to take my wife's car to work, not having Honey Bear to use.

I drive a stand-up forklift for a living, not fabulous or glamorous but it pays for the cosplay. For a few years now, I have hidden from the violence that follows me as an Inventory Clerk. I made my way as quiet as I could through the office to my dojo and hall of armor. A huge room in the back of the office, I should say man-cave. The office is covered in geek related collectables, comic books first appearances, movie posters, signed by the entire cast, hang on the walls and enough toys to make a toy store jealous.

VWORP tick tick VWORP bbuuzz

I push back the secret door, the bottom of the back-wall bookshelf and the lights automatically turned on. I stepped in the center of the room. I turned to the North and bow, then did an about face to the South bowing again, repeating to East and West. I lit the incense in front of a framed picture of the Celtic tree. I kneel down on one knee, my right arm bent behind my back the other bent at a right angle in front of me.

"To all my Gods, above and below, may my faith strengthen you." I named off the four pantheons that share my faith equally. I finished my prayer with "Manannan mac Lir with you my spark, mine soul, will sail. Morrigan, the battle crow, my destiny awaits your embrace."

I looked up at the clock and stood. I centered myself with a breath beginning my morning Kata. After an intense workout I went to jump in the shower and found my backpack, sitting on the sink. My little sister's rocks, I shuffled around in the bag, my wallet came out first, then my cell phone, and last I pulled my extra pair of glasses out of the bag and smiled. *Don't need those anymore.* Liz must have had it cause of the other Dragon Con stuff in it.

Putting my glasses on the counter, I thought out loud, "I wonder where else those vicious little sprites bit me at?" My body shivering at the thought.

On the way to work my phone finally had enough of a charge to turn itself on. It chimed over and over trying to catch up to the missed calls and texts. As I pulled in the parking lot of DSC Logistics it finally shut up. I scrolled through the text messages first.

I found Tasi's messages and opened it, a few 100 pictures he took during Dragon Con trying to load. I scrolled down pass all that until I got the last message.

"Liz told me about the tornado.... Hit me up after you get back from Oz," Tasi wrote.

I smiled and texted him back right before I clocked into work, "Not Oz, Asgard."

I went to my desk and logged into my computer. I printed out my dock sweep and got to work. After I isolated all the inbound errors, pulled all the rechecks and finally got all the research finalized two hours had past. I was heading back to the office to email my results, when my lift RF unit pinged

"...Dano come to the office…" the message read on the screen.

I walked up to Ms. Danny, "What's up?"

She ducked her head down and whispered, “Two Atlanta Detectives are in Jerrod’s office.”

I tilted my head like Scooby Doo my inner voice, “Ah, ooh Shaggy...”

Jerrod spoke from his office, “Dano!”

I answered, “Yeah man.” And stepped into his office.

Both officers stood, one with his hand already extend in a handshake he pronounced my full name in a question.

His hand waited as I took it, “Yeah man.”

The first silver bracelet locked once over my wrist and he spoke, “You are...”

Yank snag Click Smack

Before the handcuffs click again I moved stepping in then out, my hand slipped from the cuff. I grabbed the cuffs darting to the other officer locking his left wrist tightly. The first cop twisting to stop me, I punch him in the elbow twisting back. On reflex he grabbed his elbow one of my master's rules came to mind, *every strike a block and every block a strike*. His arm cradles close to him, his wrist now exactly where I wanted it.

Click Swoosh Flop Flop Flop

I dropped low and locked the other handcuff around his wrist. I reached out behind me has I took out the cops knee, his arm stuck between his legs. He and his partner flip to the office floor tangled in a human knot.

“I'm sorry, shit… you should have said you're under arrest or something.” I looked at the awkward position the two offers were in. If I wasn't going to jail before I am now. I stepped over them, “Whenever you two get done I'll be outside having a smoke.”

Before I could light my second cigarette three cop cars, lights and sirens on, pull into the parking lot followed by an unmarked car.

I called to the officers as they got out their patrol cars, "They're in the main office, glass door."

They all took off at a run except for the plain clothed officer. She walked over just as I lit my cigarette.

"You know they are going to be pissed when they realize," she informs me pulling her handcuffs out.

I looked at her with a long drag and smiled and held my wrist out to her. She attached the handcuffs as I smoked my cigarettes. The cops race back to me guns drawn.

"On the ground… on the ground." The lady cop and I just sat there. One of the detectives points his gun at me, "On the fucken ground," they screamed.

"Lieutenant," the lady spoke.

Like they had noticed her for the first time both detectives, "Captain Harris."

"I remember telling you to ask this man to come to the station at his earliest convenience," she looks at them waiting for their answers.

"He assaulted an officer!" And went to grab me.

I looked at her she shook her head with confirmation, then smiled and shrugged. I waited till his hand was over the center of my cuff. I pulled him over the concrete table, spinning up to stand. I spun Lt. Flipped to land on his back stretched over the table. I put my hands up over my head, folding my fingers behind my head.

The captain laughed at him and a few of the other cops chuckled. She stepped behind and started to unlock my cuffs. I waited for her to put them behind my back.

Instead she handed me her card, "Dano, if you wouldn't mind, at your earliest convenience," she looks at the detectives, "We have a couple of questions about your Van. Some inconsistency that need to be answered."

I stood way too fast all the guns came to bare on me again, “You have Honey bear?” I hooked my thumb towards the two detectives, “Y'all should have lead with that let's go.”

Starting towards the parking lot and pulling my keys off my belt loop. Passing the other cops still pointing guns at me.

“Freeze!” They all said.

“So, I'm under arrest again?” I clenched my jaw and stopped.

“Captain!” one of the cops says her name as a question.

Her voice called to all of them, “Tell you what, if any of you can put him in the backseat of a patrol car, be my guest.”

Like a challenge the two detectives circles me each taken their guns off putting them to the side. They nod to the other cops, 4 of them took off their utility belts. Each one had a pair of handcuffs in one of their hands. Six against one haven't had those kinds of odds since I worked that P Diddy's White party a lifetime ago.

“Ma'am?” I went to parade rest, “Permission to defend myself?” I asked the Captain.

I felt the half smile creep onto my face as Lou started to appear in my hand, as if he knew, disappearing again just letting me know that I am not alone.

Captain Harris walked over to a patrol car and sat on the trunk next to other old-time cops her voice rang, “Granted!”

Each making small wagers on the outcome. I closed my eyes in a silent prayer to all my Gods I exhaled. I tucked my keys into a pocket. Fighting cops, you need to only keep one thing in mind, all cops are top heavy. It is mandatory for all cops to wear body armor, just think cow tipping with style.

Another thing when dealing with more than one adversary, you must turn that advantage against them. Two on one, Twelve O’clock and Six O’clock.

Thud Whack BLAM

I took a step up onto the back of the first cop another step, my other foot landed on the second cop taking it in the shoulder. I leaped up pushing them towards the concrete and came down on both of them.

I opened my eyes after I had completed my summersault and I bounced to my feet in a sprint. Detective one lurched forward in a right hook.

Snag Woosh Wirl Thud CRASH

Grabbing his right wrist as it just missing my face. I ran passed him still holding his wrist. He spun in place and I kicked him into his partner. They both spilled onto the other fallen cops, they all crashed back to the parking lot. The kick left me open and the third cop fell right in my trap.

Thud SNAG SPIN WHIRL SMASH

His boot hit center of my chest with my right leg still extended. I caught his foot and looked at him when he went to draw it back, an Oh shit look appears on his face. I kicked off and spin rolled sending the cop in the air to land on the other side of me. I elbowed him in the balls. I sprung to a crouched position... searching for my next target.

"Nope I'm good," the last cop waves me off.

"Captain Harris how you know," one of the older cops asked as the young Captain took her winnings.

"1995", she began, "my older brothers were working security at 112 a 24-hour nightclub in Downtown Atlanta and got in way over their heads."

She was interrupted, "The twins?" the cop next to her held his hand as high as he could over his head.

She nodded, the other cops where now on their feet, while I took a smoke out. "He didn't have tattoos back then," she said I inhale the nicotine into my lungs. "My brothers were in the back parking lot of the club dealing with a problem, when they were jumped. Forced to their knees, guns point blank. They had my brother's dead to rights."

She looked at me, “Saved their lives, put twelve men in the hospital,” pausing, “three more in the morgue. He asked my brothers if they were okay and just walked away. Dano, you can just follow me to the station.” She calls to me.

I didn't realize I was in parade rest I hit my cigarette and nodding to her walking to my wife's Jeep.

“He would do unimaginable things for his people. They would say when my father would ask them at breakfast,” the Captain ended her story.

Pulling into the police station I hung up my cell phone and parked the Jeep a few spaces away from Captain Harris's car.

She pointed to the garage when I was getting out of the Jeep, “Take the elevator down to level 3 and detectives…”

I was already walking to the garage before she said level 3 so whatever the Harris brother's little sister said I couldn't make out.

Honey bear, blood spray paints two different patterns of impact. All the windows blown out, burn marks arch all over the van. Next to the van was Lou’s Honda Civic the tree trunk stump protrudes from the hood. The question started.

“You want to explain,” one of the detectives spoke pointing to the crushed trunk of the Honda. It covered in the dark sludge of Lou's blood.

“Attorney,” with my single word the two detectives lost their shit.

“You're not under arrest so you don't need a lawyer,” one of them yelled.

The other took his cue, “Just a few routine questions.”

Turning to leave, they both hurriedly stepped out into my path. I put my hands behind my back my feet shoulder width apart, “You’re going to cuff me or I'm walking out of this garage. Either way you'll still be left with questions.”

They stepped aside without removing my hands from behind my back as I passed between them walking to the stairs.

DING

The elevator opens from across the garage and Capt. Harris emerges.

“Ma'am, when you're done with Honey bear,” I stopped at the exit door, “please… contact me,” the door closed behind me before she could answer. I raced up the stairs cellphone already in my hand I called Cindy. I started the Jeep, orders given, I hung up the phone. Liz was already on the way to check out the kids from school as I pulled out the police station.

Glamour

Glamour refers to a magical spell, an illusion said to create a more attractive appearance. Gradually became known as a glamour. Most magical beings and supernatural creatures have some sort of Glamour magic and have no need for a magical item. After the Accords, Glamour became Law and all supernatural beings must be glamoured in front of the mundane.

Ironniesous O'Keeffe

Chapter 10

"Family meeting," I called out right when I walked in. I am very up front with my kids, "The police are very interested in what happened during the storm and where we've been for the last few days."

Alex spoke first, "If you have anything to ask me, see my Dad."

Nathan spoke over her in a deep voice, "Your Daddy said it was okay to talk to us."

Alex with her phone already in hand, "Well, let's call him."

"Outstanding," I smiled.

"Can I bake a cake?" We turn to Alex all at once.

I and Cindy look at each other.

Liz starts to do her happy dance, "caaaaaaaaaake," she sang.

I rolled my eyes at Liz. Her antics causing a chain reaction, each kid one by one starts to copy her… "Cake, cake," they sang and danced.

Cindy and I say together, “Let them eat cake,” as we raise our arms high.

They all cry, “CAKE!” and marched to the kitchen.

Kara looks up at me before joining the others, “With frosting, Daddy, cake is not cake without frosting.”

“Of course, with frosting,” I kissed her forehead.

She dances off, “cake, cake…”

I look around puzzled. “Where's Thor,” I asked thin air.

“Out of frosting,” Liz's voice came from the kitchen.

I grab my keys heading for the door, “Babe, let's go.” Cindy grabs her purse and I meet her at the door, “Liz.”

She looks up over the couch next to Nathan.

“Watch the kids,” I tell her.

She looks at me, “Where's Thor?”

“I asked you that,” shaking my head.

I closed the door to open it right back, “Alex.”

Alex calls out, “Don't let Auntie Liz burn down the house.”

I smile at Liz.

She rolls her eyes at me, “Asshole.”

I managed to close the door exactly when the couch pillow hit.

While at Food Depot I confide in my wife.

“I'm telling you the storm changed us…,” and she doesn't hear a word I say. We walk down one aisle and then to the next.

Cindy stops and I run the cart into her. “The storm you said,” backing towards me pushing the cart to one side.

"Babe?" I asked her.

And her hand touched my arm. The super old lady in one of those handicapped scooters slowly made her way towards us vanishing, replaced by a wrinkled old troll. I flinched my arm away and the old lady was back. She touched me again as the old lady passed by and the lady blurred just for a second then focused to her true form. The old troll lady smiled horribly at us.

I dipped my hat, "Ma'am."

Her scooter finally rounds to the next aisle.

"What the fuck?" my wife exclaimed.

I hugged her.

She looked up at me, "You sounded like one of those comic books you read."

Shrugging my reply, "I didn't think you were listening."

At the register Cindy grabbed my hand in a death grip while I was unloading the cart. Pulling me towards her my fingers screaming in pain.

"What what what?" I pleaded.

I looked at my wife then to the cashier who just a minute ago was a pimply faced Korean kid. Now the only thing the cashier had in common was the pimples. A frog like humanoid the same height as the boy was ringing us up. I put my arm around Cindy not letting go of her hand and proceed unloading the cart one handed. I noticed a steak in his back pocket.

Before I could stop myself, "Is that a steak in your pocket, or you just really happy…to see me."

The frog-boy blushed, "What…"

"Dude you have a raw steak hanging out your back pocket," I pointed as I said this, "I couldn't resist."

He reached back and held it out, the pocket lint and hair noticeable, “It's my lunch,” his tongue wiping out licking his eye. Then jammed it back in his pocket, not getting the joke at all.

Later that evening after dinner Alex and Liz are back in the kitchen pulling stuff out of cupboards. More noise than a Lynyrd Skynyrd concert comes from kitchen. Baking a cake in my house is a very loud endeavor. I sat in my geek cave listening to the Dresden files on Audible. Just about to light up the pipe Odin himself gave me when Cindy and Liz started screaming for me to come in the kitchen. The tone of their voices said someone had just cut off a finger. I see Alex floating a foot off the ground, finger painting the kitchen wall with chocolate cake batter.

Cindy went to our oldest daughter, reaching for her, “Alex my love child,” she said softly.

Alex blinked, “Mom.”

Like a balloon popped, she fell out of the air and I had her in my arms before her toes touched the tile floor. I carried her to her room laying her on the bed, noticing she was sound asleep.

I pulled the blankets up over her, “Rest, love you.”

She whispered to me rolling over, “Love you more.”

I walked back into the kitchen. Liz had bright yellow sticky notes stuck all over the mural of cake batter. She looked at me like she was doing something wrong, I read the nearest yellow note out loud.

“Hercules, Greek Demigod,” an arrow pointing out to a dead warrior dressed more like a character from the movie 300 but with a lion's pelt for the cape. The finger painting was so detailed I could see Hercules's eyes rolled back in his head behind the dented helmet. Liz continued each of the fallen gods from mythology had a yellow sticky note. By the time she was done some had multiple notes.

We just stood in front of the mural for a while saying nothing.

Breaking the silence, “History major,” she said shrugging her shoulders.

I answered shaken my head, “OCD.”

The Indian stands in the middle of a battlefield the only one not with a sticky note. Bodies of God's from every pantheon lay dead or dying around him. Liz pointed, “He's definitely Native American.”

I took a sticky note from Liz scribbled on it then stuck it to the wall with LOU right next to the Indian’s head…

Scribble scribble THUD

BADGUY??? The yellow sticky note said.

I don't know how many hours went by studying the mural reading those sticky notes over and over. I was still sitting at the kitchen table smoking Odin’s pipe, the cherry glowing red hot when my wife walked in rubbing the sleep out of her eyes.

“You work in few hours,” and kissed my head. Shuffling to the fridge, “What's your plan,” she asked me.

I hit Odin's pipe still lost in thought. She closed the fridge and came over rubbing my back. Looking at Lou stuck in the mural, blowing out smoke I answered her.

“Kill him,” I gritted my teeth.

Frog Folk

A typical frog folk stands 2 to 3½ feet tall and weighs approximately 30-70 lbs., although the very old and particularly powerful hunters might stand and weigh twice that. A Frog folk head and body appear similar to those of a giant frog, but its hands and feet look humanlike. Frog folk skin color varies dramatically depending on their environment, ranging from the brown-splotched green of swamp grippli to vibrant blues, yellows, and reds of rain forest-dwelling tribes. Frog Folk rarely wear clothing.

They don't have Glamour of their own so must require an enchanted item to go out in the Mundane. They usually climb the nearest tree and hide upon spotting other humanoids or any other creature deemed dangerous. To be accepted among them is difficult but once you have befriended one, they are very loyal.

Light-hearted and cheerful, they value familial bonds and the simple pleasures of food, games, rest, and shiny objects from the outside world.

Other humanoids sometimes perceive relaxed frog folk as blasé, even lazy, but a relaxed frog folk might snap to full alertness at a moment's notice.

A Bullywug looks more like a toad than any of the other subspecies. They are much more vicious. Their skin color is usually brown, black, or green. They will attack and eat intruders in their territory.

Angus, Minotaur of Minoa

Chapter 11

I woke up to my cell phone alarm, I lifted my head off the kitchen table. *Shit*, I had fallen asleep in the kitchen. Stretching, my bones and joints groan in protest at the sleep commendations. I looked at the mural as I was shooting it the bird. I headed to the shower to get ready for work. When I pass the mural, Lou disappearing and the little yellow sticky note floats to the floor.

You ever have one of those days when you knew you should have called in sick, yup I'm having one of those days. Work has pulled me in seven different directions, but my brain keeps rewinding the last couple of days. I wait as long as I can calling Cindy around 9:45 am.

She answered after what felt like forever, "She's fine, she crawled in our bed after you went to work and went right back to sleep."

"So, you kept them all home from school then." I was asking but already knew the answer.

Cindy, "I thought that's what you want me to do."

"I did babe, go back to sleep," and a hung up instead of getting back to work I went outside to have a cigarette.

I find the two detectives looking through the windows of my wife's Jeep. Man, if these two keep showing up I really need to learn their names, so I lit my smoke as I walked over.

“It's unlocked,” I said.

They both put their hands on the butt of their weapons turning, word of advice you should never scare someone that you know that has a loaded gun.

They both said, “We could have shot you!”

I noticed that they don't take their hands off their guns though. These guys are super nervous.

“So, who speaks first?” I grin a half grin because Star War does that to me.

But before they can answer my question my cell phone interrupts. Looking down at my cell phone caller ID I see it’s my wife. I hold up my index finger in the universal *belay that* to the Officers.

Answering my phone, “Yeah babe.”

Cindy in a blur of information, “Flying horse, armored lady and she said only you can accept it, or something like that.”

“I have a package. Okay babe, yep...” hanging up the phone on her.

Detective Starfish, “Flying horse?”

I went from smiles to stone ass cold, “What do you want?”

His partner Detective SpongeBob actually had something to say worth hearing, “Your Van has been released from impound.”

I waited for him to finish but detective Starfish pulled a card from his pocket thrusting it in my direction.

Now Detective SpongeBob finished, “Give it to the on-duty officer.”

Without looking at the card I tucked it away. My phone chimed, glancing at the screen, a text message.

"I want a flying horse..." from Liz.

I texted, "NO..."

In the middle of pushing send I was already headed back towards the building.

"Something strange going on," SpongeBob commented to Starfish.

Having to take another disciplinary point from my LM for leaving early, damnit wishing Jerrod my GM was here. Two days in a row I've bailed, oh well. Standing in my LM office while he bitched that I went on vacation came back and the police …. So… yeah I tuned him out…

Holding up my hand, "I came in here to inform you, not for your permission." and exited his office.

Walking by Ms. Danny's desk she stopped me, "What's going on?"

I winked at her, "Taken the day off, Darling."

"He's still pissed about yesterday," she added.

I nodded to her, "He might actually have ta do something besides sit on his ass."

As I head out I turned to the rest of the ladies of the office, "Ladies," bowing slightly, "Till tomorrow."

"Bye Dano," they all call back.

Winged Horses

Winged stallions have been ridden by many Gods from around the globe. The ancient Pegasus is a mythological winged horse. The Valkyrie ride winged horses from Asgard to choose souls among the slain in battle to go with them to Valhalla. Al-Buraq is a steed who carried Prophet Muhammad. Tianma was a winged 'celestial' horse in Chinese folklore. A Chollima is a mythical winged horse which originates from the Chinese classics. In Islamic tradition, Haizum is the horse of the archangel Gabriel. Tulpar is a winged or swift horse in Turkic mythology. Haizum, a heavenly winged horse, ridden by Gabriel according to Islamic tradition. Ponkhiraj, a flying horse from Bangladesh. A wind Horse in Mongolian, Tibetan and ancient Turkish traditions.

Angus, Minotaur of Minoa

Chapter 12

Pulling in the driveway, you would turn around thinking you're lost before you got to my house. It actually happens all the time. My house sits on a community road, four other homes share my driveway. Our house is the last on the driveway, considering the thick woods my home is well hidden. After passing the other houses and a dense patch of forest, it clears.

My house is what you would call a fixer upper with great bones. It has five bedrooms with three full baths. From the two-car garage all the way around the additional office and sunroom to the backyard it has a wraparound deck. Built in the 70's the wood siding is old cedarwood planks and sits on a river stone foundation.

I didn't see anything out of place. Until I saw more rainbow stones in the side yard. Parking the Jeep, I hopped out. I heard giggles first Kara and... Alex, so happy.

Swoosh flap flap ha ha ha ha SWOOPING flap flap flap flap

The gust of wind was sudden and silent whooshing just over my head. Hooves pass inches from my face. The horse neighed in joy my two daughters joined the flying horse in laughing. After having a facken heart attack I started to laugh. The horse hovering, a blonde Wonder Woman sitting in the saddle, her left arm wrapped around

Kara in the front of her and Alex with her behind she pulled the reins with her right. The all white stallion lands with a clip clop on the driveway. Tucking its huge wings back and shook its head more like a bird.

Xena spoke, "Dano, Son of the Golden Rays of Dawn. Are you ready to receive?" My brain took a break as I watched the horse trot into the grass. "Then we shall continue," her tongue clicked and the horse was airborne.

SWOOSH flap flap flap SWOOSH

I watched lost in my children's laughter.

"I want one." Came from the right.

"No, Liz you can't have a Pegasus," still looking at the acrobatic flying of the Valkyrie.

I find my wife sitting on the front porch drinking a beer, "Hey babe," kissing her forehead.

I dropped into the plastic lawn chair next to her. She handed me two things at one time, in one hand my kryptonite, ice cold sweet tea the other Odin's pipe.

"I love you," looking at her.

"I know," my wife eyes twinkling, did I mention my thing for Star Wars.

Nathan comes out and sits on the steps of the porch with some type of handheld game in his hand. "Dad, Kara did something to my game." Nathan said not looking from the game.

"I don't think she meant to, sorry kiddo," I tried to apologize for whatever his little sister did.

He paused it, actually pausing the game, if you have a gamer kid you know how monumental that is.

"No, I found her playing it this morning," holding the game up, "She just gave it back and everything is unlocked," scrolling down the menu of the game, “Everything.” He sat back down on the steps and got back to what he was doing.

Liz came out the house, “I want one.”

As the horse lands in the front yard. The horse dips it's ass down and Alex slid down. Kara giggles when she slipped off the horse, before the warrior could react the horse’s wings was under the 5-year-old and she was very softly placed on the ground. Xena took off her winged helmet and dismounted the stallion. She stood next to her winged war horse with the helmet under her arm.

“I want one,” I said.

Cindy and Liz in stereo, “Which one?” looking at me for an answer.

“Yep,” is all I could manage. Taking a huge puff from the Odin's pipe.

“Dano, son of the Crow and the Golden Rays of the Dawn, are you ready to receive?” she called from the yard.

I blew out a cloud of smoke, choking out my response, “Yeah man.”

She meets me in the center of the yard.

“Kneel,” she commanded.

I kneel before Zod, the exact same way I pray to my Gods every morning. I looked up to see Huginn and Muninn landing nearby I send them mental nod.

“You kneel before me in the witness of Huginn and Muninn,” she began.

Then bent down mimicking me exactly. Her head bowing, lowering than mine then our eyes locked,

“I, Lady Rain, daughter of Tyr kneels before you in the witness of Odin the Allfather. I pledge my sword to you and yours for my Grandfather's life twice over,” She stood.

I did not move as she placed her helmet back over her head. She reached behind her returning forward with what looked like a hand carved foot locker, a trunk, a medium sized hand carved facken treasure chest. She placed it down on the ground in front of me.

Huginn and Muninn both cry, "CAW CAW CAW CAW."

Just with my eyes telling them I know this is a big deal.

Looking down at me, "You, Dano son of the Crow and the Golden Rays of the Dawn accept this box of holding?"

Putting a hand on each side of the box lifting it off the ground but without standing.

"I, Dano, son of the Crow and the Golden Rays of the Dawn accepts this gift," dipping my head.

She mounted her war horse as I started to stand with the chest. A fog rolled in while she sent the horse up in the air. A gentle mist fell around me.

SWOOSH flap flap flap WHISSSHH WHISSST WHISSSSP WHISSSHH WHISSST WHISSSSP

The mist is replaced by the rainbow bridge. She flew the stead in a high arch then back into the rainbow, sending a splash of rainbow out.

Liz, "Baskets?"

"Yeah," I answered her watching the rainbow bridge fade away. She volunteered the kids to help, "Side of the house too," I reminded her.

Her finger came poking out the door while I walked up the porch steps. I put the box of holding on the porch in front of the chair I was sitting in. Huginn and Muninn landing on the railing of the porch as I reached for the wooden chest.

"Liz will be pissed, if open that without her," Cindy informed me.

"CAW CAW," Muninn agreed with my wife.

I looked at Huginn, he looked at me then at Muninn. He turned to look out in the yard and flew over to Nathan and promptly stealing the rainbow stone he had in his hand. I sat back, propped my feet up on the chest. Muninn joining them in a game of keep away. I lit Odin's pipe, holding my wife's hand and watched the funniest shit ever.

Box of Holding

A box of holding is a vessel to store anything in a fold of dimension/space and re-materialize at will, not to be confused with Pocket Dimension. It is also called Bag of Holding or Bag of Tricks, Dimensional Capture/Release, Hammerspace, Malletspace, and a Magic Satchel.

The user can put items/beings into a separate dimension for safe keeping, and can summon them back with relative ease. The Box has different methods of pocketing and can organize itself accordingly. Some use a box, others use a satchel, some have even used a pocket in a jacket to create mini pocket dimension to hold infinite amounts of objects inside. Others can create a floating box or simply reach behind them and pull out the item wanted.

Ironniesous O'Keeffe

Chapter 13

Joining the cleanup of the yard. We, I should say I, finally finished late into the evening with two 50-gallon drums full of solid gold rainbow stones. I clamped the lids closed, beads of perspiration flowed down my face. Wiping the sweat from my brow with my wife beater. My two shadows cawed fluttering their massive wings inpatient with me so they got the sweat soaked tank top tossed at them. Muninn floated up with a small gesture of her wings the ball of wetness smacked Huginn in the tail feathers.

"CAW CAW CAW CAW," Huginn crying from the rafters of the basement garage.

We laughed, Muninn and I, while Huginn danced down to the garage floor.

"CAW CAW," he muttered.

I scowled at him, "Whatever, you tried to shit on me."

Muninn chuckled.

I reached up to close the garage door giving the crows the look. They flew out of the basement garage and I locked it. I washed up and made my way to my office, my Batcave.

The whole gang was ogling Odin's box when I walked in. It is 3' x 2' x 2' made of really old wood with intricate designs carved into every surface.

Huginn and Muninn cawed loudly making everyone jump back from the box as I walked into the room.

"Auntie Liz tried to open it," Nathan pointing at his aunt.

Liz gave him the look, "I can't believe you."

"Now that you're done throwing your aunt under the bus, it is time for bed," Cindy called into the office from the kitchen.

Alex, Nathan and Kara all took turns whining but they eventually got up.

"Night Daddy," each one said in turn and giving me kisses.

I waited until it was just Liz and I, with one eyebrow up, "Tried to open?"

Liz gave me her puppy face, "It's pretty," waving her hands at the mural covered box.

I walked over to retrieve Odin's pipe holding it to my lips and went to light the bowl looking at the box. The box had no lock or latches so why couldn't Liz open it?

"Did everyone try to open it?" I asked her.

Liz very slightly nodded her head up and down in an affirmative guilty smirk on her face.

The lid of the box had the tree Yggdrasil with Odin hung from the branches, noose tight around his neck. Looking at it the details of carving it started to move, animated. The leaves on tree of Yggdrasil blows in the wind as Odin's body sways back and forth.

I looked at Liz and she pointed at the lid, "You saw that then?"

She pulled out some Harry Potter reference that I have no idea what she was talking about. Each side of the box had a different mural beautifully carved. I touched, no ran my fingers across the entire box, like braille. The images all moved slightly with the story of the mural. I finally decided to open it, the lid popped open with a touch. Hidden hinges held the lid back, the front of it opened like a wardrobe. It was empty, no not empty, a blackness filled the box.

Liz giggles, “Well I am off to bed.”

I just stared at the utter nothingness speechless.

She casually said while leaving, “Empty box.”

“Because you broke it,” I replied, closing it back.

I looked at Huginn and Muninn, “Any idea why the all Father would give me an empty box?”

Sitting back in my chair I took a big hit from the pipe I just remembered I was holding.

“CAWWW,” Muninn scowled at me.

I pointed the pipe at the ornately carved box, “It's not empty? Were you asleep I just opened the magic box and nothing???”

“CAW,” they both said.

“It's a facken MAGIC box,” a couple of disciples to high sitting straight up.

Cindy walks in, “Kids just went to sleep.” But before I could apologize she had shut the double French doors to the office.

Placing the pipe down I tipped the lid back on the box and opened the doors. The box had no visible bottom, no walls for that matter. A shadow of inky darkness filled it. So, I went and found my flashlight. When I tried, it actually seemed to eat the light. So only one way to find out *What's in the box,* my inner voice repeats the line from the movie *Seven*. I reached in deep into the dark with both hands. I felt the cold of the metal before my fingers touched it.

Grasping the metal object with both hands. It was a pure white helmet, a Trojan helmet complete with a Mohawk of black horse hair, but the metal was not just white it had a silver inlay etched in it, that shines brilliantly.

When taking it out of the wooden trunk it starts to glow. I felt something exchanged between the helmet and me. All of a sudden I felt dizzy, a draining sensation poured from my hands into the helmet. Overwhelmed from the weird tingling feeling in my fingers instead of putting the helmet on I set it on my desk.

ZNAP CRUSH SMACK

Like a reverse static shock, as soon has my fingertips left surface. The feedback exploded with a crack. The explosion sent me flying into the air. I felt the drywall smash and brake as I hit the wall. Falling back to earth, I bounced off the built in desk then crashed into the floor. When my eyes focused the white helmet now lay on the floor opposite from me. My head dropped back to the carpet right before I passed out, the helmets empty eyes started humming with glowing green orbs.

HHMMMMMMMMMM-M-M-M-M

Valkyrie

Valkyrie are Midgar or Aesir woman who has had magnificent powers bestowed on them by Odin. These women are responsible for watching over battlefields and collecting the best of the best warriors to make up Odin's army, which he will unleash during Ragnarok. The Valkyries' nobility is reflected in their appearance, they have perfect skin and statuesque figures. Their hair can be gold as the sunlight or black as the night. During times of peace, these women wear elegant costumes made from swan or raven feathers, but when war draws near, they donned their armor: gracefully carved helmets, shields and chainmail corsets. They might continue wearing a feather cape, or they do not sprout wings of their own to soar above the battlefields.

Today, Valkyries are regarded as wise and righteous

leaders—but during Norse times, these ladies were a bit more complicated. True, they were highly intelligent, they loved valor. These traits made them great at choosing heroes to fight alongside Odin in Ragnarok. Yet, the Valkyries had human weaknesses as well. They were not above showing favoritism on the battlefield, protecting mortals whom they loved or lashing out against mortals who they disliked. And some of them, who simply enjoyed the carnage of the battlefield, provoked fights among mortals when they got bored.

It's difficult to know exactly how powerful the Valkyries were. Most of them were mortal humans, daughters of royals or great Aesìr warriors. However, they worked closely with Odin, ruler of the gods, and they clearly had some magical powers.

First and foremost, the Valkyries influenced the fate of warriors and battles with Odin's approval, of course. Stories describe them riding horses through the clouds above an active battle. During the battle, they might swoop down to protect a warrior who shouldn't die. Or they might come down to collect the body of a fallen warrior and carry it off to Valhalla, Odin's hall, to prepare for the apocalyptic battle of Ragnarok.

Although numerous stories hint that the Valkyries have superhuman strength, they are not allowed to fight alongside human in a battle. They can only use magical powers to influence the battle. The Valkyries may have superhuman foresight as well. They often appeared above battlefields days before the fighting begins and sometimes delivered prophecies to mortals.

Finally, the Valkyrie are well-known for serving and brewing mead. Not only is their mead delicious, it has magical properties that can make men stronger, improve their memory, or heal their wounds.

Angus, Minotaur of Minoa

Chapter 14

A battlefield of Trojan soldiers raged in my dreams. Men dying by my hands, their blood running down my blade. Dancing over 100,000 corpses of my enemies that litter the ground. The heat of violence coursed through me in Battle rage.

"This day the carrion crow will feast!" I screamed.

Jumping up off the carpet floor ready to skin all of them. My knuckles white as my fist clenched. I took a deep breath trying to center myself and realized that the sun had come up. My eyes searching for the nearest clock 7:12 am.

"Fuck!" I said realizing that I was late for work.

In a hurry I tripped over the facken helmet giving myself a perfect carpet burn on my forehead. I rubbed it gently as I scanned the office, looking at the perfect indentation of my ass in the wall and all my collectables scattered around the room.

SSSSHHHHHHHHH drip..drop SSSSHHHHHHHHH drip..drop drip..drop SSSSHHHHHHHHH

I took an extremely hot shower, running the last few days over in my mind like the water over my body. My son opened the bathroom door.

"Dad, your work?" Nathan said in a question.

I opened the curtain, just a little, with a frown.

Nathan cut me off before I could jump down his throat, "I said you were in the shower. He said he didn't care to give you the phone."

I took the phone and pushed end on the phone call handing him the cell phone back. I closed the curtain, my cell phone started to ring in Nathan's hand.

Nathan answered the phone on instinct, I could hear the voice on the phone as he did.

"Just like your father, you can't follow a simple…," the voice said.

Nathan hit end on the call and said, "Asshat," under his breath.

"What?" I asked him.

The door opened, "Nothing!" Nathan called to me from the hallway.

"Boy," I called him back.

"Yeah Dad," his voice cracked.

I rinsed the soap off me as I asked him through the shower curtain, "What do you think the consequences would be for dishonoring a samurai's son?"

"Dishonoring the son also dishonors the Father, Death by stupidity," Nathan answers without a seconds pause.

I turned the water off, "Have a great day at school, Kiddo," I said as the door shut behind my son. I went to the Master bedroom to get dressed to find my naked wife pulling back her covers.

"Pink dragon," she winks.

"Yeah man..!"

Half-dressed covered in perspiration and panting I stumbled into the man-cave looking for my work boots.

“CAAWWW CAW!” Huginn and Muninn greeted me.

“I didn't ask about my phone,” I retort, “Boots, work boots?” in a horrible Swedish accent mimicking the movie Frozen.

My phone chirps and beeps as Huginn pokes it with his beak.

Muninn, “caw,” softly from under the TV's stand.

“Thanks,” I tell the bird while I put my boots on.

My phone drops into my lap 7 missed call, 11 missed text messages. I just slid it in my back pocket. My belt undone, boots not tied, not one button done on my shirt I grabbed my wallet and wife's keys.

“So, you two staying here,” I opened the door to leave and a wind took it from my hands, “or with me,” I whispered to myself as the birds flew off.

As soon as I clocked in I was ambushed. Inbound had 4 rechecks, 2 guys where in count back. I took care of the count backs right away, Login onto my lift and getting them back to work. I finally got into the front office and Nick my inventory manager was in his office on the phone with the GM Jerrod, which is only 2 doors down from his.

“He just walked in…,” I heard him say.

I said nothing walking to my cubicle. He stormed out of his office. My fingers had just touched my keyboard.

“Unacceptable, your shirt is not even button.” Nick is purple with rage spit flying from his mouth.

I looked down, shrugged and started to button it.

Nick started to say, “And I don't appreciate how your son…”

WHIISSH Whack YANK Smack GRIND

I spun around in the chair kicking him in the shin. At the same instance I grabbed him by the back of his head. His face hit my desk with a wet smack from his nose exploding. Now on one knee his nose bleeding all over my desk.

"Not a facken sound," I leaned closed grinding my elbow into him.

I stood up looking over my cubicle to see if anyone noticed. He had to try me so I smeared his face down hard, his teeth dug deep grooves into my desk. He changed his mind and whimpers. I picked up my desk phone with my free hand, holding the receiver in the same hand I dialed my son's cell phone. No one noticed anything.

"Hey Dad," Nathan answered.

I didn't answer Nathan, instead I crushed the receiver into Nick's ear. Tears welled up in his eyes as blood dripped from his nose.

"Hello Dad," I heard Nathan's voice say.

"I am sorry," a tear running down Nick's face as he chokes it out.

I put the phone to my ear, "Love you Kiddo."

"Love you more!" Nathan answered.

I hung up the phone and reached into my back pocket. Dropping my security badge and clock-in card next to Nick's bleeding face, I leaned into him.

"You have always mistakenly taken my kindness as a weakness. You will keep this to yourself." He shook his head yes as I continued, "I'm going to let you stand. You are going to go make yourself presentable so you can tell Jerrod that I gave you my resignation."

The trees rustled with a slight breeze as I came out the warehouse. With the contents of my desk and locker in a box I walked towards the parking lot and noticed a huge black shadow land in the tree next to the Jeep.

“Muninn,” I said nodding my head to the crow that sat on the branch.

I set the box down on the bumper of the Jeep, balancing it with my knee.

“Where's Huginn,” pulling my keys from my belt I ask her.

“Caw caw,” she answers me.

“He's thinking,” I smiled at Muninn, “That's facken funny.”

I slammed the trunk and lit up a cancer stick. Inhaling the glorious nicotine letting it relax me. Muninn floated up, landing on my shoulder. She stepped side to side, her feet trying to find a good perch. She was surprisingly light for such a huge bird. I rubbed my head against her, she did the same. I noticed that she had something in her beak.

“What ya got,” I asked her. She let me take it from her. It was the business card Detectives Starfish and SpongeBob. I sighed, “Honey bear.”

Thud, clack, thud, click

I looked up to see Huginn on the roof of the Jeep commander with a huge solid gold rainbow stone. He rolled it to me with his massive beak. I took the heavy stone. It was the size of a softball and flipped it behind my back sending it up in the air.

“Thanks,” I looked at Muninn and Huginn. The rainbow stone landed in my open hand, “Yeah man.”

Huginn and Muninn flew away and I started the Jeep.

Vvv..Vvv...RRRUUUMMMMMBLE.

Mjolnir

Mjolnir is one of the most powerful weapons wielded by any deity. Not only does it enable Thor to call upon the forces of the weather, including the power of the lightning, to aid him in combat. It also has other enchantment's making it a truly devastating weapon of destruction in his hands.

Forged by the master metalworkers Brokk and Eitri dwarves indigenous to the realm of Nidavellir. Mjolnir is composed of a virtually indestructible Cold Iron that will always return to Thor's hand after being thrown at a target and striking its intended mark. The blue silver blaze of energy said to trail the hammer when it's thrown is a manifestation of the forces of lightning that it controls.

There is scarcely a creature from any of the Nine Realms who can withstand being hit by this hammer. Many powerful foes of the deities have fallen before its might.

Angus, Minotaur of Minoa

Chapter 15

It was rather late in the evening the sun was low in the sky as I pulled into the driveway, Nathan and Thor in the front yard. Getting out the SUV I scanned the yard.

“We already picked them up,” Liz walking over to me as she continues, “No one mentions how much physical labor is involved keeping Harry Potter's secret.”

I just handed her a cigarette and held up a lighter.

She took it and lit her fag, “Everyone is on the porch watching the show.”

“Show?” I asked her as we made our way down the front sidewalk.

Liz smiled but said nothing.

I gave her the middle finger, then turned my left arm across my body. My right hand made a shadow puppet. I walked my shadow puppet dinosaur from right to left on my left arm. She busted out laughing.

“Facken dinosaur,” I whispered while I finished it in sign language.

Looking over I see Nathan sitting on Mjolnir arms wrapped tight around the short handle. Thor on the other side of the yard, 100s of yards away, held out his arm before him looking into Nathan eyes and waited.

With a nod from my son, “To me Mjolnir,” Thor called flexing his fingers.

Mjolnir shot from the ground leaving a wake of dust but Nathan's death grip held. As I watched my son soar all I could picture was Rocket Raccoon. The happiness emanated from Nathan's body while he held on. His face was pure and overwhelmed with joy. Mjolnir seemed to just stop in midair before it got to Thor’s hand.

I flinched expecting Nathan to fly forward when the hammer stopped. Thor just held his arm straight out in front of him looking at Nathan scramble to the top of Mjolnir. Nathan sat down on the head of the great hammer looking at Thor, a joker like smile stretching on my son's face.

“You did not even try that time,” the huge man said arm still outstretched as if the hammer and Nathan weighed nothing.

Nathan crossed his arms over his chest feet dangling from Mjolnir with the most serious face he could muster, “We should keep practicing then.”

With a twist of his wrist Thor dumped Nathan to the ground unceremoniously.

“Indeed,” he grumbled.

He tossed Mjolnir across the yard again with a thud. I tuned them out as I made my way to the front porch. Giving Alex a kiss on the head as I stepped over her while she sat on the first step. Before I could finish the four concrete steps up to the porch, Kara came off of her Mom's lap and the 5-year-old was off the top step in a single bound. I stepped back down the stairs, over Alex. I caught her with a spin and dance, her feet helicopters inches from the top of Alex's head. I hug her to my hip and like a baby monkey she latches to me.

Cindy asking me when she walks into the house, "Ya hungry?"

I smiled up at her with Kara attached to me, "Of course."

Made my way back up the porch steps. I put Kara down and she tore after her mother. Thor is trying to explain to Nathan about something.

Nathan interrupts, "If I concentrate any harder I'm going to crap my pants," he explained in frustration.

"Shit, will wash off," Thor retorted.

Then reaches under his WWE championship belt and takes a pouch from underneath. Thor takes the small leather pouch and pulls the drawstring apart. The huge man bent low as he takes Nathan's hand turning it palm up. He tips the contents of the pouch out. A small sliver of metal rolled into Nathan's hand. Thor tucked the pouch away and pulled a dagger out in a swift motion cutting it off a lock of his red hair. He then with a gentle touch cut a lock of Nathan's hair and placed the dagger in his belt. Taking the hair in his meaty fist he braided it with care chanting something to it that I couldn't make out, but I could see a spider web of light being weaved into the hair while he braided. Thor takes the piece of dented metal from Nathan and attaches it to the braided hair still chanting. Wrapping the hair around the metal he gestures to Nathan to turn around. He loops it around Nathan's neck tying a knot. He holds the knot with his left hand and reaches down with is right stabbing his thumb into the very point hilt of his dagger. He presses his thumb over the knot and I watch the spider webs of magic close the circle. Thor stood grasping Nathan by his shoulder and patted him making Nathan look like a bobblehead.

Cindy sneaks up to me kisses my cheek and whispers, "Love you." Then louder for everyone to hear, "Food will be ready shortly!" handing me Odin's pipe.

"Ditto," I told her returning her kiss.

She smiled knowing I used a reference to Ghost. Kara popped up with a glass of sweet tea I kissed her on her head. Not long after we all sat on the porch eating steak with sticky rice and thumbakhoung, a really spicy papaya salad. While we ate dinner, I told them about quitting work and getting Honey bear out of impound. After we drank 2 gallons of milk to cool are melting faces from the heat of the thum.

Thor and I retired to my office, AKA the geek cave. Cindy and Liz must have cleaned up the debris and even rehung my stuff to cover the butt print.

I pulled the screen down then turned on the projector and the Western Digital media box. Thor lounged on the pink couch waiting as the 10 ft screen came to life as the Marvel Comics movie logo lights the room. We sat passing Odin's pipe between us never saying a word and watched the movie.

The kids came in and out of the office during the movie as quiet as they could trying not to interrupting the silence. I turned the lights on as the credits rolled in and opened the French doors into the sunroom.

He squinted from the blinding lights, “Heimdall,” he whispered thru gritted teeth.

So, I changed my hypothesis, the lights were not the reason why he was squinting. I looked out the sunroom windows it was completely dark outside.

“Liz, rainbows are fractures of light cast through raindrops,” asking as I opened the glass doors of the sunroom walking onto the wrap around deck.

Liz sitting in the old leather lazy boy her head down scanning her phone she looked up, “You can't have a rainbow at night.”

I looked up at the night sky, “And we are way too south to see the Aurora Borealis, the northern lights?” I ask.

She walks out onto the deck, her mouth just hung open. The lights bent and turned like huge brush strokes across the sky. With a rush of air, the pressure changed and my ears popped. Then the northern lights changed with an invisible paint brush the colors arched to the ground. Heimdall walked out the northern lights bridge.

SSSWWWOOOOOOOSH FFWWISHH FFWWISHH FFWWISHH

"The Bifrost," I heard my mouth say.

Heimdall brushed his arms, "That shits cold!" he rubbed his arm faster to get warmth.

The northern lights faded while I stepped down the back deck, "Heimdall, what's up?" we bro hugged.

Cindy walked out the sunroom throwing a beer to Heimdall, "That's pretty," she said looking in the yard.

I pointed into the house towards the office, "Thor inside!"

Heimdall popped the top of the beer and downs the whole thing and goes to find Thor. Me and Liz gaze at the backyard, moonlight twinkling off the lawn. The breeze made the grass wave like water, the rocks sparkling silver.

"Moonstones," I said picking up the solid silver lump.

Liz picked one up holding it up to the moon. The silver actually started to illuminate in her hand she giggled then frowned, "I don't want to…" then she stomps off in slow motion.

It was in the backyard and darkness shrouded it, "We can clean it up in the morning."

Liz clapped… My eyebrows went up, "How old are you?"

She turned on me, "Now, ain't that callin' the kettle black," in her best Southern Belle imitation.

That broke me, laughter echoing out of me. We went different directions as we walked in the house.

I found Thor and Heimdall on the pink couch, "You are not a blonde pillow biter." Heimdall said comforting Thor.

Thor looked at me, bolts of lightning actually sparking from his eyes. He stood up slowly at his full height towering over me. I have a massive IQ and an even bigger stubborn streak. I wasn't going to back down because he didn't like the movie. He clenched his jaw looking down at me.

ZZAP…

Hephaestus

Hephaestus was the Greek God of fire, metalwork, stone masonry, forges and the art of sculptures. He was the son of Zeus and Hera and married to Aphrodite.

He was the only ugly god among perfectly beautiful immortals. Hephaestus was born deformed and was cast out of heaven by one or both of his parents when they noticed that he was imperfect. In some accounts, he was said to be the son of Zeus and Hera; in others, he was the son of Hera alone, conceived in order to get back at Zeus for bringing forth Athena.

He has his own palace on Olympus where he made many clever inventions and automatons of metal to work for him.

He was a smithing god making all of the weapons for Olympus and acting as a blacksmith for the gods. His forge or workshop was located under a volcano, and the work he did within it caused frequent eruptions. He was the workman of the immortals: he made their dwellings, furnishings, and weapons in his workshop. Hephaestus had three assistants who helped him with his work.

Hephaestus manufactured the aegis or shield that Athena is known for carrying. The arrows of Eros, known also as Cupid, were fashioned by Hephaestus as well. The gold basket that Europa, daughter of the King of Sidon, used to gather flowers when she happened upon Zeus in the meadow. Hephaestus crafted the armor that Achilles wore in the Trojan War.

Hephaestus's ugly appearance was the reason Zeus chose him to marry Aphrodite, but despite this she had many affairs with both gods and men. In one story, Hephaestus builds a tricky invention which catches Aphrodite laying with the ARES, the god of war, trapping them both in the bed to be laughed at and ridiculed by the other gods.

He is similar to Athena by giving help to mortals – in his case the arts. It was believed that Hephaestus taught men the arts alongside Athena. However, he was also considered far inferior to that of the goddess of wisdom. He was a kind and peace-loving god.

Angus, Minotaur of Minoa

Chapter 16

I immediately remembered naval boot camp and being stunned with a Taser gun to qualify for guard duty. I hit one knee from the biggest electrical shock ever. Both men started to laugh.

"Ha ha ha… Ouff!" Heimdall fell off the couch, he was laughing so hard.

Thor was bent over holding his stomach with laughter, "You thought I called Heimdall cause movie," he explained between breaths.

I crawled to the lazy boy and shot them both a bird. I waited till they were done that seemed like forever.

Heimdall pulled himself together, first clearing his throat, standing at attention. "The Cold Iron War Helmet forge with Mjolnir given, but no story told."

Thor stood and pushed him back into the couch playfully, "You and story time."

He made his way to the opposite side of the office picking up the solid white Trojan helmet. Placing the helmet on the coffee table in the middle of us, brushing his fingers across the black horse's Mohawk.

Magical Viking runes appeared to glow on the white surface of the helmet. They pulsed a fluorescent blue. Ancient Greek and other glyphs magically manifested a bright canary yellow getting brighter and brighter.

"I forged it, using Mjolnir," Thor says as he sits next to Heimdall, purposely taking up most of the large faded pink couch.

"Hephaestus, do you know of him?" Heimdall asks me ignoring Thor.

I gave him the look like he must be joking but I answered him, "The Greek God of the Forge. He made all the of the Greeks greatest weapons."

I held out Odin's pipe to him, Heimdall took it. He placed it to his mouth and took a huge pull on the pipe. I watched the flame of the match being drawn into the bowl. As he exhaled the smoke rolled in the air forming a bull. The smoke bull stomps the air in challenge and charges towards the wall. The smoke bull hit the wall and with a puff the bull is gone.

Heimdall looks at the pipe, "Good Shit!" and hands it to Thor. "So, our big friend and I are exploring Troy. By exploring I mean we were," tapping Thor. "What would Perun say?"

Thor, blows out smoke rings and in a really good Russian accent, "Getting shit Bottomed."

Heimdall chuckled, "We were so very drunk, at a Bar in Troy."

"Shit Bottomed!" Thor corrected.

"Well?" Heimdall continued, "I gestured to this balding older man covered in dirt. You see the extra-large dwarf over Thor's beer came spitting out like a fountain when he turned to look.

"He has to be the ugliest dwarf I have ever seen!" Thor roared.

"This ugly dwarf is married to Aphrodite," Heimdall said in a gruff man's voice.

“You should have seen Thor's mouth hung open no words came out. My bar stool must have moved because I found myself on the floor, ok I was laughing so hard snot bubbles were coming out my nose. After a formal introduction and a full barrel of mead Hephaestus told of this cold iron ore that was solid white and no hammer could forge it. Thor had struck bargain with Hephaestus that his hammer could,” Heimdall pauses and takes Odin’s pipe from Thor.

Heimdall took a long hit of Odin’s pipe, blowing out cotton candy blue smoke.

“Hephaestus shook his head, no, he didn’t agree with Thor,” Heimdall paused changing his voice ruff, “*You know nothing, it takes more than muscles and a big hammer.*”

“Then teach me,” Thor says quietly folding his arms over his chest as he leans back into the couch.

I looked at Thor then back to Heimdall as Heimdall handed me Odin’s pipe and continued, “When the sun rose the next morning I went home to Asgard and Thor stayed behind. I watched as Thor learned how to forge raw iron. When Hephaestus deemed him ready he explained to Thor that there were three ways to make a magical weapon. The first way, and easiest is to use ore that already has magic. Second use an ordinary weapon and imbue it with magic. The third and the strongest is to do both. Hephaestus then shows him how to take one of his ordinary blades and imbue it with magic. Hephaestus etched symbols and runes on the blade chanting in Greek.”

“Hephaestus would inspect all the weapons, shields, and armor Thor had made. All the weapons displayed in front of Hephaestus, the grumpy old God would just nod,” Heimdall pausing his story to reach over to take Odin’s pipe.

“Thor went to work, months flew by before Hephaestus was satisfied. He showed him how to fold magic into the very metal itself. It took Thor many years to master the last.”

Heimdall made his voice gruff again to imitate Hephaestus, “When the next full moon reaches its pinnacle we will start.”

"Daddy," Kara walking in dragging my blanket behind her, "I'm not sleepy." She climbs up Thor by trying to pull the heavy comforter. Thor's eye wide, his hands went up and he froze solid, I could swear he was holding his breath.

Kara curling into a ball like a tiny kitten she looked at the mountain, "Uncle Thor," she yawns. "You finish your story now," and drifted back to sleep.

I got up to take her back to bed but before I could Thor had pulled the blanket off the back of the couch and wrapped the blanket around her.

"Sleep little one," Thor whispers to Kara. Then started to rock her as he started the story where Heimdall had left off, it played out like a movie in my head.

Hephaestus and I stood under the night sky, clouds covering the moon. We had just stepped out of a very thick wood into a small meadow. I walked to the center of the clearing and saw nothing. Turning to Hephaestus finding him still at the edge of the meadow. The clouds chose that moment to reveal the moon. Bright beams of moonlight cascaded over the meadow. Moonstones dotted the field. The earth cracked, whole sections of the meadow jetted up. What I had assumed were small moonstones in fact huge moon boulders carved in glyphs. Below my feet the ground folded and I found myself rolling down stone steps. Finally, I came to a stop, I stood only with a bruised ego.

Hephaestus walked past me, "Welcome to my secret Forge and Armory." The stairs opened to a great Hall lined with unbelievable things.

Hephaestus stopped in front of an empty spot on the wall. He reached in his apron pulling out a ring of keys talking to himself looking at each key, "nope, nope, not that, nope... ah."

He slides the key into the stone wall, with a turn the ground closes up blocking the moonlight, but before the last rays of light disappeared veins of orange red light crisscrossed across the walls brightened. When the stairs had closed the other end of the hallway had opened Hephaestus waited, back lit by a river of lava. The forge was a comfortable size. His anvil set steps away from a lava waterfall that spilled into a river of lava that flows under the floor. It was hot but I should have been cooked alive.

"Now what did I do with," Hephaestus mumbling while he went through cabinets on the opposite side of his workshop. He pulled out a box with wheels, "ah," and wheeled to his work bench.

"Brontes, Steropes, Arges!" Hephaestus screamed.

The three-cyclops rumbled in, I sighed, glad that he had told me about his hidden helpers. Steropes yanking on a chain that looped down from the ceiling stomping his foot. A stone forge pushed out the lava waterfall. Brontes grabbed two log sized levers pulling one down and it.

clicked clacked

Then pushed the other up with tongs Arges put the cold iron ore into the forge and starts to chant. Steropes pulled a different chain making the lava flow over the forge, his foot stomping and started humming different deep tones joined. The melody ran together with his brother's chant. Brontes moved activating a different lever adding a click clack to orchestra. He was also controlling the temperature of forge.

I put on Mjolnir special gloves and held Mjolnir to my lips, "Sing!"

Arges pulled the white-hot ore out placing it on the anvil. Hephaestus struck his mallet, sparks showered him and his voice gave words to Arges grunted chant. Mjolnir hit sending lightning bolts across the cavern. Without skipping a beat Hephaestus hit the ore. It's all about rhythm, like a heartbeat. The song was doing two things, it kept us in sync physically and pound magic into the ore. We are Gods so without rest we pounded and reheated, pounded and reheated. For 42 days we beat the cold iron ore into a square billet. We rested for 2 days and Hephaestus couldn't wait any longer. Hephaestus insisted we must fold it 42 times.

After pulling the hot metal out of the forge we would shape the cold iron folding it. Arges would dip it into Moonstone dust and place the billet back into the forge then onto the anvil. After the folding process is finished the fun really begins. The metal starts to speak to you with the rhythmic banging of metal on metal. Magic flooded the chamber Hephaestus and mine own twisting and braiding around us.

We knew that this was no sword. While we formed the solid white metal into the war helmet I lost track of the days. Never have I demanded so much from my muscles. All of us looked at the shell of the war helmet sitting on Hephaestus tool bench steam rising from the rapidly cooling metal.

Hephaestus and I took turns after that. Each etching magic rune, glyph, or symbol on it. We put every Battle Magic spell on the helmet we knew of and some we just made up.

Before the other started we would run liquefied Moonstone in the grooves of the etching. Then quickly quenched the war helmet hardening the magical silver instantly and binding the magical spell to the solid white Cold Iron. The combination of Norse and Greek magic created a war helmet with no equal. Every spell and enchantment calculated precisely to enhance the wearer. Him nor I could figure out how to close the circle, to give the magic its spark, its soul. I left Hephaestus that very day with no regrets. I had learned a valuable skill and have another great tale to tell. Hephaestus however was not pleased with his beautiful paper weight.

"Going, going, gone," a little voice interrupts. "Give me one sec," I told Thor and Heimdall making my way to the kitchen. Sticking the chocolate milk in the microwave. After 30 seconds I was heading back into the office.

"Sit up monster." Kara sat up in Thor's lap and took her warm chocolate milk from me.

Heimdall puffed on Odin's pipe like a choo choo train, "Shortly after the Cold Iron War Helmets completion it was brought to MT Olympus and placed before Zeus. He decided that it was too dangerous for any God or man to have such power. Zeus's declaration condemned the magical Greek Norse helmet for destruction. Let me tell you," Heimdall hands me the pipe. Blowing big rings of smoke.

"They freaked the fuck out when a single mortal stormed MT Olympus. Proceeded to pimp slap Ares's and walked off with it. See the helmet being made of Cold Iron no magic could track it. They spent centuries hunting it with no avail."

"How Odin get it," I asked.

They both shrugged. I reached for the white and silver helmet.

"We cannot be here when you put it on," Thor stops me with his booming voice.

I pulled my hands back like it was going to bite me.

"There's rules," Heimdall explained.

I looked at Heimdall, he tipped his head to me, "Evening."

Thor placed Kara on the couch, she had fallen back to sleep and handed me her chocolate milk. I held the empty cup Thor left with nothing said when Heimdall's horn clinked on his back tapping a soft rhythm. The sunroom was cast in a dancing blue and green light as the Bifröst opened.

SSSWWWOOOOOOOSH FFWWISHH FFWWISHH FFWWISHH

A heartbeat passed after the northern lights dimmed and faded away. I looked at my sleeping baby girl and I slid the helmet on my head. Facken nothing, I pulled it off and really took a good look at it. The war hood was beautiful, running my fingers across the glyphs and runes.

TTZZZ TTZZZ TTZZZ

When my fingers touched the surface of the helmet I felt the magic, like spider webs crawling on my skin. Pulling my hands away I stood back.

Getting my nerves under control I placed my hand like a Jedi Knight and tensed the muscle fibers in my fingers. Not just flexing my muscles I flexed my will.

SHUSSHHH SSSSSSWISSSH SHUSSHHH SSSSSSWISSSH

The Norse runes reached out with blue ribbons of magic like tendrils. The ribbons twinkling with tiny writings wrapped around my fingers. Hephaestus's magical glyphs grew golden hair made of light, its locks slowly twined between my fingers. Placing my other hand next to the helmets side in a very Buddhist monk fashion. Closing my eyes slowly as my eyelids shut I centered my will. I inflated my lungs as I did so just like the air I inhaled the magic into me. I opened my eyes to see the magical hair and ribbons wrapped up my forearms. Watching the magic trace my tattoos as it continues its advance up my arms. I let out the breath I didn't know I was holding picking the war hood up.

"To all my Gods, I give you my faith, my strength, my life. For I pledge to fight the darkness that resides in my own soul, so I may fight alongside all of you. My destiny is the Morrigan's," as l placed the magical helmet over my head I whispered.

Taking my hands away the magic gripping tight to my tattoos. It stretched like hot Taffy then snapping individually. Feeling the two different magics crawling down my shoulder. Holding my arms out like a brain surgeon, watching the magical ribbons and hairs flow through my tattoos. The Superman soundtrack playing in my mind I see the magic starting to connect, no bonded with itself. Through the helmet eye holes, I scanned my arms all my ink was glowing as the magic flowed. Turning my right hand like I was waving in a parade looking at Panthro from the Thundercats tattooed on the back of my hand the magic danced in his eyes.

WHIZZZZT ZZZZT ZINNG WHIZZZZT ZZZZT ZINNG

My entire right arm is covered in a Samoan tribal tattoo, a story of me flowing behind two Japanese style Koa on my upper arm and shoulder, then finishing on my chest. The ribbons and hairs of magic rolled over me, the light from my tattoos shining yellow and blue through my clothes. I pulled my shirt up. The magic had worked its way across my chest down the samurai on my left rib cage and side. Then on the right rib cage a realistic crow shaded with a sutural Polynesians tribal design hidden in the feather patterns lights up yellow with more of the golden hairs of energy.

Blink blink TWANNNG TNNNNG DDDDAAAAARROOOMM

Then, like Iron Man, a translucent holographic Bio screen appears but it was in Greek, literally, well it was also in Old Norse to be fair. Then the HUD display went all facken Matrix. Runes and glyphs went from yellow and blue to green, then screamed across the HUD. My desktop computer started flipping through the internet on its own, my surround sound speakers blaring Powerman 5000, "When Worlds Collide". The laptop on the other desk turned on and started to do the same. The lights in the office flickering and then the pain struck me.

BZZZTT..SNAP BZZZTT..SNAP AAAHHHHHHHH BZZZTT..SNAP BZZZTT..SNAP

The two magic that were flowing around one another collide in fantastic green explosion. So intense was the agony I tried to scream but nothing came out of my mouth. Desperately trying to pull the helmet off I tripped over the coffee table. Now on the floor my body flopped like fish out of water. Nothing I did helped me to get the cold iron war hood off my damn head. The pain just increased I clawed desperately at the helmet.

"Daddy," Kara voice rang.

I tried calling to her, tell her to stay away. Kara's little hand touches the helmet and then it really gets intense.

"Be still!" she says.

Every muscle flexed in my body like you see when someone is being defibrillated.

Kara tells me matter factly, "It just needs an update Daddy, like Nathan's game."

I started to sweat profusely. It ran down my face stinging my already teared filled eyes. I felt something crawling into my right ear.

POP…

Pain shot down my neck, my eardrum screamed a single note. The pressure increases as I felt searing hot liquid dripped into my ear. I screamed and this time the sound rips out of me. Then the blackness surged over me like a tidal wave making my muscles go limp. I naturally assumed the fetal position, feeling like acid was eating me from the inside. A light breeze cooled my face and a tiny kiss brushed my forehead.

"Night Daddy," Kara said as I felt her tuck herself into me.

Sleep overwhelms me as the world fades to black.

Cold Iron

Cold Iron carries an inherent significance with magic. Anything made out of it will be imbued magical, good or evil, or just incredibly strong, never to lose its edge or to be broken. The rare Iron was held in esteem for sacred metallurgical fabrication of weapons, musical instruments and sacred tools.

It forms from meteorites that have traveled the cosmos gathering magic from different worlds as it went from galaxy to galaxy. Not all meteorites become Cold Iron. Cold Iron is not just iron it has other rare metals from around the galaxy infused with cosmic magic. Each chunk of Cold Iron is different like a fingerprint, its own personality.

Crafting meteoric iron is Older than Dirt. Iron from meteorites has been used to make tools and weapons since the

Ice Age. The Meteor Iron tools, weapons and other items were strong in their own right but they soon realized that some of these had great magical abilities.

Contact with Cold Iron causes immense physical pain to Faé creatures, and as a result the metal is often used as a way to determine if somebody is a Faé in glamour. Cold Iron also disrupts and impedes unicorn magic, something that has led to a lot of speculation in-universe about unicorns' exact relationship with the Faé.

All the weapons of the Gods from around the universe are made of this magical metal. The legendary sword Excalibur was made of Cold Iron, Thor's Hammer, also Cold Iron, and Neptune's Trident the list goes on and on. King Tut had a Cold Iron dagger found in his sarcophagus.

Angus, Minotaur of Minoa

Chapter 17

"Sir, your oldest daughter needs Sir's attention…," a thick Irish accented man said in my ear.

I didn't actually jump up, considering my inner voice has a serious multiple personality disorders. But when did Liam Neeson from Rob Roy move in, I asked myself?

"I assure you, Sir. I am not this Liam Neeson," the Irish voice said reading my very thoughts.

That got my attention with a quickness. I bolted up right to find I was still on the carpet floor in the office. Kara had covered us up and slept soundly. The facken coffee table was shattered, I looked at the clock on the back wall of the office 12:12 am. I frantically search for the source of the voice and we're completely alone. Peeling Kara from me as gently as I can, not to wake her. I covered her back up kissing her as I stood. Wiping my brow in consternation I pulled my shirt off to inspect myself as if looking for ticks. No magic blue, yellow, or green for that matter, my tattoos all seem normal. Rolling my shoulders, feeling that familiar crack and pop somewhat eased my tension. Since I found us alone I scooped Kara up in my arms wrapping the blanket and her into one bundle. Walking through the house without bonking something or bonking her is a delicate ballet in the dark. Making my way out of the kitchen and into the downstairs hallway I noticed the light from under Alex's bedroom door. She stays up late every night so it doesn't concern me. Faint music seeps out into the hall, she must be drawing. Heading to my room knowing if I put Kara in her bed she will just end up in mine anyways.

After I tucked Kara in I sat on the toilet, smoking a cigarette listening to Alex's music whisper through the wall. What the fucking hell was going on. I crushed out my second cigarette lighting a third. I looked at the cigarette smoke burning from the tip. Fuck I thought… double fuck shit damn... it's all real. Opening the bathroom door, I turned and knocked on Alex's door but didn't really wait for her to answer.

“Hey, What ya….” And I was speechless.

WHURL WHOOSH SPLASH ZIP SPLATTER SSWWOOOSHSHSH WHURL

She floated in the middle of the room orange magic whipped around her. Her head was tilted back arms splayed out to each side of her like a bad Exorcist movie. She must have been practicing her cosplay makeup, her face was streaked blue and red over pale pale white. Without knowing how I knew, the story of my life, I just know things that I've never been taught.

WHURL SSWWOOOSHSHSH SHUSSHHH SHUSSHHH

But I knew Alex's orange energy was some form of caster magic and to never interrupt a casting. I watched as the orange clouds form ancient ruins like floating lines of text dart around the room.

SCRATCH ZIP WHURL SLOSH SPLASH SWOOP ZIP WHURL

Pencils, pens, chalk, paint brushes and makeup brushes fly from wall to wall. A mark here, a stroke there and very detailed drawing cover's two of Alex's bedroom walls. All of her posters and pictures still hung on the walls. The enchanted items had just painted over them. The dresser that rested against the wall had received the same. Making the dresser vanish in the mural. The chair and the corner lamp, her book case on the adjoining wall are all masterfully blended in. Taking in the full image. The Indian from I-20, the same Alex drew in the kitchen. He stood on top of the world. Locked in Battle with a Godzilla sized Wolf the world tree Yggdrasil burning behind them.

KerBOOM FAWOOSH tinkle ping smack splash SNAG

With a wash of orange magic like a flash bang grenade blasting out in all directions from Alex. Moving before thinking I have Alex in my arms the Caster magic sparks showered us. I put her down on her bed.

BZZZTT..SNAP BZZZTT..SNAP BZZZTT..SNAP BZZZTT..SNAP

Her magic arching from her to me snapping and popping. The current arcs through my tattoos turning those arc points orange then fading to green.

BANG, clinking, SMACK, splash SPLASH splish TINK PING CRASH

Gravity taking over the now unenchanted items.

"Alex, baby girl," whispering to her sitting on her bed beside her. I brush the hair out of her face, "wake up," her eyes just fluttering orange magic glowing under her closed eyelids.

"She had another one," Her mother's voice came from the doorway as if it had been a nosebleed and no big deal.

"SON of A MonKEY!" Liz's voice although clearly said big deal.

I placed my thumb on Alex's face running my thumb across her brow like I did when she was still in her crib, tears filling my eyes. Fear turned to regret to rage at my impudence, "Great and Terrible things baby, Daddy's going to fix this."

Cindy came to our side placing a soft hand on my shoulder, "Go have a smoke," taking my place with Alex on the bed. As I walked out the room towards the kitchen, Cindy's voice came at a whisper "Hi, my love child."

I passed the kitchen puffing away on Odin's pipe. Like Sherlock facken Holmes, this Indian I have concluded was the key. Big plot twist I know. He might not be the source of our new circumstance though. So, I intended to ask him... physically ...first chance I get. I stared at the now clean, no blank kitchen wall and the hole Lou left.

Liz and Cindy came in the kitchen blank faced. I exhaled a huge puff of smoke from Odin's pipe already knowing, "She's not waking."

Their heads sunk in the negative. Liz broke the silence first, "Thor or Heimdall?"

I cut her off, "Rules… remember."

Cindy came around my right side, "Did you get a new Bluetooth earbud?"

Stopped in my tracks with the abrupt change of topics, "No!" I answered sharply.

Then unconsciously touched my ear sure enough I must have left my Bluetooth in again. I left it there with a shrug. Hopelessness overwhelmed me.

"Sir, if I may," the Irishman spoke in my right ear.

Pocket Dimensions

Pocket Dimensions are spaces that are too small or too easily accessible to be truly considered a separate Pocket Realm. They are referred to as small extra bubbles of space that are attached the Tree of Yggdrasil. Much like an actual pocket, they are often used for some extra space where you can get things Bigger on the Inside. A smaller example of this is a Bag of Holding. Hiding place, transportation, bank vault, Pocket Dimensions can do them all. They also can serve as a small, Secluded World with its own ecosystem and lifeforms.

Ironniesous O'Keeffe

Chapter 18

"Sir, must put the helmet on." he finished.

I looked around frantically, "Fuck that!" I told the phantom voice. "Let me guess," I looked from Cindy to Liz, "You don't hear him do you?"

Liz tapped her right ear indicating my own ear. Jamming my fingers into my ear desperately trying to dislodged the device there.

"Time is urgent, Sir. If Sir would forgive me, I must insist." the Irishman's voice rings in my ear.

Informing Liz and Cindy, "It's the helmet, it's talking to me!" pointed to my ear.

"Sir, my name is Ironniesous O'Keeffe, Bastard son of Manannán mac Lir of the Tuatha De` Danann, my mother was Atalanta of Sparta," Liam Neeson introduced himself. "If Sir would allow me. Alex is lost in her own vision, Sir." I was already walking to the office before he was finished. Looking for the Greek helmet and not seeing the antique. "Sir, the pink couch," he informed me. The helmet is radically different.

As soon as I looked at it *Taskmaster*, a *MARVEL* Comic Book supervillain, came to mind. Then as I looked at the solid white helmet, Red Hood Batman's second Robin, Jason Todd's helmet also came to mind. Like the Red Hood helmet, it had a counter line that traced the front. The war helmet was solid white with strong emotional eyebrows giving the mask an organic look to it. Silver lenses covered the mean mugging eyes.

I ran my fingers across a silver bezel that creates a counter line drawing a continuous line that starts at the back of helmet cresting over the forehead. The line runs down and over the center of each silver lensed eyes. It continues down the porcelain white metal across the helmet's cheek making a frown line for a mouth and then traces back up the helmet's cheek completing the circle.

Starting just under the frown line tracing the chin of the white helmet, a silver rebreather jutted lower than the muscular jaw line. The shape of the ventilator gave the helmet the appearance of having a goatee with a silver grill.

Picking the Cold Iron War Helmet up off the couch and the silver channels started to glow fluorescent green. I held the helmet up to looked into the silver lensed eyes.

Turning it from side to side. The left side of the helmet was molded like a skull, with a silver inlay under the cheek and down the jaw. The other side was the same but had an *Ironman* style earpiece that protruded just slightly.

"Nice to meet you, Irons." Flipping it around in my hands I pull the helmet over my head.

blink..blink VAROOOM HHMMMMMMMMMM SWOOOSH..

A full body pulse shook me as magic surged down me through my tattoos. The pain and light show was brief. The glowing magic fades from the tattoos. The HUD appears in the helmet, or in front of my eyes, magic is well magic.

A satellite image of the surrounding area and a map draws itself, "It is an old way, Sir." Grabbing my keys and slamming my feet into the boots that Thor had given me. Irons informs me, “Sir, keys will not be necessary.”

I didn't even put on a shirt as I went straight to Alex. Walking through the kitchen the ladies just watched me discombobulated. Draping the blanket around her better. Tucking it in under her, picking Alex in my arms. She didn't even budge and a tear ran down my cheek. I carried her into the kitchen.

Liz stepped in front of me. Her face very serious, “Where's in the blue blazes am I going?” as she pulls my keys from my belt and putting them on the kitchen table, “And what's up with the white skull helmet?” she finishes.

Already moving past her towards the garage, my voice sounding mechanical through the helmet, “Panola National Park, the one between hear and Stonecrest Mall.” My lovely wife opened the door to the garage and reached out to hit the garage door opener.

She turns to me, pulls me down to look me in the helmet eyes. I could feel the emotions held there, “Make this right,” she orders me.

“Great or TERRIBLE things for the ones I love,” I answered her. The helmet making me feel like *Darth Vader* with the way it modulated my voice.

Liz had slid by us and had the back door of her gerbil car open, waiting. I dropped into the backseat of her car and Alex's magic spikes. The orange magical runes buzz the inside of the car like killer bees sending all the cars electronics into frenzy.

Irons choice to speak up, “Sir, I did inform Sir that Sir did not need one’s keys.”

“Fuck, witches, wizards, casters... their magic affects electric current!” I explained to myself out loud. Then an idea hit me.

“Sir, that is ill advisable,” Ironniesous tries to warn me.

See I had remembered how her magic reacted to my tattoos pulling my left arm from under her. Years ago, I had her and her brother take a sharpie marker and they signed my forearm then Tasi ran the ink. Taking Alex's hand I placed on the tattoo of her name,

"Mine," I breathed in.

The pain was instant I could see her name glowing bright orange under her hand. The lights in the car returned to normal with my will I pulled the rest of the daughters' caster magic into my tattoos.

With teeth greeted, "To me," my face red agony I called the last of magical runes.

My ink was fluorescent orange with the very edges blending with green. The engine starts. Liz slams it into drive and drops the hammer.

I could feel the difference in the orange magic. My tattoos burned my skin like the ink was made of acid. Slowly the orange glow turned to a glowing green then fades completely, the pain sticks around for a while longer.

We finally pulled in the parking lot of Panola Park. I got out of the car with Alex cradled to me. The HUD actually lit up a path for me to follow,

"Run!" Irons told me.

Without even considering Liz still in the driver seat. I took off at a full sprint. The parking lot turned to a gravel trail under my feet. The HUD trail turned off the gravel and the woods stole the light. The hood's HUD display changed and the darkness lit up. I ran, pushing my legs as hard as I could, trees flew by me. A meter ticks down in the corner of the house, distance from, another indicates speed of 16 mph. The fastest man recorded ran at 28 mph, I have to run faster.

"Sir, if I may?" he asks.

Before I could answer my tattoos all started to glow green. My magic lit up the forest leaving a comet's tail behind me. Pushing off the ground with my left foot I felt the magic push with me as my right foot extend out. The magic reached out.

The magical green energy looked like a desert heat mirage. The magic grabbed the ground ahead of me and pulled my foot towards it. When my other foot touched the ground the magic pushed off the ground even harder. My left foot extends and its magic pulls me forward. Right, Left… I pump my legs faster. I was running at inhuman speeds with the magical green energy pushing and pulling across the forest floor. The HUD trail cuts right and I juke with a push of magic sending yards down the trail.

WOOSH

My feet hit the leaves. All the while the speedometer advanced, 22 mph, 30 mph, 36 mph, 42 mph faster and faster the numbers climbed. I slid to a stop, when I say slid, try a 20 ft skid mark about 3 inches deep. Pulling Alex away from my body, I checked on her, still out like a light. The HUD display trail was gone.

"Where?" I asked in frustration. A green holographic image appears of a triangle of trees with distance marking from each. It spun slowly revealing the trees up close oak, maple, and a pine tree. The holographic was so detailed. Information about the trees appeared all around the holographic images. Separate details became visible on how tall each tree was and how far apart they were.

"You're telling me we have to find those exact trees, those exact ones down to the circumference…. in a facken forest of trees?" asking Irons.

He didn't answer for what seemed to be forever. "Please sir, if you would be so kind enough and set your daughter down just for a moment," Irons asking me in a very polite tone.

Looking for a place to set her, I put against one of the granite stones that litter this park being so close to Stone Mountain.

Irons starts to explain what I need to do, "Kneel down and place both of the backs of my hands on the Earth. Making sure my tattoos actually makes contact on the ground."

My magic flows out my ink and into the ground creating a perfect circle of glowing green energy. "Sir, pull your hands back now," Irons says.

For a minute the circle does nothing,

Kerfump...

And in a single wave it spreads out 360 degrees. The magical energy scans the woods expanding farther and farther away. As I walked over to Alex on the right lower corner of the HUD display winks on, location found. The holographic image overlays a satellite image of the park, it was a perfect match.

Teleportation and Portals

Teleportation is the use of magic in the transfer of matter or energy from one point to another without traversing the physical space between them. It can instantaneously transfer all the mass off the practitioner and whatever it is touching from one location to another without physically disturbing the space in between. Its limits cannot exceed the practitioners own magical spark.

Portals or doorways to other place is too simplistic to convey these extraordinary magical gateways. They could take many forms, from holes in the ground, to a grove of trees, to mirrors, to large magical constructs like the rainbow bridge that's big enough to sail an Aircraft Carrier through it. Places linked by a portal include but not limited to different spot on the same world or other worlds attached to the Galactic Trees of the universe. Sometimes they aren't about traveling distance at all, but instead are about traveling through time. A portal can also link the past or the future. A portal can also cross planes of existence, such as heaven, hell or other dimensions. Portals are similar to the cosmological concept of a wormhole.

Ironniesous O'Keeffe

Chapter 19

I wrapped Alex up a little better, brushed her hair away from her face. I pulled the helmet off, my tattoos dimmed and the darkness approached. I leaned over tucking Irons under my arm pressing my cheek against Alex's cheek. Then I kissed my still unconscious daughter forehead. I stood, an emotional volcano about to erupt. I put Irons back on and my tattoos instantly turned green. I picked up Alex. Ducking my head in concentration I pulled, trying to pool my magic inside me.

Instead of willing magic from inside myself to manifest the magic came from everywhere, the ground, trees, the bugs, the animals. The magical energy floating through the air like glowing musical notes. The magic swirled into me like a facken train, from all sides jumping into my tattoos. Like a track star in the Olympics, I crouched slightly and launched myself forward.

CRACK... WOOSH

The HUD speedometer 55 mph, 70 mph, 84 mph… and pushed harder.

"Sir, would Sir enjoy some music?" Irons asking.

I just nodded yes, expecting harpsichord music. Legends from Score blasted inside the helmet and the world blurred as I ran. My trail behind me glowing with musical notes of Gaea's magics.

I slowed down this time instead of just jamming on the brakes. Relaxing my muscles, I walked into the clearing in between the triangle of trees. The extra magic dripping off me like sweat returning back to Gaea. The music fades to be replaced by nature's own music has the breeze blows through the forest.

"It is an Old way, Sir, like a combination lock," Irons' Irish accent chimes in.

The holographic image appears looking straight down at it. A pirate like map with glowing footsteps appears and overlays it. 17 steps counter clockwise around the oak. I straight line to the maple, 37 steps clockwise around it. Then to the pine 12 steps clockwise, 12 steps counter clockwise around the same tree.

Then back to the oak, closing the magical circle, then 4 steps counter clockwise, 20 clockwise. As I made my way around each tree completing each magical mini circle the air would pop, wine then click as if imaginary gears locking in place.

I got about 10 steps around the oak, the night sky fades to day. By the time my foot takes the last steps around this 500-year-old oak tree the sun has replaced the moon. Standing with Alex clutched to my arms to see that we're standing what looked like the Shire from *Lord of the Rings*. Rolling hills of green, a single grass covered Hobbit hole sitting smack dab in the middle of the triangle of trees. The trees are a hell of a lot farther apart than I noticed.

I started for the Hobbit hole and Irons spoke, "Sir, he is a very dear friend of mine, do not be frightened, Sir."

Scared, I thought to myself of a Hobbit.

Irons reading my mind again, "Sir. Sir is no Hobbit."

Passing two different well taken care of pig pens we made our way closer to the Hobbit hole. The hill that made up the Hobbit hole was more like a mountain. The massive trademarked circular door loomed over me. The top of the door at least 6 ft above my head. The door knob was as big as my freaking head, lay in the center of the door. It started to turn before I even knocked, so of course my asshole puckered, just a little, not in fear but in anticipation.

The door opened and was immediately replaced by an eight feet tall silhouette. The huge shadow emerged shrouded by a thick burlap robe with a hood covering his head complete. A thick scarf was wrapped around the creature's face only revealing its eyes.

Sam Elliott's voice deep and manly spoke from under the hood, "It's been a long time, Ironniesous."

My mouth opened to say something but instead Irons' Irish voice projects from the helmet, "Aye. It has, me laddie, it has," in a way more relaxed banter. "My friend's daughter here would be needing your assistance," Irons tells the shower curtain.

Moving slightly to one side pointing to the interior, "Put her in the study, my old friend. I will see what I can do, it's through there."

I followed his directions placing Alex on the oversized loveseat.

SSSSST FIZZLE Swoosh

Taking off Irons and putting him on a side table next to the loveseat. The biggest facken Hobbit I have ever seen covered in facken tarp pulls out a pair of bifocals and tucks them on under his hood. Kneeling he begins to inspect Alex very carefully his massive hood moving side to side.

Taking his spectacles off before standing up and taps them on his teeth, "I will need a few things."

Without another word he leaves the room. Turning another chair to face Alex it screams as I scratched the wooden floor.

From the hall, "Why is your ass about to disgrace my chair, when you should be following me?"

Irons, "Sir, she is safe."

My ass hovering inches above the chair ready to collapse. Refraining reluctantly, I walked quickly to catch up. Walking through the super-sized Hobbit hole we passed a living room with a flat screen TV, I pointed to it as we passed in question.

"We head to the library and gallery, not the living room," he spoke avoiding the TV comment.

Coming to the end of the hall to a closed door with multiple door handles placed around the door like a steampunk Stargate. The door knobs sit at 8 o'clock, 10 o'clock, 12 o'clock, 2 o'clock and at 4 o'clock like numbers on a clock. He reaches for 10 o'clock with a turn... the door opens to a huge library covered in old manuscripts, scrolls and ancient books mixed among the new volumes. The only spots not covered by literature had beautiful paintings or sculptures there.

He started gathering different items from different areas of the library. A white feather quill and a dust covered sketchbook bound together by human hair.

"Da Vinci's sketchbook," He says as he handed me both. He moved on, rummaging through a ben of scrolls.

"There it is!" Handing that to me while he moved on down his mental checklist. A silver knife and a wooden chalice where next. I bobbled the plain wood cup, almost dropping it and everything else I was holding.

The shower curtain stops clearing dust off a box of candles to look over at me, "Careful with that, it was hand made by a carpenter friend of mine."

Carefully I readjusted to make sure I had it, "I'm good."

With the crate of candles, he walks past me and into the hall. You know the automatic doors on Star Trek that close right behind them, well the library door did the same. No sound as soon as I stepped out and into the hall it just closed. By the time I caught up to him he was unwrapping Alex from the blanket with motherly gentleness. He picked her up placing her on the floor in the center of the room. The walking stuffed trash bag took everything from me and neatly arranges them a few feet away from Alex running horizontal.

He picked up the silver knife handing it to me, "Draw a circle," pointing a few feet farther out, "But do not close it."

Taking the knife knowing what to do I stood a couple feet away from them. I pressed the blade under Alex's name on my forearm and drew a deep red line under it. The blood flowing free from the deep cut in my arm I started to walk in a circle letting it drip to the floor.

He held the feather close to his face whispering, “Wake up William.”

Then he took Alex's index finger and poked it with the silver tipped feather quill. The big white feather soaked in her blood like ink. I was about halfway done with my circle making sure my blood made a solid line on the floor. Mr. Shower curtain took Da Vinci's sketchbook, opening it he set it on Alex's chest. Then placed the feather quill across the empty pages and stepped out of the circle. I only had about a foot to go to complete the circle so I just stood there, blood flowing down my arm, dripping from my fingers. He walks to me taking my bloody arm, holding it over the wooden chalice and squeezes, so blood flows freely filling the cup.

“Light all the candles from the box,” he says releasing my arm. He pours just enough to close the circle. Dips his fingers in the blood and his hooded face just looks at me.

“Oh… candles,” I reassure him that I heard him and noticed one of those coffee table doilies that your Great Aunt puts across her table.

Snagged it up I wrapped it around my arm to stop the bleeding and reached into my pocket. Opening the cigarette pack, I pulled out my Bic lighter and a cigarette. Lighting my cigarette without even asking I filled my lungs with that beautiful smoke. Just start randomly placing candles around the room and lighting them as I went. While I lit 189 candles, yes I counted, Trash-bag-man had drawn runes that I didn't recognize around the edge of the circle.

He stands when he does then he unfastened the shower curtain to let it drape off him to the floor. Definitely not a Hobbit.

Clip swoosh flap

Imbued Items

Magic when used for enchanting or imbuing can take on a property that allows it to bind and interact with the inert material. Enchanted items are items taken from everyday life; a broom, weapon, armor, clothing, a candlestick or other sparkless things and imbue it with magic.

A Magical Being can attach magic to the object and that object will contain magic from the moment it is created until the moment it is destroyed or another magical being removes the magic. Enchanted items have magical powers inherent in them. These may act on their own free will or be the tools of the being whose hands they fall into.

Magic items are commonly found throughout all the realms. They could also be used by Mundane against the supernatural and against magic itself. The enchanted item may even give magical abilities to a Mundane lacking in them, or enhance them physically.

Da Vinci's sketchbook, Shakespeare's feather quill, George Washington's Masonic Bible, King Arthur's Sword.

Angus, Minotaur of Minoa

Chapter 20

A fucken Minotaur, the walking shower curtain is a Minotaur. I was frozen, a real flesh and bones Minotaur.

More bull than man he was mostly a rich creamy brown with some dark brown patches here and there. White tufts of hair freckles around his massive jaw like a 5 o'clock shadow. His stomach and chest are pretty much hairless considering he's a bull man. His legs completely bull like, down to the hooves and tail. He's wearing a leather kilt thing and shoulder armor that harnessed under his arms.

The Minotaur unties the scroll and unrolling it he begins to read it out loud. I can't even come close to the language he was speaking. He read it over and over again, the candles flames flared up all at one time. Yellow magic burned hot from the candles. The yellow hairs of Greek magic wove through the air.

The feather quill magically stood straight up then started to write and draw onto Da Vinci's sketchbook with Alex's blood. Alex's orange magic whipped out of her like a hurricane, it bounced off the protective circle in waves. The Quill scribbled faster in the sketch book pulling the orange magic into the feather.

The Minotaur rolled up his scroll, “The spell needs time,” retying the ribbon around it, “I have some sweet tea in the kitchen.”

“Two of my favorite words,” I tell him, “Lead the way!” I grab up Irons and follow the big guy towards the kitchen.

Walking in the kitchen the Minotaur was pouring a second massive mason jar full of sweet tea and hands it towards me. I set Ironniesous on the butcher block island and took a huge drink from the nectar of the Gods, you can say I have a thing for sweet tea.

“Now, Ironniesous, I think it's time you introduced me to your new bearer,” lifting his glass of ice tea he gestures towards me.

I spoke first, “Nope, none of that… father was grandma, shit,” I reach my hand out, “Dano.”

The Minotaur took my forearm in an old-fashioned hand shake, “Angus.” Sitting on a bar stool I looked at him like he was full of shit. He smiled, “Ironic isn't it?” We both laughed.

I pulled out my smokes, showing Angus in permission and offering at the same time. He took a cigarette and held it to his nostrils, smelling the tobacco held inside the paper. Lighting my cigarette then holding the flame out to light his. We just enjoyed the cigarettes in silence for a time, savoring the taste.

I finally broke the silence, “Okay, one of you needs to fill me in …. Legends say you died? Are there multiple Minotaur or just a Minotaur? And where the facken holy hell are we?”

Angus blows a ring of smoke out, “My home, most of the herds lives in India. But some hide amongst the cattle of Texas,” pausing to take another drag from his cigarette. “I am The Minotaur from Greek mythology.”

“Killed in the labyrinth,” I said not waiting for him to continue, but was getting a little bit chilly, no shirt on and coming down from the adrenaline rush. So, I crossed my arms over my chest making me look like I was questioning him unintentionally.

Angus's head looked to the floor, "For so long I had wished that he had. Instead I was given to Ares as a slave, entertainment for the God. The pretty boy chained me, whipped me, beat me without hold, until I passed out. I woke to the same, years on end. Until I woke in the middle of the arena on MT Olympus as he spoke it came to life for me."

Ares stood in all his glory. His tan skin and short jet-black hair glistening from the sun. He only wore a pleated leather kilt held up by a lavishly adorned belt, which left the rest of the War God's 6'3" frame armor less. He just grins as his eyes started to fill with black ink. The muscles of his shoulders straining against his skin as the tree vine sized veins in his arms turn black.

Ares on the other side of the coliseum, black horns growing from him. As the horns created armor his voice boomed, "If you can walk out these doors." Ares pointed to the wide-open door behind him, "Freedom... is yours." A Trojan helmet, complete with a huge plum, forms from the horns in between his hands. Putting it over his head, his eyes turning to black fire... the plum on his helmet erupted into black flame, "Pledges, Ares... the God of War."

Every day from sunrise to sunset, we battled. Some days with just our fists others with sword and armor. On and on the cycle repeated. Then late into the afternoon Ares and I locked in hand-to-hand, applause came from the stands of the coliseum.

clap, clap, clap, clap, clap echoing

Ares and I broke our holds with a violent shove then started to circle one another. We both kept one eye on each other with the other scanned for the source of the clap, clap, clapping. A middle-aged man sat in the stands, his feet propped up the row of bleacher sets in front of him.

"So... What we wrestling for?" An older man with a short gray beard with hints of black in it and speaks in the heaviest Irish tongue I have heard, but spoke in perfect Greek.

"Freedom," With hate in my voice I answer before pretty boy could.

"Him or yours?" he asked standing up.

"His," Areas growling,

"Wasn't talkin' ta ya, laddie," The Irishman hopped down to the colosseum arena floor pulling his tunic over his head, letting it drape, to reveal Celtic tattoos that covered most of his body. With a twinkle in his eye the Irishman walked towards us, but looking at me the entire time eyes locked. "So how do you propose ta do that?" he asks me.

"By walking out those doors," pointing to the open doors on the opposite side of the coliseum I explained.

"Is that all." he smiled a wicked grin. "You just have to walk out those doors," the Irishman points over my shoulder. "Well... we'll just have to walk out together then," he walked right between Ares and me heading to the doors. Then paused, "You comin', or what?"

Huff BOOOMMMM Puuffff

Ares went to leap and smash this reckless mortal but when he did he found all the leather he was wearing had bounded together. The God of War fell to the coliseum floor in a cloud of dust. Flopping and flipping Ares trying to free himself.

The Irishman winked at me. We walked out those fucking doors without a word. Then he asked me my name and I couldn't answer him, never had someone asked me my name. He shrugged, "Well, Angus... My name's Ironniesous."

Daddy

Alex's voice… snapped me back to reality and I sprang into action, running from the kitchen.

Angus

The Minotaur is best known as an ancient Greek monster, half-man and half-bull. The beast is most famous for dwelling inside a labyrinth where he devoured dozens of human sacrifices each year. The ancient Greeks depicted the Minotaur as a creature with a man's body and a bull's head. Minotaur's actual appearance is less human and more bullish, only his muscled stomach and arms are human, although he does manage to walk upright on his bull's legs.

The Minotaur was a bloodthirsty, mindless monster. He killed innocent, unarmed victims and feasted on their bodies. It's possible that the Minotaur was not so monstrous; he might even have been viewed as a hero by the people of Minoa.

Thor

Chapter 21

Angus is fast, like facken super-fast cause I was only a cent-a-meter away from breaking the protective circle. When he pulls me back by my jacket, causing me to crash to the floor on my ass.

"Thanks, "I tell him.

He nods leaning over to rub the dry blood away, gently dissolving the circle. Looking at myself, *when did I put on a jacket?* I shrugged out of the 15th century sailor's pea coat and tossed it on the back of randomly placed chair in the study. I looked at Angus and back at the white and black jacket and I couldn't remember putting on the jacket.

Angus saw the bewildered look, "You were cold."

MMM..

Alex started to stretch knocking the feather pen and sketchbook made of magic parchment tumbling to the floor, "Daddy..."

I looked at Alex then to him, "She will still need rest, sit by her, reassure her everything will be alright," Angus tells me. "Lie to her,"

I mean mug him. He shrugged, “It's what parents do to protect their children.”

Walking to Alex, “I have never lied to her before, I will not start now,” I picked up the fallen things, placing them to the side. Sitting on the floor next to my daughter, “Hey you.”

I filled my daughter in, telling her about running like the Flash with her through the woods, the biggest Hobbit hole, and the Minotaur Angus. She drifted in and out of sleep, I picked her up off the floor.

“The couch in the living room is very comfortable,” Angus informed me.

He was right the couch was and it was Minotaur size, facken huge. Angus moves a pillow under Alex's head, while I recovered her. The huge bull man flops into an oversized lazy boy, and drops the sketchbook and feather quill on the table next to his chair.

“Alex must stay here... with me,” Angus putting his massive finger on the sketchbook, “Her magic will get stronger. These will help her channel it,” Angus said. The feather quill popped up and the sketchbook opened on its own. Angus in surprise pulls his hand away.

SWIVL SCRIBBLE SWOOP SCRIBBLE

The feather floats across the page as Alex's orange magic flares. We both looked at Alex, she was sound asleep but I could see her magic seeping from her. The Quill falls softly to the parchment.

Angus holding the very detailed portrait up, “Ring any bells?”

I just looked at the drawings. The orange of Alex magic fades to sepia brown and black. Under the man's eyes the only hints of color. The entire parchment was drawn as an old playing card, the eight of spades. Across the face of the card a detailed portrait of a cowboy instead of an eight spades.

“Doc Holliday,” I said to Angus.

Of course, I know who that is. Other folks think Jesse James or Billy the Kid is the shit, not me. The number one gunslinger from the old west is hands down Doc Facken Holliday.

Angus studies the picture, “I concur.” He paused to stroke the thick hair on his chin thinking.

I do the same not in thought about the image of Doc Holliday but of Alex… I clenched my jaw looking at Angus, “Look I need your word, I want your word… you will do whatever...”

Whoosh SRATCH scribble swoosh scratch scratch

Before I could finish the feather quill leaps up lashing out at the sketchbook. The violence of motion knocked the sketchbook out of Angus hand. We watched the two items fight like alley cats across the floor. Then it was done before I could even turn to check on Alex.

Angus picked up the feather quill setting it on the table next to him. I looked at the sketchbook, the parchment was actually cut in some places. A zombie Native American warrior sat cross legged with a dead child in his lap. A huge demon cheti danced above his Mohawk.

I looked at Angus.

Ripping the picture from the sketchbook Angus started out towards the living room, “If you ever refer to me as Chewbacca I will stomp on you.” With those words I felt his magic close around me and Alex.

Irons’ Irish voice talking in my ear, “Sir, Sir is headed back to the library. We’ll keep a watch over her, Sir.”

On the other chair the white and black 15th century sailor’s pea coat. Its hoodie had a pattern that made it look like it was looking at me, I swore I left in the study. Irons, my helmet looked up at me from the seat. I shrugged, maybe Angus brought them from the study. I gave Alex a kiss heading to the library. Halfway down the hallway Angus walks by me, with a huge book in his hand, pieces of old parchment used as bookmarks. He walked past the living room towards the study.

In my best Batman's imitation, "To the Study, Robin," wiggling my fingers up in the air.

Angus sitting at his desk, his glasses propped up on his nostrils, face down in the huge book. I pushed one of his bull horns out of the way so I could see what he was reading. He thumbs through a couple pages and starts to read out loud.

"Single Navajo kills everyone and displayed the scalps off all the children nailed to the front gate. All of the US cavalrymen had their hearts ripped out," Angus skips down the paragraph. "Connor and I investigated fully coming to the conclusion that this Navajo medicine man could walk through different planes of existence at will." Angus leans back in his chair closing the book and starts tapping his glasses against his teeth, "I wonder if this Navajo is the same Indian known as the killer of the white man's Gods…"

Looking down at the almanac I can only make out 1817-1917 case files.

"Keepers of the Hidden case logs, I borrowed it from their library," matter of factly Angus answering my curious look. Putting his glasses on top of the book, "Tell me everything."

So, I did, the magical tornados, Odin, the Navajo, and Thor walking out the rainbow bridge, all of it.

Life Debt

A life debt is a magical bond formed between a magical being and the magical being whose life they saved or swore an oath to. The one who owes the debt to the other would one day be obliged to repay the deed by doing something beneficial to the said savior. Such a bond can be formed between even the worst of enemies, regardless of the involved parties wished it or not. As this bond is magically binding, the indebted could commit the repayment without acknowledging it, or even against their will. Some debts are passed down and very depending on the particular magical being.

Angus, Minotaur of Minoa

Chapter 22

After we had chained smoke, my entire pack of cigarettes researching this Navajo. Angus snored fast asleep in the lazy boy so I put a blanket over him that I found in his study. I checked on Alex, sleeping peacefully, without another episode. I pick up Irons off the chair where he had been a sentinel over my daughter.

"You ready?" I ask the helmet.

"Whenever Sir wishes to depart," Liam Neeson replies.

Making a quiet get away never seems to work out for me. With Irons tucked under one arm and my boots held in my other I didn't notice the white and black sailor's pea coat on the floor.

YANK SMACK TING

With a clatter of the metal helmet hitting the floor, I looked up to see if Alex or Angus had woken. Neither moved a muscle still both sleeping. Sitting up off the floor I untangled my legs and feet from the sleeves of the coat. It was like trying to take off a wet pair of jeans, kicking and pulling to free myself. The dark gray triangles on top of the leather hood seemingly to squint at me.

A sleepy Sam Elliott, "Don't forget your jacket," and Angus rolls over pulling up his blanket.

"It's not my jacket!" tugging it off me and tossing I proclaimed.

“Tell him that,” Angus snorts his reply.

Like the face hugger from Aliens the pea coat ran across the floor right at me causing me to instinctively crab crawl away. The sleeves had ripped apart at the seams giving it four legs in the front. The hind legs of it forms from the bottom of the jacket.

“What the fuck!” sounding like a pubescent teenager I yelp.

The 15th century sailor’s pea coat from my nightmares slides around me gripping my bare skin with what feels like little suction cups. Without putting my arms through the sleeves, I was just wearing the jacket sitting on the floor. I stood looking myself over, running my hand down the sleeves, softest leather ever. The jacket reminded me of a video game my son played *Assassin's Creed*. The coat was a fantastic multi layered Captains pea coat, which even *Captain Jack Sparrow* would be proud to wear. I sighed in acceptance to my defeat and my magic flared, just for an instant. The jacket shivering, like it exhaled in a hiccup, then relaxed around me.

“Sir, if Sir is finished putting on his coat,” Irons says with a hint a cynicism in his voice. “Sir did mention that Sir was ready to depart.”

I waved my middle finger really close to the helmet’s eyes. Leaving him on the floor instead. I walked over to Alex checking on her one last time. Leaving her was hard, I took in a strong breath through my nose, smelling her being, not just her physical aroma.

I swooped Irons off the floor on the way out of The Minotaur’s Hobbit hole.

“Sir was that really necessary,” he asks me?

“Yeap,” I told him as I closed the front door as quietly as possible.

blink..blink VAROOOM HHMMMMMMMMMM SWOOOSH..

I took in a breath placing Irons over my head. Just small goose bumps danced across my tattoos. The combination lock was easier the second time and I was back in Panola National Park.

"Sir, music while run or would Sir prefer a story," he asked me as the HUD display came to life highlights the path home.

I closed my eyes trying to recall what I did last time to access the Speed Magic. This time when I exhaled, I let everything go, just let it wash away, the anger, pain, and sadness. I just held like that, not breathing until my cup was empty. I crouched down in a sprinter stance, digging my fingers into the very earth. Inhaling I pulled from the earth itself, tattoos glowing bright. I let the magic fill my cup until it was spilling over the sides.

"A story," I answered him. Releasing the magic as I pushed off.

KABOOM... ZZZZOOOOOOOOMMMMMM

"How... About... the one on how you got stuck inside this helmet?" I asked.

"Sir, that particular story is not what I had in mind," Irons stated to evade the question.

"Okay," I'll tell him. "Whatcha have in mind," letting him off the proverbial hook, for now.

"It was 1685 off the coast of Africa two battle hardened Ship Captains wage war on one another," Irons said as he actually showed me.

Aboard the pirate ship Amy, Captain George Dew yells over the musket blasts at the youngest member of his crew, "Cut us loose!" The 9-year-old boy already in motion dancing between the two ships starts cutting Amy away from the slave vessel. Edward already 5' 5" was going to grow up to be a big man someday, chopped the moor lines while ducking the many other fighting sailors.

Huge octopus tentacles slither between the two ships and wrapped around the other ship. With splinters of wood exploding the octopus squeezes the slave vessel. Edward is sent crashing to the other deck of the ship. The Kraken continues to crush the ship as Edward dodges sailors and tentacles alike. From the belly of the slave ship Edward could hear the slaves screaming.

With a massive ejaculation of water, the bow of ship is snapped off. Without hesitation Ed jumps down to the lower decks to save the slaves, still shackled, from drowning. With the slave ship rapidly sinking he tried to move as quickly as he could until the bulkhead and deck explodes. Tentacles smash the timbers to dust as the ocean floods in, filling the compartment with water. With no time to get a full breath of air, Edward panics and begins to drown.

He managed to swim through the broken hull of the slave ship but right as his feet cleared the jagged timbers, his breath ran out. He thrashed and kicked his lungs filling with water. His arms frantically swam in circles as he choked.

He felt the sharp prickly pain first, then saw a baby kraken wrap its tentacles around the boy's hand running up his arm as the small kraken swims to the surface of the water. Gasping for air he swims back to his ship.

The juvenile kraken saved his life but leaves perfect circle lesions all up and down his left arms and hands. For the next two years until Captain Dew and Captain William Kidd sacked Guayaquil Ecuador, Edward and the baby kraken became inseparable.

1704 Edward stands on the deck of his own ship as the storm rages all around him. His thick black beard being blown over his shoulder from the gale force winds. His leather Captain's hat pinned securely to the rag tied around his head, to ensure that the hat Captain Dew gave him would not fly away.

"Captain, the ship can't take much more!" his first mate yells over the storm and crashing waves.

He just ignores the man scanning the water, until finally he sees the one mast size tentacle break through the waves.

"Found you," he whispers. He watches through the storm as more of the Kraken's tentacles emerge from deep. He briefly looks at the suction cup scars that dotted his arm knowing.

Then yells, "The hunt begins! To your stations! We have magic to harvest!"

"Sir, the two kraken's tale, are one and the same," Irons returns to his normal tone of voice. "The jacket, Sir now wears," Irons paused for just a couple of brief seconds then continues, "is also the same kraken, Sir," Irons finishing with.

"No shit!" I blurted. "Hank... I'm going to name you Hank, after my oldest daughter's favorite movie from when she was a baby Disney's Pixar "Finding Nemo". Well the second one, never mind."

"Sir, is not going to parking lot. Sir's sister, Liz was already informed and is waiting at home," Irons mentions as I noticed that we were not going in the right direction.

Coming to super hero stop in my front yard sending a rooster tail of dirt in the air. I pull Irons off walking up the front steps.

"Wonder what time is it?" I ask myself.

"4:20 am," Irons answers.

Spells

Magic spells are not just wished to life, it is cast with action and purpose. Contrary to popular belief, most spells don't actually require the waving of a magical wand or a focus, a practitioner can use words or songs or just their will. From simple snaps to complicated hand gestures, all movements of the hands are used to harness magical energy and produce magical effects.

But a spell needs something more than hand movements and the proper knowledge of its circumstances. Along with the physical aspects of magic, the psychological aspects of magic are crucial to properly performing a spell. Magic is based on how powerful the spark is within a practitioner, much like the willpower of your soul.

For a spell to work, it has to be done from the heart. It is a focused intensity, a clear view, an unwavering sureness. The practitioner has to have no doubt that the spell will work, and needs to intend to do that spell wholeheartedly. Therefore, a practitioner cannot simply be forced to do a spell.

Angus, Minotaur of Minoa

Chapter 23

Waking up on the living room couch my face jammed between the cushions. I wiped the snot and drool from my face making my way to the kitchen.

"Coffee I need," yawn, "Coffee!" I explained to myself out loud.

KaThud

Then I was walking face first into the wall. Nope I blink I rubbed my head from exhaustion not a wall of sorts. Thor was holding a cup of hot coffee tenderly, not to spill it. Walking by him I took it, sitting down at the kitchen island. A quick smell of the caffeine goodness and I took a big gulp.

"You can start with who the fuck is the scary Navajo," I look at Thor drinking his coffee.

He did not answer just looked at his coffee. I took another drink of his coffee. He slowly made his way around the kitchen making another cup of coffee.

"Your daughter is well?" Thor asked but does not wait for reply "Good, good that is good," putting his empty cup under the tap. "The

Navajo medicine man turned Skinwalker is called Iisxiinii 'Ana'i Haashch`eeh," punching numbers on the microwave. "Killer of white man's Gods," pressing start.

Angus was right, the information in the Keeper's log book and this Skinwalker is the same dude but I kept it to myself. I notice the time on the clock when Thor retrieves the hot water, 6:12 am. Less than two hours of sleep no wonder I'm so tired. Out the corner of my eye a faint glow of yellow and orange was coming from the hallway. I leaned over to see down the hall from where I was sitting.

ZZTT ZZTT WHOOSH

The linen closet door under the stairs, flying open and Angus comes walking out his Hobbit hole hallway clearly visible behind him as the door shuts. The look of an insanely intense college professor creased his bull face. A stack of different book and accouple scrolls of varying widths extruded underneath his arms.

"To the Batcave, Robin!" I proclaimed as I watched Angus walk past me and towards the office as if he knew exactly where to go. Thor didn't even seem to notice Angus's entrance or exit. He just turned stirring his instant coffee.

"You refer to the geek-cave, as Cindy would say," Thor walking to the office as he said it and facken drops his coffee to spill all over the office carpet. Thor squares off against Angus. "What is this Greek half breed doing here?"

"He's kinda like my…," I started to say but Angus gave the eat shit and die look. I gave Angus my best I'm innocent expression, "I wasn't going to say Chewie."

I looked at Angus's bull face as I swore Sam Elliott from the Netflix show The Ranch said, "Then by all means!"

Walking around the statue Thor had made of himself, "Alfred I was going to say Alfred," I backpedaled. I looked up at Thor and pointed to the coffee stain on the carpet, "Cindy and Liz are going to trip their shit when they see the facken carpet. You spilled it, you clean it."

"GGRRRUUUMMBBLLE," Thor looked down at the carpet grunting.

Angus opening each book to specific bookmarked page laying them on my desk. He pulls a smaller wrapped up parchment out, unrolling it flat it's actually two pieces of paper. Laying a piece of parchment between two of the books. First was the picture Alex drew of the Navajo sitting on the ground, the other Angus had revealed was another of Alex's, but I haven't seen it yet.

Tap TAP Tap

It was a picture of an Indian medicine bag with an odd symbol for an Indian to use on a traditional medicine bag, three black feathers and a broken carved horn. He pointed out the black and blue horn it reminds of a carved elephant tusk but has a narwhales spiral growth ring, by tapping on the paper.

"This!" Angus pausing to look at the books he opened, "The horn of Indrik protector of The Holy Mountains in Russia... and this symbol." He points to the medicine bag. "The Leviathan the alchemy symbol for sulfur also the mythical whale from the Bible and other myths all included an underwater supernatural creature.

TAPPING TAP TSP

The feathers, well there are three black feathers with no visible markings making them nearly untraceable but not impossible to research," he concluded.

FLIP flutter

Angus went to the third book and opened it onto the desk rapidly skimming through the page, "1815 Fort Glenn Arizona was attacked by the native Indians. 352 people massacred men, women and children. A negro, the only survivor was questioned and repeatedly said that it was just one Indian." Pulling out the largest scroll a rubbing of a Viking rune stone and started to translate.

"Be warned for man that wears another's animals face lives in the Newfoundland!" Thor pauses, "And now he comes for Odin!" Like thunder a deep rumble came from Thor still looking at the coffee stain on the carpet.

“No!” Angus replies. “Iisxiinii will be too busy with getting THESE back!” holding up Alex's drawing of the 3 things I had cut from him during the fight on I-20.

SSSSHHHHHHHHHH drip..drop SSSSHHHHHHHHHH drip..drop drip..drop SSSSHHHHHHHHHH

Caster

A caster of magic, wizard, enchanter, mage, magician, sorcerer, warlock. Are broken into two categories, Wizard or Warlock both are known as Casters.

Warlock is an older word than wizard, coming from the Old English waerloga, which means oath breaker.

While wizard comes from the Middle English word for wise. Wizards generally use magic in the pursuit of knowledge. They are good Beings with strong moral codes who also offer wise advice and assistance. This moral code affects their magic greatly.

A Warlock, on the other hand, can and will use their magic to destroy and kill. Battle Magic was created by Warlocks.

Wizard and Warlock are typically used to refer generally to male practitioners of magic. Witches referred to all women who practiced magic. This is wrong, Witchcraft is a different faith entirely. There are male and female Casters just like there are female and male Witches.

Angus, Minotaur of Minoa

Chapter 24

SSSSHHHHHHHHHH drip..drop SSSSHHHHHHHHHH drip..drop drip..drop SSSSHHHHHHHHHH

In the shower the water as hot as it would get, my skin red from the scalding water. Leaning against the tile with my forehead not even remembering when I got in the shower.

“Dad, there's a Minotaur in the kitchen asking if you want bacon and Thor just left,” Nathan's voice comes through the door of the bathroom.

“Yeah man!” I called out to him.

I took a little longer than I should have in the shower. Walking in the kitchen in my towel to find Angus cooking bacon and eggs for everyone. Liz and Cindy at the table gossiping about something, Nathan and Kara fighting over a mobile device of some sort, and Alex… face down plowing through her food. I couldn't help but smile pulling out a bigger chair for Angus, we all ate.

“The guy at Chevron is a Jin,” my wife's way of small talk.

Angus asks her if he had said what region he was from and I tuned all them out just watching everyone eat. My mind only coming up with one conclusion to our problem. Excusing myself from the table still in my towel caught up with family and went to get dressed for war.

But instead of going to the bedroom I went to the office. I pushed the bottom shelf ducking in my Dojo and Temple to my Gods. I grabbed the clothes Thor had given me in Asgard pants and shirt. Pulling the thick gray leather pants up, the belt self-buckles. The sleeveless light gray shirt fits like under armor.

I pull a set of dog tags from the wall, one tag is mine the other is my father's father, well my step dad's dad, but if you ever called him anything else then my father I'd John Wick your ass, and drop them over my head. Next to the dog tags hung a white with a black pattern desert scarf stained and tattered. Folding it and tying it around my neck.

I ducked out the secret door, back into the office before I stood, Hank was wrapping himself around me. I have never liked guns they always felt distant in my hands. I pulled a folding chair over to another bookcase and pulled a row of books out that are attached to one another. A dust covered Winchester not much different than the one the lead character has in Jurassic World. Hopping down I check the lever and the optics.

cha-chuck...click

"You're going to need more than a single shot rifle, Cowboy!" Angus informs me from the office door as the hammer falls on the Winchester.

"Yippee ki yay yea," flipped the rifle, spinning it around onto my back. As I did this the belt Huginn and Muninn had given me compensate creating a separate bandolier. "You know that facken zombie Indian called me the same," reaching under a Batman statue searching for the button.

click, pop

"I've been thinking this guy can't be tracked or one of these Gods would have found him," Snapping my fingers together trying to remember, "What you'd call them Keepers of the Hidden? Wouldn't those guys have taken him out by now?"

I reach down into the concealed drawer pulling out two different 1911 checking each one. I put one in the bandolier across my chest pirate style. The other 1911 was place in a cross draw position tucked into my belt. I shoot a million times better with my right hand then my left, so why would I want to put a gun that I have to pull with my left.

"So, let's figure a way to find those three items and let that mother fucker come to us!" holding my closed fist up like I had a great weapon in my hand. Lou manifests into wicked Battle Axe, "And cut his fucken head off!" With my point across Lou disappears.

"I will need your daughter's help," Angus says.

From next to him Alex says, "When do we start?"

"Now," I say.

They get to work on some sort of circle on the floor of the sunroom, taking with them all the books and scrolls into the sunroom.

I pick up my lighter and cigarettes.

"Sir, Sir doesn't need his lighter to light Sir's cigarettes," Irons says in my ear.

"Show me!" I said out loud knowing he could read my mind.

Irons begins, "Just like when Sir pulled the magic from Gaeia to run. Sir needs to pull your magic into the tip of the cigarette…"

In concentration imagining my magic spinning the molecules of air right above the cigarette. The tattoos on my wrist and the back of my hand glowing green. The cigarette tip flared green and then red bringing it to my lips.

"Neat trick," I smiled to myself and exhaled the smoke.

"Extraordinary," Irons and Angus say with general surprise at the same time.

I take another hit from my smoke, "You and Alex ready?"

Angus just nodded, "There is no guarantee this'll work," he tries to prepare me.

I walked into the sunroom Angus had used orange spray paint on the sunrooms wood floor painting a three-ringed circle around Alex. Purple glyphs and runes traced the inner and outer rings of the circles. I looked at Alex in her eyes as she sat on the floor.

"She's got this," I say as I sit just like her outside the circles.

Alex closed her eyes, "Find what is missing," she whispered to the feather quill.

The quill jumps to Da Vinci's sketchbook. It started to draw a forest covered slightly in snow with a staircase made of stone with years of moss growth. A massive rune stone with Norse glyphs carved into it sat under a tree at the bottom of stairs.

"It may take some time to narrow down that Rune-stone, but not impossible," Angus says, but I already had an idea.

I got up to grab two pairs of socks and my boots. Sitting on my bed sliding my foot in one of the boots.

"Heimdall!" I say out loud, "If you can pull yourself away from whatever you're doing ya think you could take a look at it?"

I feel the pressure first like right before your ears popped. Opening the window and a fine mist floats in the air on this cloudless morning.

Coming out the bedroom into the hall I notice the linen closet door under the stairs was open. Pecking around the door to see if it was the closet or facken Angus almost runs me over coming back through the door, stopping suddenly to look at me.

"Ironniesous once told me it," Angus puts on an Irish accent that's worse than mine. "Angus me boyo, it's always better to be the attacker, the aggressor… than to be crawling backwards, cowering behind fear. That's not how a fight is won. Perception and the will to act." He reaches behind his back pulling a round shield with a crescent notch in it.

“A Spartan shield was made not only to defend the soldier but let soldier use the opportunity to turn defense into offense,” Angus tells me handing the shield to me.

I just took it flipping Captain America style onto my back, the shield was really light weight but had no wobble. It sat perfectly over the rifle. The crescent shape made the stock easily accessible. The belt of burden adjusted itself to hold the shield across my back.

Angus in his normal voice, “It was Ironniesous.” Pausing, pulls out a rolled parchment from Alex's sketchbook so of course, I thought it was some new vision she had but it was blank. The left top corner and bottom right corner had glyphs set in a right angle, the top right corner had nautical compass, the needle being redrawn, the left bottom corner had numbers 1, 2, 3 and 4. He showed me then rolls it back.

“Do not lose this,” Angus chides me but instead of giving the scroll to me he gives it to Hank and it disappears inside jacket.

“Sir, What Sir's daughter draws. A copy Sir will receive,” Irons filling me in on the blank parchment.

“Angus I need you,” I tried to ask him.

“I'm not holding your hand,” Angus cuts me off, “I will be too busy warding your home and teaching your daughter to control her magic.”

Kara running into me full force bouncing off me to the floor. I look at her and she has Irons on her head making her look like a bobble head. I pick her up still wearing the helmet.

Before my foot hit the front porch, Alex and Nathan wrapped their arms around me and I stopped, giving all three of them a huge hug. Liz looking at us like a lost puppy so I wave her over to join. Putting my arms around all four of them I squeeze hugging them tighter.

We all went outside together and stood on the lawn in front of the rainbow bridge.

“Okay, you're Daddy has to go to work,” Cindy tells the kids.

I put Kara down. The helmet jiggles on Kara's head like a bobble head. I give my wife a big kiss as she shuffles the kids and Liz into the house.

She hands me an extra pack of cigarettes and Odin's pipe. I put the cigarette in some random pocket and tucked the pipe in my belt. "Love you," as she looks at me telling me that I better come home with just her eyes.

"I will…" kissing her forehead.

Before I stepped in the rainbow I knelt on one knee placed Irons to one side of me with both hands I scooped up earth and dirt rubbing it in my hands like soap.

Clap Clap Clap Clap clap

I smacked my hands knocking the loose debris off in puffs. Praying to all my Gods to grant my enemies a quick but painful death. It's an old tradition I picked up in the desert when I was a young man. See just a light coating of dust or dirt keeps your hands from sweating. I picked up the white helmet.

blink..blink VAROOOM HHMMMMMMMMMM SWOOOSH..

Irons slides on my head like an old friend, his magic flares sending a single wave down through my ink and the HUD display appears. Walking into the rainbow bridge this time was like the ice bucket challenge as I stepped through.

WHISSSHH WHISSST WHISSSSP… WHISSSHH WHISSST WHISSSSP

Ratatoskr

Ratatoskr is a squirrel who carries messages along Yggdrasil, the tree of life. The most regular subscribers to his messaging service are the wise eagles who sits at the top of Yggdrasil and the hungry dragon, Nidhoggr, who lies coiled among the tree's roots. Ratatoskr relishes the chance to ferry an insult between these two mighty beasts, and by doing so, he is continually stirring the animosity between them.

Scurrying up and down the Norse tree of life is Ratatoskr, a giant red squirrel with extremely long ears and a taste for mischief. Ratatoskr may have big responsibilities as a messenger for the gods, but he doesn't accept his duties meekly. This crafty squirrel puts his own spin on his role.

Thor

Chapter 25

WHISSSHH WHISSST WHISSSSP… WHISSSHH WHISSST WHISSSSP

It really does feel like a dry waterfall when you step inside the rainbow bridge. At the end of the rainbow I found myself standing in the very same place Alex had drawn during her fingers casting. I lean over and brush snow from the 3 ft rune stone.

“We're definitely not in Kansas anymore,” informing myself as I start up the stone steps.

“Sir, Ratatoskr,” Irons warning me.

Getting to the top of the stairs a 4 ft tall red squirrel stood on two legs chewing on a nut. A Norse version of Rocket Raccoon crossed with Pikachu spits out what he had in his mouth. With no sound he digs into his full mailbag strapped over his shoulder. He pulls a folded letter out holding in his paw. Have you ever really watch a squirrel move? They take hyperactivity to a whole new level. A normal squirrel is six inches tall and twitch constantly, try watching super squirrel stand still long enough to hand me a letter.

“Chittering, chitter, chitttt, chit,” Ratatoskr tail twitching.

“From Thor,” I asked?

“Chit,” Ratatoskr confirmed holding it out to me.

“Yep, opening it now, thank you,” I tell Ratatoskr as I took it and started to unfold it.

“CCHHitter chit,” Ratatoskr says puzzled.

I look back at the squirrel, “Yeah man,” and started to read.

“Chitter chat chitter?” Ratatoskr asks me.

I nodded my head that I would and folded up the note putting it in my back pocket. I took a blank parchment from the squirrel that he offered me to write on.

chuck chuck chuck

Ratatoskr had a pencil in his mouth and took the pencil wiping it off on my pants.

When I was finished with my note. He shoved it in his bag with a chitter. He wiggled his big ears and bounded away up into the canopy. I just watched Ratatoskr hop from branch to branch.

“Why is everything so big here?” asking myself out loud.

I didn't super speed and go running around like a chicken with my head cut off, if you don't have a destination it's best to take it one step at a time. I just walked through the endless forest on the very well-traveled path from the looks of it.

The path wound through the woods as I walked. The forest finally opened wide to let in the sky.

I walked out the tree line and was no more than a yard from woods when I was surrounded by tall green grass.

Not far off in the distance I could make out smoke.

“Sir, Sir does not know if that is a friend or foe. Sir did mention that, Sir was not in Kansas anymore,” Irons warning me.

“By Odin’s pipe or by Lou’s tip, makes no never minds,” shrugging my reply.

I started to hear small results of leaves and noticed the shadow track me from the forest. Then Irons' HUD started tracking the movement, marking it with a green targeting outline, making me feel like RoboCop meets Iron Man.

"Sir, Sir is being stocked," He tells me as the HUD appears.

"Yeah man," bending over near the tree line and stomping off a good size branch off a fallen tree. "Fetch!" and the stick sails by the last green outline of movement.

Crash, crash crunch, snap

A facken freight train of joy barreled out of the woods, a gold and red dire wolf, the wolfs tail swings back and forth.

"RrrrRuf!" she says with the stick in her mouth.

I took the stick, "Of course." Throwing it deep into the woods again.

The dire wolf pounces on me with her excitement it's huge head immediately goes submissive. I take her chin and lift it so her muzzle is eye to eye with me, "You're a good girl." I pet her roughly with both my hands and noticed the collar and cringed. A shriveled human hand carved with runes hung from her neck.

"Whoof Yelp!" she responded with licking the front of my helmet with attention to lick it off my head. Her head darts towards the campfire and her master.

"What's your name?" I ask as I massaged her neck with both hands.

"Yelp whine," tucking her tail between her legs.

"No name…humf?" I petted her head. "Whatcha ya think about Lana?" I ask her.

"Grrr ruff!" looking at me with surprise. I just nod my head yeah and she starts to hops up and down. She then runs in circles around me skids to a halt turning to me.

"Ruff Rufff!" super-excited trotting off to find her master.

"You sure?" teasing her on as if she likes her name.

She turns running behind me, pushing me toward the campsite with that big melon of hers.

"Ggrrrrr!" she insisted.

"Okay, Lana, quiet pushing," I told the massive wolf.

She walks on my right side the entire time it takes to get to the campsite. Her tail like a pendulum on a clock was steady as I petted her as we walked. When we walked into her camp her demeanor changed into guard dog. Her tail goes rigid and all her hairs bristle on her back. She whines to me and I winked at her, that it was all good.

She disappears into one of the four large tents ahead of me. I sat next to the flames letting the heat wash over me, Hank absorbing the heat spreading it evenly, instant heat blanket. Looking at the dirt around the fire Lou materializes in my hand, as a walking cane I start to trace patterns in the soft earth while I waited.

CRACKLE BURN FAWOOSH

Talking Animals

Before the Accords all kinds of animals like bears, rabbits, wolves, snakes, owls, lions, tigers and all the Mythical Creatures could talk. Over time those languages were lost to man and Gods. Each creature has its own dialect, not many Magical Beings in this day and age can understand one animal or Mythical Creature besides all of them.

Angus, Minotaur of Minoa

Chapter 26

I leaned back against a tree as I sat on the ground. The fire just in front of me. Four tents spread evenly apart that made a half circle around the campfire. The path that I had fallowed out the forest was about twelve yards beyond the tents. To my right was the way I had come, to my left the way I needed to go.

Lana the red and gold dire wolf prances over to me and lays her big head over my legs. Then with a thud, plopped down on the ground next to me. I rubbed her behind her ear.

"Your name, stranger?" Clint Eastwood asks me from the other side of the fire.

He was only about 5" taller than me but he was wider than a set of double doors. He held a still bleeding troll's head in his one leather gloved hand. His other arm ended at the wrist, rested on the hilt of his sword. The bangs of his long pure white hair were pulled tight behind his head. His white beard and mustache hugged his weathered face. A jagged scar ran down the left side of his face from his hairline to his jaw disappearing beneath his beard. He drops the trolls head into the fire. Unintentionally fluffing his blood red fur cloak and hood as he does so. The thick red fur droops over his massive shoulders and is clasped in the center of his chest. A brass wolf's head with rubies set in the eyes holds the stained and ripped cape around the Asgardian Forest Ranger.

"RuuRuffffff gruff!" the wolf barks at her master as he rolls his eyes at her.

I pet her massive head, "She already gave you my name." The wolf chuffs at him in a see I told you so moment.

"Well Ironhood," stopping to confirm my body language that was my name, "My name is Gustav of the Red Capes." He sits opposite of me frustrated in the way his familiar was acting. "What brings you to the edges of Asgard?"

SHIVER SWISHHH SHIVERS SWISHHH SPAT!

Alex's scroll oozes out of Hank like the Venom symbiote from Spider-Man into my hand from under the sleeve. I enrolled the parchment handing Gustav the magic paper.

"Have you seen this guy or any of the following?" I asked him. Then the picture automatically charged to the picture of the medicine bag, the demon horn and feather, "Or know anyone who might?"

"I have not," the one-handed man told me handing me the scroll, "But they should be returning from patrol soon. You are welcome to wait."

"Your hospitality is a generous gift," I nodded to him. "You mentioned you're a Red Cape?" asking him.

"You have not heard?" I shook my head no, cutting his question off.

He began with his mission, "We guard the gigantic, ravenous wolf Fenrir and vow to kill him before he kills the All Father in Ragnarok. We all carry brass horns," tapping it the little horn hung on his belt. "If the great wolf ever breaks his bonds. But the wolf has slept like a forgotten volcano. Just like Tyr son of Odin gave his hand to bind the great wolf, so we do the same." He holds his stump up, "to bind our animals to us."

“GGGRRRRR!” she rumbled.

“An initiate must capture his own familiar and break its will. Animals are marked using the same blade we use to cut the runes into our living flesh,” trying to continue but his wolf glares at him.

“WOOFF, RRRuf ggrrrrr!” protesting her view of her tormentors. The hand that hung from her neck illuminated bright blue and she whined in pain. She crawled over to him whimpering.

“They have to completely obey their master,” and pets the wolf with one hand.

I have magic site, eat your heart out lion-o, so I concentrate on them both the blue line of magic starting to appear. The magic getting more in focus and defined. Norse magic looks like ribbons of runes made of blue light. Like a dog leash, it ran from the mummified hand around the dire wolf’s neck to the stump of Gustav left arm. I reached out with my mind, imagining I had a magic facken pencil eraser rubbing as hard as I could.

“Sir,” Irons whispered.

Then I noticed the spot where I was erasing. The rune was faded, clenching my jaws under my helmet I erased even harder. It was gone, the ribbon was still there, but the glowing rune was gone. Like dominos the runes on each side of the one I had erased faded away. Holy shit, I erased the runes on the magic ribbon.

The huge canine felt it first stretching all her muscles out in a backbend of relief. She brushed her body against him in a pet me please attitude. He just brushed her away, so she turned her huge eyes to his. He didn't even acknowledge her as her fangs ripped off his face.

SINK SPLURT..splurt GURGLE CHOMP CHEW SPLURT SPLURT..splurt

Tyr

Tyr is the Norse war god, but also the god who, more than any other, presides over matters of law and justice. His role in the surviving Viking Age myths is relatively slight, and his status in the later part of the Viking Age may have been correspondingly minor but this wasn't always the case. Other kinds of evidence show us that Tyr was once one of the most important gods to the Norse and other Germanic people. For example, in the Sigrdrífumál, one of the poems in the Poetic Edda. The Valkyrie Sigrdrifa instructs the human hero Sigurd to invoke Tyr for victory in battle. Another Eddic poem, the Lokasenna, corroborates this picture by having Loki insult Tyr by saying that he could only stir people to strife, and could never reconcile them.

But the most compelling evidence for Tyr's role as divine jurist – and a heroic one at that – comes from the tale of The Binding of Fenrir, the only surviving myth to feature Tyr prominently. The dreadful wolf Fenrir was only a pup, but he was growing quickly. The gods feared for their lives, so they endeavored to tie up Fenrir in fetters from which he couldn't escape. When Fenrir laid eyes on the chain that would eventually bind him, he was suspicious, and declared that he would only allow the gods to put it around him if one of them would stick an arm in his mouth as a pledge of good faith. Only Tyr was willing to do so.

Angus, Minotaur of Minoa

Chapter 27

Fountains of blood sprayed as she ate. From the left side of the dirt and rock path a white arctic fox the size of a Great Dane bounced out of the woods, then a gray dire wolf strolled down the path towards the campground. A few moments later three Red Capes strolled down the path. They talked and laughed to each other still oblivious.

First thing I noticed about the three was a Viking battle axe with runes carved into the arch of the blade. He was a barrel of a man, his blood red cape was torn completely in half making it look like a fur shawl. A great big wooden shield was strapped to his stump. He laughed hard and loud pushing a much skinnier man that walked on his left.

The skinny Asgardian's red hood fell back from his face. His head was completely bald and covered in tattoos. The tattoos ran down his clean-shaven jaw.

The last Red Cape stood at least a foot taller than both the others. The stump of his right hand had a three foot double-edged broadsword extending off it. It was lashed and strapped to his forearm gauntlet. His brown hair was cut short and jagged. The man's face was square and hard a two-day old beard covers his jaw. His red cape only hung from his left shoulder.

Why is everything so big here, I thought to myself, of course the giant tractor trailer sized brown bear chose that moment to lumber into view.

"GGGGRRRRRRRRRRR!" The gold and red dire wolf looks up, her master's head still in her mouth, the body limp. With a plop the dead body dropped from her mouth, she turned to me in fear, "ggggggrrrr."

"Go!" I winked at her. She leaps over the fire rubbing her huge neck and shoulder on me letting me know she would stay.

Lou materializes as a small blade and I slip it under the collar with a flick the dead hand falls away. With that last bit of freedom, she turns to the right and ran. I sat waiting for the three Red Capes watching the gold and red dire wolf disappearing down the path I had come from. The scent of blood had the two canines at the campsite in seconds. The Red Capes all at one time look towards there camp.

"Yelp, Yelp bark yelp!" Lana cries then screaming in terror from the right.

The three Red Capes stop. Making a defensive circle searching the tree line and the path to my right. The gray dire wolf and the white fox blast pass me on the way to intercept the new threat. I hadn't taken my eyes off the three warriors. Each had drawn a shield that covered the stump of one arm the other a battle axe, sword or a spear. They moved with fluid precision always scanning as they stalked my way.

CRASH, SNAP, YELP, snap whimper whine…

The forest went still no one even breathed.

"RRRROOOAAARR!" a feline demanded.

Jumping to my feet, my hands relaxed, ready. I scanned to my right as the three Reds did the same. The brown bear rearing up on his back legs towers over the big men.

Smash CRACK smack

"RRrrrrrROAR!" the cat demanded again.

"Wwwhhiinnee, Yyyeeellllpppp!" the two canines screams as they bounded into view.

My asshole puckered as the arctic fox red with wounds and the dire wolf with his ear torn off and face gashed opened retreats behind the three Reds.

"RRRROOOARRRRRRRRR!" the bear challenging.

The HUD started tracking movement past the tree line running perpendicularly to me. I watched turning my body to track the movement and the three Reds turned to consider me. The dead body of their brother clearly visible to them now. His face half missing, looks at them, his one eye dangling from the socket.

"You die," the spear point aimed over his shield, at my heart, the smallest of the Red Capes proclaimed, even though he is at least 7 inches taller than me.

"RARrrrrr Growl!" came from the flank of the Red Capes high in the treetops.

BLAM CRASH RRRUUUMMMMMBLE

Before they could spin to face the sound. The brown bear, its mouth open in a silent scream, crashed end over end into the forest. Clouds drifted lazily by the morning sun as the trees snapped and branches broke. The shadows of forest growing dark, a single cricket chirps a warning.

All eyes on the massive hole left by the fallen bear. Muscles tighten as we waited for something to spring from the tree line. A light fog rolls out the forest.

"RRARrrrr rrRoar!" the big cat explained padding down the path from behind the Red Capes blocking my view.

Click Clack

My Winchester rifle was pressed against my cheek, exhale, and squeeze.

BOOM

The three Reds in mid turn looked at the cat whipped around towards me.

Click Clack

Pulling the gun up, I aim.

BOOM

Click Clack BOOM

I stood in one spot timing every squeeze leading my bullet so the Red Cape that blocked my shot would move just enough. Finding my rhythm.

BOOM BOOM BOOM

I didn't yield until my rifle rang empty with a click. The saber tooth lion just shook its massive body like it was wet, not a drop of blood fell from the beast, and it tilted his head back.

RRrrrrrROAR RRRRRRRROAR

Mythical Creature

A mythical creature can be described as a creature thought not to exist and possibly possess mystical and, or magical powers.

An example could be the unicorn or griffin. A mythical creature is not to be confused with a cryptid, which is a prehistoric animal. The Tasmanian tiger is an example which was hunted to extinction, yet it's a cryptid because people have seen it.

Most mythical creatures resided from other realms. A creature does not need magic or be magical to be a mythical creature.

Other names for a mythical creature are mythical beasts, fabulous beast or legendary creatures, mythological creature.

Angus, Minotaur of Minoa

Chapter 28

THAWACK SLASH SWOOSH YYYEEELLLPPP gurgle gurgle gurgle

A saber tooth cat the size of a large rhino with 3 foot teeth leaped into action. Asgard seemed to be full of these super-sized creatures. The tiger landing on one of the Red Capes with a crunchy smack ripped the man in two then sprung back into the woods as the torso hung in its jaws. The arctic fox cringed curling up struggling for breath. The mummified hand around its neck was choking the life out of it. In that second the tiger had the fox in its teeth shattering the fox's spine and was gone again.

I don't remember backing up but I abruptly stopped when I stumbled into the tree behind me as I watched. It looked like a multiple car crash on the interstate. They're massacre was at 100 mph, brutal and over in seconds.

SLASH SWOOSH YYYEEELLLPPP GURGLE CRASH RRRUUUMMMMMBLE SSHHHUUUUCRACK gurgle gurgle gurgle gurgle gurgle CHOMP CHEW CHEW CHOMP CHOMP CHEW

Frozen like a deer in headlights I watched the tiger drag the dire wolf's mangled remains over to a comfortable spot and begin to eat. All I could think about was Animal Planet's show When Animals Attack. You watch this hunter feet from a lion, rhino, hippopotamus, he has a gun but the hunter just looks at it and does nothing. See the hunter's brain is running the physics and mathematics formulas in that second, caliber of bullet, and distance from target, speed and mass of said target. Then his feet say fuck that and he runs for dear life. Since I had already tried bullets and wasn't carrying a facken rocket launcher it was time to sneak away real quiet like.

The beast still shrouded by shadows a silhouette of carnage. The tiger inhaled deeply through its mouth, brings the air over its scent glands on the roof of its mouth. So, it not only could smell my scent it could facken taste it. The tiger licked the blood from one of his fangs shifted his shoulders. With a snap, pop the beast cracked its huge neck right before looking at me.

Sliding around the tree my feet scream fuck this and I immediately trip over the roots, tumbling face first. Scrambling on hands and knees to right my balance enough to facken get my legs under me. The tree trunk exploded behind me as the beast went through it not wanting to go around it.

KARACK BOOM SMASH

As the 500-year-old tree came crashing down. The green light of my magic started to glow from underneath Hanks sleeves. Time did that slow-motion thing. The HUD display blinked, all the optional information highlighted with distance and probabilities.

Time snapped back, a hail storm of branches rained down on me. Irons HUD lit up like *Dance Dance Revolution*, left step, two steps forward, hop right. I came out of the canopy at sprint, running on the trunk of the tree as it fell.

THUDDDD

The impact sending the forest into an upheaval of cries. I hit the forest floor in a dead run heading deeper into the woods. I pour on the speed. The trees get closer and closer together as I run. I'd juke left than right barely missing the tree trunks as I pass.

RUMBLE SNAP CRASH snap snap

The falling tree had barely touched the forest floor and its leaves erupted but I heard nothing. A rustle of leaves and a whispered snap of twig is the only indication that the tiger had landed right behind me.

SSSSMMMMAAAAACCCKKKK CRACK SMACK SMACK THUD thud thud

My body took a 90-degree left turn while the rest still wanted to move forward. I was suddenly crashing end over end. The shield that hung across my back took most of the giant paws impact. I reached pulling the shield to bare while still crashing down to the ground. Skidding on my shoulder the shield is hit again before I came to a stop. Breaking a trail of tree branches with my backside I roll to a stop. The mid-morning sun peeks through the foliage. I stand placing the shield in a guard position squaring myself off. The sun beams shine down like a spotlight over me. The silhouette of saber tooth tiger paced back and forth waiting for his mouse.

“I'm up for suggestions,” I inform Irons out loud just in case he stopped reading my mind.

“Sir, Sir could utilize the canopy in Sir's retreat. With the enhanced probability,” Irons stops mid-sentence, “Dance Dance Revolution as Sir kindly referred to it.”

The cat's ear poked up and its head tilted slightly listening to every word. The sun dips behind the clouds as my spotlight fades. The saber tooth cat strikes. I leap frog over its huge melon landing on its back. The huge cat bucks like bull spring boarding me off its back. But it's exactly what I intended, my tattoos flare up and I push with my magic launching myself high into the treetops.

SWISHHH CRACK THWACK SNAP SNAG

Landing gracefully on a branch, yeah right. I over shot crashing down and through the first branches grabbing on to one with dear life, I climbed up to my feet. The forest floor hundreds of feet below.

“Facken giant dudes, giant facken birds, facken giant dogs, now facken giant facken trees,” I mumble to myself as I started to jog along the tree branches. Worried about falling I pictured Irons' HUD holographic balloon shaped footprints and palm prints magically clinging me to the tree trunk. It stuck to the branches as lunched myself from branch to branch.

Crash Smash, Crash Smash

The canopy shakes as the saber tooth cat leaps up the trunks pinballing his way up to the treetops. The HUD displayed the next branch over so I side stepped. The branch that I was just occupying was gone, the cat had broken the trunk of the tree so I followed the idiot's guide to free running, parkour, from branch to branch in the treetops. The saber tooth crashing from trunk to trunk. Splinters rain down with the cannonball force of the cat's huge paws. It's claws grip deep and the bark explodes.

SWIPE CRACK SNAG RIP SNAP SWOOSH SWIPE CRACK

As I avoid near miss after near miss Irons and I start to flow. Just like when I used the speed magic when I super run I started pushing off with the magic and pulling the next branch to me. Keeping the magic around my hands and feet in green soap bubbles that would envelope the tree. Like you would see in an infomercial the big bubble wand and they make this long 9-foot bubble that's as big around as a small child, yeah that one. I would blow the magical bubbles up with just enough magic, careful not to burst my own bubble, pulling, gripping and pushing with every fiber of my being. “Timber” by Pitbull started to play.

Getting a handle on the combination of speed magic and the clinging magical bubbles around my hands and feet. I learned the magical bubbles of my green magic could be harnessed and utilized in different ways. The next tree trunk had a U shape arch to it due to what looked like a lightning strike. Still moving at 72 MPH in a blink of an eye I imagined Tony Hawk from my youth hit that high arch off the halfpipe. I let the bubble roll freely still gripping the surface but surfed across the branch like waves on the ocean. The clinging grip became more of a hover-slide effect. Eat your heart out Disney's Tarzan I think to myself running through the canopy… With the less effort of what I wanted my limbs to do but more instinctively moving them, I poured on the speed.

SWISHHH spring SNAP snag Woosh ZOOM

I called on nature's magic to fuel my flight. Musical notes of magic from the forest surge through me and into my tattoos. Magical energy pulsed through my tattoos in time with the beat of the song I was listening to. Making me look like a living EQ. Feeling like Obi Wan Kenobi letting the force flow through him, I imagined letting Irons and the magic guide my actions and we hit Warp Speed. Ha… see what I did there snuck in a Star Trek… never mind, I was moving at considerable amount of speed when I noticed that the saber tooth lion was gone. No longer crashing through the canopy behind me.

"Fuck! That means?" and I started to look down.

KARRACK

Gravity Magic

Gravity Magic allows practitioners to utilize gravitational force as a form of offense and defense magic. Practitioners who possess the ability to utilize such magic are able to generate these elements from their wands, vessels, hand gestures, or with there will alone and manipulate them. Practitioners can create, shape and manipulate gravitational forces hypothetical elementary particles that mediate the force of gravitation. To push and pull targets, create spikes from ground or manipulate earthen materials such as sand, clay etc. They can bend gravity to cause some objects to fall toward another object instead of the earth.

They can repel and attract matter and energy regardless of its mass or move objects in a manner similar to telekinesis. Practitioners of this power can increase gravity to crush or immobilize opponents, decreasing it to render them defenseless, or surrounding one's body in a gravitational field to amplify physical strength. The gravitational force can also be used to cling to any surface.

Ironniesous O'Keeffe

Chapter 29

The branch that I was running on breaks with a sudden snap when the weight of the saber tooth cat landed on it. I fall a foot or so landing on a branch below me springing me up to dart from the trunk of the nearest tree.

Still running through the leaf covered tree tops keeping one step ahead of the cat. I was tired of running, it was clearly not working, so I had to figure out plan C. The saber tooth cat attacks me exactly at the moment. Its claws passing under my boots as I dive into a hollow trunk of a great oak.

OWWWW zzziiiipppp SPLAT

I fall into the hole, the trunk of the tree turning into a sandpaper waterslide. I get ejected out the hollow tree trunk. With a graceful face plant I scramble on my belly. I crawled on my elbows, popping up on my knees. I leaped to a run the sunshine bright overhead. I was running in a small clearing, grass had just started to sprout. A tree stump with roots bigger around than a fifty-gallon drum lay directly in the center of the little meadow. Diving over one of the massive roots like TJ Hooker, I lay flat and hold my breath. Nothing, not even a soft panting of the cat's breath. With my right hand I lean very slowly up to see over my left shoulder. My eyes barely making over the lip of the root and my right-hand sinks to my elbow.

PPPRRRIIINNNNGGGGG

Breaks the silence as my helmet smacks the root. I had sunk elbow deep into a cavity under the stump. I could feel air on my fingertips. Wiggling my fingers like jazz hands the dirt crumbles away. Pulling my right arm free I grab my shield with my left. I dug with the shield like a dog for a bone. Deeper around the root, cramming the shield in the earth over and over. Shoving the shield under the root for another scoop of dirt it slips disappearing. With my bare hands I dig pushing myself into the earth. Falling into the hollow space under the huge stump. My shield breaks my fall. My eyes don't have time to adjust to the dim light because the green glow of my magic illuminates the stump's walls. The center of the fallen tree is bigger than I expected.

"Sir, Sir's plan C is to hide," Irons whispered. Knowing he could read my mind I replied silently plan C is always to hide.

It was like a carved out mini-cathedral inside the hollow tree stump. A wooden pillar sprout from the floor to the ceiling as thick as my leg. The huge hollowed out roots of the tree became dark foreboding tunnels shooting off in random directions. Getting to my feet the ceiling was still a foot over my head.

SHIVER SWISHHH SHIVERS SWISHHH SPAT! SPAT! SPAT! PLOP

Hank spits the scroll out on the dirt floor like it was dip. The rolled-up paper flops around the ground like fish out of water. I snatched up off the floor and untied it. It was blank as I unrolled but the magic parchment came to life when I finished extending the paper out fully. I am looking at it when the ink lines start to appear in a Celtic knot pattern, three-black feathers, inside the details of the knot a crow flies. I knew immediately two things; I'm looking for the feathers and whose feather it is. The compass in the corner of the parchment, its gears and cogs start to click and tick. Like old stop motion cartoons, it flickered with every movement of the gears. The animation speeding up making the compass move fluidly. Now I knew the direction.

So, I dug my way out from under the tree. With no signs of the huge saber tooth cat I reached for Irons.

STTTTT FIZZLE swoosh

I took off the helmet letting the afternoon sun heat my face. Opening the scroll to check the compass sure enough the needle pointed the way pulling my cigarettes out I magically lit it as I put it to my lips. My lungs filled with the smoke and I relaxed. With Irons tucked under my arm I smoked my cigarette scanning the forest and started to walk in the direction the compass indicated. The forest felt different when I passed the tree line. The connection with the feeling got stronger as I walked. Woodland animals like facken Snow White came up to inspect the strangers. I almost tripped a couple of times with those little bastards underfoot.

Groarrrr gurgle gurgle gurgle gurgle

My stomach letting everyone know that I was getting hungry.

CRACK

Hank snapped out like Indiana Jones's whip. A fat gray and white bunny wrapped in its tentacle dead from either from the strike or from strangulation. Hank tucks the rabbit away with the speed of a frog's tongue. It happens so fast it was if the Bugs Bunny had just vanished.

“Sir, Sir does like roasted Bugs Bunny,” Irons Irish voice chimed in.

I kept walking until the sun hung low when I heard the flow of water. So even though it was a little bit out of the way I made my way to the sound of a good-sized creek. I set up a small campfire along the stream. Gathering dry sticks in a bundle from up and down the banks of the creek. Dropping the fire woods, I grabbed the nearby rocks creating a circle. Only a short while later I had the sticks broke and laid in a teepee shape in the stone circle, with two Y shaped bigger branches on each side. I reached for my lighter.

“Sir, Sir does not need Sir's lighter,” Irons reminds me.

It took more magic to get the fire started but it didn't take any more thought than lighting my cigarette. So, it took me awhile to figure it out.

CRACKLE snap pop

With the fire burning I took out Odin's pipe.

Puff..puff Puff

"All right spit," I informed Hank holding my hand out.

SHIVER SWISHHH SHIVERS SWISHHH SPAT! BELCH!!!

The bunny landed in my hand, gutted, skinned and a little slimy. Hank shivering a burp, I laughed. So, after washing it off in the creek I roasted the fuck out of Bugs Bunny. I love how on TV or movies it only took a 30 second montage and wham bam, thank you ma'am, foods cooked, try 30 minutes. While I waited I did an inventory on my supplies and checked my gear. When I go to clean and reload the Winchester.

"MMM…," and I tossed the brass shells up in the air and caught them again.

I pulled bullets out of my pocket knowing I had to reload the rifle and found it already reloaded. I put all my gear back on and checked on Bugs.

I ate watching the sun set and the moon rise… and seeing the earth in the evening sky. I don't remember how long I sat there I even think I dozed off for a little bit. Okay I know I fell asleep cause I opened my eyes to see that the campfire had burned itself out. Stars filled the night, the moon and earth hung high in the sky.

blink..blink VAROOOM HHMMMMMMMMMM SWOOOSH..

Battle Magic

Battle Magic manipulates magical energy to focus solely on combat; Mental, physical, spiritual and conceptual ones, including the force behind attacks, defenses, tactics, etc. Battle Magic concentrates around seven different incantations of magical spells. Warlocks will usually master two or three of these types of spells. Each one of these spells are complicated and takes years of knowledge to use, let alone in stressful combat situations.

Enhanced senses allow a magical being the ability to use any or all of their five senses to god like degrees, allowing them to see, hear, feel, smell, and taste things that mortals cannot.

Magically enhancing the practitioner skills makes them think faster than a normal human.

Regeneration is the powerful magical ability that allows a practitioner to regenerate and heal both damaged and diseased bodily tissues and organs.

Magically enhanced endurance allows the practitioner to never feel fatigue.

Magically enhanced agility, provides the practitioner with superhuman, reflexes, flexibility, and speed. It allows them to perform incredible feats, such as long-distance leaps with little effort, inhuman flexibility, and moving at speeds faster than the eye can see.

Magically enhanced durability, granting immunity to attacks that can easily kill a mortal. This power is a limited form of invincibility.

Magically enhanced strength increases the physical strength compared to that of an average human. Super strength usually comes down to the individual depending on their species, age, size, and even magical skills.

Angus, Minotaur of Minoa

Chapter 30

The night comes alive with sounds, I slide Irons over my head absently looking at the earth floating in the sky. The HUD highlights immediately.

SHIVER SWISHHH SHIVERS SWISHHH SPAT!

I pull open the parchment checking my direction. With perspective again, I roll the parchment up. Standing in the chilly evening air I stretched. The musical symphony of the night became a solo of just the crackles of the fire and the trickling of the creek.

Splish Splash splish Splash…

Lou was in my hand as a wicked bone machete blade and I reached for my shield. Needing as much visibility as possible I stepped into the ice water of the creek. In my ear Irons started to play "Believer" by Imagine Dragons

SPLISH SPLOOSH SPLASH SPLISH SPLOOSH SPLASH SPLISH SPLOOSH SPLASH

With a splashing of elephant sized paws, the saber tooth cat charges towards me from downstream. I hold my ground with the shield held tight. Louisé morphed into a bone spear now resting in the crescent notch. The HUD ticks off the distance between me and the lion. Time slows when I inhaled the magic, intending to gather the magic from the forest around me like I had before. What I got was a blast of supercooling magic pulled from the very water I was standing in. My tattoos flared bright neon green with a blue outer tint, the magic boiled out my ink in puffs of blue steam. I planted my feet digging them into the creek bed. Snapping back to reality as the splashing water from the huge cat rained down like a thunderstorm. I will my magic into the shield with my faith that it can stop the facken Juggernaut from the facken X-Men dead in his tracks.

BABOOM SPLOOSH

With the impact a shower of blue and green magic exploded. My feet dug deeper into the creek bed with force of the saber tooth cat's collision. The force of the detention of magic hurled the giant cat a hundred yards back downstream and I stood there like Wyatt fucken Earp at the O.K. Corral.

RRROAR GRRRROOOOAAANNN Yank yank

Shaking the water from its fur the saber tooth lion noticed Lou sticking out its shoulder. The cat trying to rip Lou out with its mouth, I drop the shield. Pushing with my magic I stepped on top of the water like it was the shore. Running across the surface of the creek locking eyes with the cats. My right hand pulls the 1911 from my chest, my left-hand reverse grabs the hilt from my belt. Extending my arms in front of me I let the hammers fall.

BANG BANG BANG BANG BANG BANG BANG BANG

I empty both clips into the cat's face. I let them fall from my hands to the water but heard no splash as I was already moving to pull my rifle. Slowing my pace only yards away.

The Winchester sang in my hands.

Click Clack BOOM

Every shot, I took another step towards the cat. My feet firmly landing on the surface of the water. My magic screaming with emotions as I unloaded my rifle. The smoke from the gunpowder floats across the water surface like fogs. The smoke slowly reveals the Lions bloody face staring dead at me. It was crouched low in the water only five feet from me.

"Ggrrrgggrrrrrr," the lion grumbles softly, shaken its massive head like it had a fly in its ear. Bringing its eyes back to bare on me, his bullet ridden face healing.

Keeping eye contact with the huge cat I reached to put my rifle back over my shoulder and found my shield back in place. "Oh...we've just started this dance," with confidence in my voice. Pulling more of the water's magic into my tattoos. We sized each other up like two gunslingers. We circled each other.

The saber tooth lion's light tan fur bristles with anger. All of his muscles flexed along his Ford F150 sized body in anticipation. As we circled I saw that the saber tooth lion was covered in red geometric designs painted on its fur. Around the lion's neck, multiple collars of claws and different kinds of teeth were mostly hidden from view by his mane. Braided in his tangled mane of hair are many different styles of feathers and small bones. His whip like tail covered in red finger-paint ends in a tuft of white fur with three eagle feathers tied to the tuft of fur.

With every step the lion took Lou, he dug deeper into the saber tooth lion's flesh. The reflection in the water danced from the glow of my tattoos. The water surface glowing bright blue with every step I take. With an upheaval of water, the lion swiped his claws across the spot I was just in. I ran up the spray of water like it were stairs pivoting my body. I went to my belt and sure enough my pistol that I had dropped in the creek, its handle slid into my palm. Now to test theory number two. I racked the slide of the 1911 completing my turn in midair aiming with a two-handed grip.

Blam Blam Blam

Three bullets struck the saber tooth lion in the back of the head.

Swoosh Smack

Impossibly fast the lion turned and batted me out of the air. Rolling with the blow I turned towards the lion landing on the creeks rocky shore still firing my gun at him. He leaps at me from the water I rotate to catch the next blow with my back.

SMASH SKREECH

Its massive claws rake across the shield. I call Lou back to me as I let the inertia of the blow spin me around.

Stab SNAP swish..swish swish..swish CRACK

Lunging up, Lou morphed, turning to a super-size icepick. The blood flowed freely from the saber tooth lion's neck as I plunged Lou repeatedly to the hilt. I heard my left arm break before I felt the pain as the lion crushed it in his jaws. I was shaking over and over, the motion so hard my shoulder is dislocated and launched into the air.

splash splash splash splash sploosh

Skipping like stone over the surface of the creek. With my right arm I push myself out of the icy creek water, my left arm hung loosely to my side. My fingers sunk into the creek bed as I tucked my body lower in the water. The magic from the water pooling with mine making the entire creek glow with blue and green magic.

Whiiissshhhh KaRack Boom

Its huge mouth wide as the beast came out of the sky to finish me off. My right hand shot forth grabbing the saber tooth lion's massive canine, sweeping my legs counter clockwise.

The drops of water falls upward as I looked the lion in his eye as I broke his facken tooth off. The lion's mouth still open as he faceplants into the water.

SPPPLLLAAASSSHHHH

I stand as the lion finishes his splashdown. I make my way out the creek. The first rays of sunrise hinting over the horizon. Dropping the tooth in the water.

Sploosh

Practitioners

Practitioners can focus raw magic to jump incredible distances in a city block and land safely. They could leap frighteningly tall heights and long distances. Now combine it with other forms of magic and you can cover extreme amounts of distance in miles. In antiquity normal people believed that the Practitioners were flying.

Ironniesous O'Keeffe

Chapter 31

I fumble my 1911 out from the bandolier, collapsing on the rocky shore on my knees, I turned. My left arm flopping loosely, my right arm shaking as I bring the gun to aim. It was gone. The facken saber tooth lion had vanished without a sound.

Still on my knees I looked around for a large rock. Seeing one not far from me. I very painfully made my way over to it. Pressing my left shoulder into the face of the rock, I rotate my shoulder grinding and pushing until I felt the spot.

SMACK, POP.. SSSSST FIZZLE Swoosh BURBLE HURL

I rip off my helmet just in time, vomiting from the pain. My left arm was still broke but at least it wasn't dislocated any more. Getting tunnel vision as I puked. With Batman like determination I made my way to the water's edge to wash the throw up off me. Needless to say, I'm not Batman and I stumble, trip then roll into the creeks refreshing water. I roll over to my right emptying the rest of the contents of my stomach, then onto my back. Turning my head, I watch the chunks wash away. As I look at the vomit floating away with the current, firefly lights shimmered across the crest of waves.

Zip-Zitter Zip-Zitter Zip-Zitter Zip-Zitter Zip-Zitter Zip-Zitter

My eyelids fluttering open, close, lights on, lights off, lights on… some kind of purple blue light had landed on my chest as if it were an island. Focusing my blurred vision on the light a purple with neon blue markings sprite was crawling under my jacket. More sprites flew over to land on my left arm all proceeding to crawl under my sleeve. The bites were sharp and painful as they tore into my flesh.

SHIVER SWISHHH SHIVER SWISHHH

I felt Hank tense in retaliation ready to crush or maybe eat the sprites.

“It's okay, they have to set the bone first,” reassuring Hank as much as myself. The intensity of my injuries overwhelming me as I lay in the shallow water.

KaRACK AAAAAHHHHHHHHHHHHHH

Waking up on the shore, Hank wrapped tightly around me. Irons’ HUD blinking to life. Fact, I took off the helmet dropping it over there looking at the place it should have been. Fact, I passed out way over there looking at the creek sitting up with no pain I get to my feet.

SHIVER SWISHHH SHIVERS SWISHHH SPAT! SPAT! SPAT!

I hold my hand out, Hank slides the scroll into my open palm. The compass needle steady pointing to the feather. Rolling up the parchment Irons’ HUD highlights.

“Sir, plotting direct route complete. Playing Sir's music,” he tells me.

Reaching up to adjust my helmet for no reason, I post my body pooling just my own magic, my ink sparks to life.

WWWWWOOOOSSSHHHHHHH

The forest flies by has the speedometer ticks faster and faster 112 mph, 138 mph faster and faster. The trees gave way to monolithic rocks, the ones you see in Arizona. Just like the tree tops but this time I was going to do it not Irons. I felt him going to say something but he refrained.

Imagining pockets of big soap bubbles of magic around my hands and feet. I envision smaller bubbles near my knees and elbows. Small vacuums of pressurized magic appearing into reality. Now with the manipulation of the skin of the bubble I could create a vacuum to the surface of the rock. Eat your heart out Peter Parker. Releasing the vacuum pressure resulted in my propulsion up the cliff walls, no spiderweb needed. I'd grab with the bubble of magical energy then I'd pop the bubble exploding me upwards. With the same aggression I took with superspeed I scaled the rock. In seconds I had reached the top and was sprinting across the peak. I ran towards the cliffs edge and created a super charged magical bubble.

KERBOOM WWOOOSH...

With an Incredible Hulk explosive leap, the rock shattered with the force of the ruptured magical vacuum bubbles. Arching my body as if I was a professional snow skier I soared.

THUUUM pitter..patter pitter..patter pitter..patter KERBOOM WWOOOSH…

Landing a mile away I ran above the tree line from huge monolithic pillars of stone to the next. Leaving puffs of shattering rock in my wake.

THUUUM pitter..patter pitter..patter pitter..patte SSKKKIIDD

I stood overlooking a clear strip of land, a simple log wall dividing it right down the middle. I was still miles away but from this distance it reminds me of a power company clear cutting through the forest to run electrical cable. The wall stretched as far as the eye could see.

pitter..patter pitter..patter pitter..patter KERBOOM WWOOOSH

Taking a few steps back from the edge I take a running leap. In a freefall without a parachute I pull my shield keeping my arms tucked in. I don't spread my body out to make more surface area to try to slow my descent. I came down like a facken glowing green comet.

SNAP, CRACK, snap snap, CRACK

The foliage screamed as it struck my shield. The ground raced towards me. I grabbed the side of the shield and placed both feet in the middle of the shield focusing a magical bubble around my feet that encompassed the shield.

BOOM ting swish CLI..clacked

With an explosion of debris I hit the ground like a comet. Standing with dust cloud settling around me, I stepped on the edge of the shield to pop it off the ground and into my hand. With a twist and a spin of my wrist, I fling the shield to rest on my back.

I walk into the clearing to find a log wall made to keep out King Kong. Each post bigger than a giant redwood. Old Viking runes as tall as me, carved deep, completely covered every log. The cross beams of the wall carved with reliefs of wolves.

"Sir… The wall was built with two different magic spells. Sir, one that redirects any physical attack across the entire surface of the wall. The other, Sir, is to take its vast stores of potential energy and anything that comes in contact with the wall change that potential energy to kinetic energy," Irons translates for me.

SHIVER SWISHHH SHIVERS SWISHHH SPAT! SPAT! SPAT!

Hank shivers and spits the scroll out, I snatched it out of the air. Unrolling it to find me looking straight up into the open jaws of a monster wolf about to eat me, total Jurassic Park, T Rex eats lawyer.

Elemental Magic

Elemental magic is one of the most powerful forms of magic. Air, Water, Fire, and Earth magic are the classical elements, though the magic of electrical manipulation is usually considered a form of elemental magic as well.

Few magical beings are capable of controlling one of the elements fully, usually taking several lifetimes to understand completely. Those who have studied these elements and mastering them are called Elementals. These practitioners are considered to be among the most powerful magical beings.

Ironniesous O'Keeffe

Chapter 32

How to climb unclimbable wall, you don't, and before you say dig under it. Do the math that would take weeks to manually dig a tunnel under a wall that pretty much touches the sky. I walked the wall looking for, ah, there a crack in the log from it settling over time. With everything in Asgard on an epic scale the cracks in the timber are overlooked. Carefully without touching the sides of the fisher sized cracks I made my way through the wall.

The other side was damp and gloomy. Fog hovering six inches above the ground covering the open field. Just beyond, laid a forest of shadows.

The Dark forest had no animals as I walked for miles until I reached a giant lake. The lake shore feels like the ocean. As the thick fog rolls onto the shore with the sound of the crashing waves. But way in the distance I could make out the crest of the other side or maybe an island.

SHIVER SWISHHH SHIVERS SWISHHH SPAT!

Checking the compass on the magical parchment, the needle points straight across Lake Erie. I wade into the shoals drawing the water magic into my own.

WHIRRR WHISK TTZZZ TTZZZ WWWOOOOSSHH S-S-S-S-S-SLOSH

Taking my first step I picture the blue and green magic pulling together as one. Freezing the water for that second my foot touched the surface of the water. Then instantly melting when I moved that foot away. The water wasn't turning to ice, more like blue and green glowing Jell-O. During the battles I have been doing this stuff on instinct all emotional driven. To just use one emotion to control the magic was difficult. But I needed a crash course on multitasking my magic, literally to get my feet wet or I guess the point would not to get my feet wet.

PITTER..PATTER PITTER-PATTER PITTER-PATTER

I made good time across the ocean sized lake. The island is Hawaiian sized, but felt like zombie pirates were going to attack any second. I had goose bumps on my goose bumps. The fog just got thicker and thicker as I made my way into a bamboo jungle. Every sound echoing in the silence. Moving with caution picturing the fucking bamboo spider from King Kong, I reached for my shield and Lou materializes in my hand.

"Fuck you giant spider," I whispered.

Following a small stream trickling down the hillside I pressed forward. Till I finally stood at the highest peak of the whole island and the view was amazing.

SHIVER SWISHHH SHIVERS SWISHHH SPAT!

Dora the explorer song I'm the map, I'm The Map started looping in my head, as I called the magic scroll to my hand.

RUMBLE RRRUUUMMMMMBLE SSHHHUUUCRACK

The earth broke away under my feet with the sudden earthquake. Grabbing at the edge I watch the scroll fall down the fisher I was attempting not to fall in.

SSWWOOOSHSHSH

Huge plumes of hot steam erupt from the ground. It's a cave I realized as I stuck my head down the jagged steam vent. Climbing down, the ground of the cave was a slime covered mud and the fog smelled like dead skunk that's been rotting awhile. Scanning the cave by the light of magic tattoos I searched urgently for Alex's magical parchment. Irons' HUD changed and the cave lit with night vision. Looking over, to see the scroll hung from the ceiling by a long dangling piece of slime.

RRRUUUMMMMMBLE SSLLLUURP

Soon as my fingers wrapped around the magic scroll the floor shifted, another earthquake. No, it felt like one of the moving sidewalks they have at the airport. Then the walls started to collapse in.

"This ain't a cave!" yelling as I turned to look for a way out.

"Sir," Irons say's as the HUD highlight beams of sunlight leaking between the cracks.

CRACK SHATTER KAPLOW

Dirt and moss of the cave breakaway when the cave floor lurches up it's a massive tongue. So, in my haste to get the fuck out of dodge I didn't see something jetting from the cavern wall. I came crashing to the floor as I was clotheslined off my feet.

YELP, WWHHOOOF WHINE

Echoing through my whole body as the cave's jaws opened wide. Falling from the mouth of the cave looking back over my shoulder, still falling, to see a rusted broadsword hilt protruding from the now roof of the cave.

KKiiDDOOOSSSHHH

Splashing down in a small pond. I swim to the surface debris hitting the water lake hail. Sheets of earth slide off the hill. Trees and bushes crashing to the ground exploding with the impact.

Swimming under the water I realized I was diving into a lake of drool water. Resurfacing on the opposite side of the drool pool I crawl onto the shore. I watched the hill become a wolf. The mountain sized wolf shook earth from its black fur coat making visible gray fur markings. But as soon as the giant wolf stretched, angry yellow and red magic lines tightened, around the wolf's body.

“YYYYEEEEEELLLLPPPP!” he screams in pain.

I bounced like a basketball with his impact to the ground. A single piece of golden yarn wound and twisted around the wolf. The wolf's fur and muscle were burnt and smoking where the magical golden yarn touched. He was only taking shallow breaths as I walked over to him. I could feel his pain through my magic. My tattoos burned in remorse. I brushed the caked dirt from his huge eye. He flinched back causing the magic yarn to tighten and burn him again. Like a dog at the local animal shelter that was beaten its whole life.

“Shhh, easy, I'm not going to hurt you,” not just telling him with my voice but also telling, no, reassuring him through my magic.

“HHUUFFFF wwhhoof, grrrr!” he declared muffled by the sword in his mouth.

“Heard that one before have you?” I tell him as I take my shield from around my back laying it on the ground. Hank pulling himself off, my jacket draping himself over a nearby limb. I pull Irons off placing my helmet on top of Hank.

SSSSSST FIZZLE Swoosh

My magical connection severed from the helmet, my tattoos fade to normal. Removing the belt of burden I placed the belt with all three guns still in there holsters on the shield. My left hand snags my pants holding them up. I ran my fingers across the magical yarn, burning my flesh as I did.

“Might not be able to do anything about this,” pulling the yarn from the wolf's burnt flesh. My own flesh burning as I let the yarn go. “But it looks to me like ya got something stuck in your teeth. That I could probably help out with.”

“Woof,” he exhales his eye searching me for answers.

"Cause you already had a chance to eat me and didn't. So, I figure I owe you one," I answered him. "You're going to have to sit up for this," informing him with regret.

He sits up and I just think about the children's book *Clifford the Big Red Dog*. His head the size of a four car garage looms right above my head. He slowly lowers his head, massive teeth inches from me. I can only see the hilt, a pus ridden tumor has grown around the sword blade.

"Fen… remember when I said I wouldn't hurt you," pausing just for second while Lou materializes. "I lied," grabbing the hilt as I cut the tumor away.

"WHIMPER…………………………………….. YYYEEELLLPPP… **HHHHOOOOOOWWWWLLLLLL**!"

Fenris

Fenrisúlfr, Fenris, also known in many sources as the mighty Fenrir Wolf. He is the ultimate canine fury, a wolf with a godly powers.

He is one of three monstrous offspring of Loki, the Norse god of mischief and the frost giantess Jötunn.

Fenrir went off to carve a niche for himself in the lore and legends of the Asgardians. In one of his many adventures Fenrir fathered two other wolves that featured prominently in Norse mythology, Sköll and Hati. Upon reaching adulthood, Fenrir ran freely across the terrain of Asgard, rapidly growing in size and strength.

Certain prophecies known to the deities foretold that Fenrir would become a major threat to the deities upon reaching his maximum size and strength. So it was decreed by Odin, king of the gods, that the majestic wolf was to be bound so that he would be unable to eventually wreak havoc on the godly realm as predicted by prophecy.

However, this goal turned out to be easier said than done, as every single time a chain was forged for the purpose of binding Fenris, the powerful creature would break free. On several occasions larger and stronger fetters were created but each time the supreme lupine broke them.

Growing fearful of Fenris obviously increasing power, the deities went to the diminutive, subterranean dwarves, natives of the realm of Nidavellir who are the masters of the forge. The dwarf blacksmiths were commissioned by the deities to construct a tether that would actually hold the grandiose beast. Out of the dwarven forge came a thin, fragile looking yarn that they christened Gleipnir. This rope, the dwarf smithies insisted, would successfully bound the Fenrir Wolf.

To succeed in getting Gleipnir around Fenrir, a contingent of the warrior deities chose the strategy of appealing to the giant wolf's ego by daring him to prove his prowess yet again by allowing himself to be bound by the thin cord. Then breaking himself from it, which the warriors insisted he was too weak and would not be able to do.

Suspecting a trick upon seeing the fragile-looking string, Fenris allowed himself to be bound, but with a stipulation one of the deities must place their hand into the great wolf's enormous maw. If the tether did indeed prove to hold, then Fenris would bite off the God's hand if not set free.

Of all the deities only Tyr, the god of war, had the courage to make this sacrifice. True to the words of the dwarves, Fenrir discovered that he could not break free from the enchanted cord, as hard as he pulled, the tighter it seemed to bind him.

Fenris proceeded to bite off Tyr's right hand. As a result of being successfully bound by the deities in this manner, Fenris swore vengeance trying to bite at his captures and was stabbed in the roof of his muzzle with a broadsword.

Ironniesous O'Keeffe

Chapter 33

Covered in slimy puss I threw the blade to the ground. It had started to rain while I was doing doggy surgery.

Wwwhhhiiinneee SLAM GGRRRRIIINNNDDDD

Fenrir yawns, opened his mouth fully then snapping it shut for the first time in a millennium. Grinding his teeth together the massive wolf smiled. I petted him behind his ear and leaned against him as the rain fell harder. The dirt washing off his fur mixing with the slime washes away from me. Like a monsoon the rain continues as the sunsets. The rain wasn't cold in fact it was warm and when it hit the cool ground a blanket of dense fog started to form.

The sunsets and the last of its light fade. Fenrir looks over, his ears perked, listening far off into the distance then he slumped back down with a grunt. Figuring that I was not going anywhere till at least the rain stopped. Tucking me and my gear under Fen's ear I took a nap to the sounds of falling rain and his slow breathing.

"GGGGGGRRRR Whhooofff," he rumbled.

Blinking the sleep away, "Timmy's stuck in a well." Then way off in the distance, little more than a whisper I hear it a small brass horn. "Fuck, Red Capes," I muttered.

“RRRrrr Chuff Chufffff,” Fen states the obvious

“Let's just say I had a hand in one of them maybe getting his face chewed off,” shrugging my shoulders. The rain had stopped, “Fen, ya hungry? I'm facken starving. Hank… please tell me you snagged something to eat?”

SHIVER SWISHHH SHIVERS SWISHHH SPAT! SPAT!

Hank quivering and seized, like cat with a hairball, two nice sized skinned rabbits plopped to the ground.

It took much longer to get the campfire built because every time I stacked the wood Fen would whufffff with an exhale of breath. Throwing a big stick at him after the fifth time feeling like one of the three little pigs. He facken loved that.

“Chuff chuff chuff!” he laughed.

Building the campfire again and try to light it with my magic. Getting just a little bit of smoke. So, it took a while to figuring out that the wet wood was all in my mind and didn't matter, after that mental wall broke the fire burned bright. It doesn't seem as long until the rabbit was ready.

I cut small pieces of rabbit holding it out. Fen would tenderly take it from my hand. Chewing every tiny morsel.

“Fen… tell me a story…,” I asked him while I took a bite of the rabbit.

BBBUUUURRRR..Bbbrr...BBBUUURRRRR

Horns, that's plural, meaning multiple horns echoing in the night air and closer this time.

“RuuRuffffff grruff whoofff woof,” he begins his tail. As he nuzzled towards me, his magical bonds flaring slightly. Images and emotions, taste and sound followed his words.

My father watched from a far at my failures at hunting. Day after day I would go out and hunt the nearby forest or meadow. Day after day I returned hungry. One day my father calls me to his side.

"I should get my son a spear. For he hunts like a man and a man needs a spear to hunt." Loki tells me.

"I'm no man!" I growl sitting on the floor in protest.

Then as my father walks from me, "Then why does my son hunt like one?" With that said he starts to walk away. His footsteps tapping on the floor turned to paws padding. Loki, my father, had morphed to a dire wolf. Yipped to me to follow him.

"HUmmmfff mmmmm," Fen whined interrupting his own story. "Wowoof," he continues.

He first showed me my nose and what wonders it could smell. As we sniffed every Asgardian ass we could find. Oh, the glory we had that day. He said my next lesson would be at the next full moon and to learn everything my nose could teach me. By the light of the moon my father taught me how to hunt and track.

"RRUFFF!" and both his ears perked up in alarm.

"Yeah man, I hear it," looking into the darkness of the bamboo jungle. "That's not horns."

DRUM DRUM DRUM..DRUM

Drums a faint rhythmic...beat. *Tot tot tot...* slow like a heartbeat. Fen pulls at his bonds causing the magic yarn to burn its retaliation. Standing, I scanned the shadows as walked over to calm Fen. The drums beat changed heavier and faster.

Then a whisper, "Cowboy."

Skinwalker

According to Diné legends, Skinwalkers are accomplished medicine men or witches who reach the highest level of priesthood but choose to use their powers for evil rather than good. Skinwalkers take the form of an animal for the purpose of inflicting pain on others.

The initiation procedure is pretty tough—all prospective Skinwalkers must kill a close relative. Once a prospective Skinwalker passes that test, he gains immense magical powers, including shape-shifting abilities. These abilities enable Skinwalkers to turn into any animal they choose, though their top choices are usually foxes, owls, coyotes, wolves, or crows—the most feared or revered animals in Navajo mythology.

The Carib tribes, Kanaima is an evil spirit that possesses people and causes them to turn into deadly animals and/or go into a murderous rage. Assassins, or Carib people seeking revenge for a slain relative, sometimes invited the Kanaima spirit into themselves by taking certain drugs or conducting certain magic rituals.

The Stikini are sinister monsters from Seminole folklore. Originally they were evil witches or medicine men, who transformed themselves into animal-beings. By day they still resemble Seminole people, but by night, they vomit up their souls (along with all their internal organs) and become undead animal-monsters that feed on human hearts.

Though Skinwalker lore goes back into ancient Native American history, stories of the evil sorcerers still circulate today. Witnesses report seeing or hearing them knocking on windows or doors, peering through windows, or otherwise trying to frighten and inflict harm. Skinwalkers in all the legends are immortal.

From Angus's Library

Keeper of the Hidden, case file notes

Keeper Doc Holliday, Vampire

Chapter 34

From the silence, tomahawks fly at me in slow motion as Lou materializing in my hand. The hilt morphing in my hand as it started the arch as Lou became a bone whip. With a snap of my wrist trying to do my best Indiana Jones.

KRACK TWURL blink..blink VAROOOM HHMMMMMMMMMM SWOOOSH..

Lou reached out taking the three tomahawks in a single motion. Drawing back, I spin Lou around me in those few moments Hank had brought me Irons. With one hand I slid my helmet over my head. Hank, my living pirate pea coat, slithers around me covering me in his almost impenetrable hide. With a snap of power, Irons channels magic through my tattoos, the magical light burst out of all my ink.

I take a fencing stance one arm holding my pants up the other held Lou straightforward, the arrows whistled towards me. In the smallest of moves my arm flicks up, left, then spinning my wrist counter clockwise while I step forward. I pull back in the guard position Lou's needle like blade facing the sky, 8 arrows fall to the ground.

Irons enhanced optics was streaming a 360-degree view of my surroundings, highlights and info on key elements around me," Sir, tactical combat vision active," Irons informs me.

Kicking my shield off the ground. I looped my arm through my belt in midair letting my pants fall. My magic belt of holding sprang to life snagging my pants and creating all it's wonderful pockets and holsters. Grabbing the airborne shield with my left hand as I put my arm through the belt. Spinning the shield to rest on my back.

From the darkest shadows of forest, the 7 ft tall Indian warrior emerged. His Mohawk making him feel even bigger. He wasn't adorned with the armor like he was in our first encounter on I-20. He had no shirt or shoes just a pair of simple leather pants. Red war paint was drawn with extreme details all over his body. His charcoal white gray skin stuck to his muscles when he moved he was that ripped. He was not much older than me when he died, I realized as he stepped out of the shadows. We started to circle each other just like me and the saber tooth lion.

“Ah, fuck,” I whispered to Irons. Irons’ HUD highlights all the red markings on the Indian. Then a holographic image of the saber tooth lion appears highlighting its red stripe pattern on the lion's fur.

“Sir, Sir is right, the markings on the saber tooth lion and the Indian match,” Irons states.

The palm of my right hand resting on the hilt of my 1911 tucked into my belt like facken Buffalo Bill. He started to blink and my hammer fell.

BANG BANG

In a military trained stance, I had my weapon cleared and double tapped him on the head before he finished blinking. His head shot back at a complete right angle with the impact of the bullets. He just tilted his back down and looked at me. He grumbled while grinding his teeth together. Holding his palm out he spit into his hand, then held it towards me spilling the two bullets onto the ground.

“ggggrrrrrRRRRRROOOOOOOOOOOOOOO!” Fen protesting and Irons pushed play filling my ear with the perfect soundtrack.

The two of us crossed the yards between us in seconds and “Drowning Pool Bodies” plays inside my helmet.

BOOM ting swish Ting SWISHHH Ting SWISHHH SMACK BANG BANG BANG BANG click

My shield takes the impact as we collide. He slashes and cuts at me with a magically conjured tomahawk. We twist and turn with each other's moves. My shield appearing to flow around me as he came from every angle. With my 1911 in my right hand I squeezed the trigger every time his tomahawk calls. My gun would click, grabbing the other 1911 from my bandolier. Empty that clip into Iisxiinii, drop. Reaching for the 1911 in my belt, which I just let fall to the ground and sure enough the hilt slides into my hand. I put so many bullets into this guy he should have just died from lead poisoning. I felt the edge of his tomahawk grab the lip of my shield. Letting him pull my shield away from my body.

Click, Clack BOOM

My Winchester introduces himself blowing a big chunk of the Indian's head off. He stumbled back a perfect hole where his cheek and eye use to be. Right where I wanted him.

CRACK CRUSH Riiipppppp CHEW

"Woof," Fen says with his mouth full.

"Dude, don't eat that!" I scowled at him. "Spit it out!"

Plop Splat

Iisxiinii lands in two halves. I give Fen a rub behind the ear when he bends lower.

"Sir, Sir does know that Sir's enemy still moves, Sir," Irons' HUD highlights the body parts as he is telling this.

Turning to watch the torso dragging itself towards the kicking legs. Fen had spit him out some distance away. I just watched as the Indian put himself back together and then stands the fuck up. From deep inside him he started to chant. He reached up touching a chipped saber tooth lion tooth that hung with many other bones and teeth on his necklace.

"Pretty sure if you hurry you can still find it," pointing in the general direction of the creek.

Clouds of ichor puffed angrily around him when his Skinwalker magic started to transform him. This ectoplasmic ichor of black and purple crisscrossed over his body, eating him, leaving a trail of transformation. His skin erupts with fur or from such a rapid growth of his muscles tearing through it. The cheti cloud of glowing ectoplasmic ichor and debris envelopes him entirely.

SWISHHH BUBBLE GURGLE RIP SWORLING WOOSH

For a moment the ectoplasmic ichor just twisted and turned, building with magic. Then the cloud parted with an explosive puff. Leaping straight at me from the ectoplasmic ichor cloud. He had changed to a facken weresaber tooth lion.

Towering over 12 feet tall he rolled his Volkswagen sized shoulder making the geometrical patterns of the dripping wet red war paint reflect the moonlight. It shimmers and twinkles across his tan fur. The werelion's mane still with random bones and feathers braided in it, not only framed his face it formed a huge rooster's tail of a Mohawk that ran down the entire length of his body. The blood red fur-hawk stood out promptly on his spine merging with his tail with the same three eagle feathers wrapped to the tip. With every purposely slow place of his giant war painted cat clawed feet, his woven hemp necklaces of teeth and claws would click together softly. He flexed his paw fingers extending his huge razor-sharp claws and grins exposing more of his 2' long fangs that dripped with saliva.

In motion already but instead of trying to dodge I went forward. Pushing and pulling with magic I moved with supernatural speed right at the charging beast. The saber tooth werecat roared its spit hitting my helmet it was so close now. Sending magic through my left hand I grabbed with it to the nearest tree yanking me like Spider-Man's web.

YANK SLASH kerplop… CHOMP CHEW CHOMP CHOMP CHEW SPIT CHOMP

Lou in a downward slash takes off the Skinwalker's arm. Magical clinging to the tree I watched the arm hit the ground. The werecat didn't even pause I wasn't his main threat. In terror I watched the Indian rip chunks of meat from Fenrir’s nose and muzzle.

Out of silent night air an army of brass horns in a symphony of hatred announces their approach as Fen begins to cry.

BBBUUUURRRR..Bbbrr...BBBUUURRRRR, HHHHHOOOOOWWWWWLLLLL... WHIMPER

Familiar

A familiar, an animal, supernatural creature or minion believed to serve a magician or warrior as servant, spy and companion, in addition to helping bewitch enemies or to divine information. The animal was often believed to be possessed of magic powers.

Familiars, from the Latin "familiaris", meaning a "household servant", were mentioned in the Bible, referring to the spirit guides of sorcerers and necromancers. Dire warnings were issued against any contact with them. There is nothing evil about a Familiar.

The Pact between the two are drastically different in magical potential. The pact is either forced domination over the creature or it is given. The Being obtains the familiar, forges a pact, and begins the relationship. The pact entails the exchange of blood to the familiar to strengthen the bond and forge the union. Also, methods of magic must be used as spiritual superglue. This is very important, the being and familiar must be bound to one another's spark. This allows magic to be shared with their familiar.

Ironniesous O'Keeffe

Chapter 35

THUD SONIC CRACK YANK shake..shake SMACK

Flinging my shield at the werecat as I leaped from the tree. My shield took him in the leg, dislodging his claws. Lou had his tip wrapped firmly around his ankle. I pulled on the whip's handle. With Fen's unspoken help, shaking his muzzle side to side the werecat crashes to the ground.

WRENCH SQUEEZE KABOOM

Fen lunges for him but the magic yarn flares bright constricting Fen with intense pain. With his one huge paw the werecat punched Fen so hard it knocked the dog out cold. Blood pours from Fenrir's ear. Reaching down to pick up his arm that had crawled to him. He holds it to his arm it doesn't heal it just stays attached. He flexes his clawed fingers then looks at me. Like facken Michael Myers he just slow walked my way.

Click Clack BOOM, Click Clack BOOM, Click Clack BOOM

My Winchester called but the werecat didn't answer. He didn't even facken notice. His left claws raked across my chest in a downwards arch, before the third shell barely cleared the chamber. Hank kept my guts from being spilled out but still felt like I got hit with a steel lawn rake.

KRACK SWOOSH SMASH

With an uppercut, the force of a freight train, his right paw followed his left. My ribs break with the force of the blow. The impact sending me off the ground. I was above the tree line as I coughed up blood. Before I had the chance to reach orbit with a massive jolt his feet smashes into my head. He landed on my fucken face intending to ride me to the ground.

BOOM

My shield on my back displacing some of the impact. My collar bone shattering takes the rest. Pushing myself, pain gauged through my leg. Grabbing at my leg first before I looked caused his third and fourth claw to pierce my hand. He dug his claws deeper into my leg. He shook me violently then proceeded to bash me like Incredible Hulk.

THUD SMACK THUD SMACK THUD SMACK THUD SMACK

I blacked out or he got tired but either way I was lying face down in a puddle made of my own blood, the world spinning. Pushing myself up on my elbow I vomited more blood, the pain was intense, I turned my head just a little to see the facken Indian getting ready to take a running start.

WHUMP THUD

Kicked in the side to crash into Fen's furry neck some twenty-five yards away. Blood pouring from my nose and mouth pooling in my helmet as I tried to get to my feet. He calmly watched me try to stand as he walked towards me. Wrapping his huge paw over my entire head he tries to crush my head like a tin can.

YANK ThaWhack ThaWack ThaWhack ThaWhack ThaWhack

When that doesn't work he rips the helmet off my head. He watches my tattoos fade of magic, then he proceeded to beat me with my helmet.

CLANK FLOP CHOMP

My nose, cheek and eye socket are crushed when he drops Irons and I to the ground.

"WWHIINNNEE!" Fen looks at me his massive head held to the side by the werecat. The lion's claws ripping through Fen's flesh as he moves the wolf in position to sink its huge teeth into the wolf's neck.

Click Clack BOOM

My Winchester blows the werecat's dick off.

"RRRRRRRROAR!" the werecat grabs his missing junk.

"Just getting warmed up," spitting out my own teeth I answered Fen. I stared at the huge zombie Indian werecat as I get to my knees.

blink..blink VAROOOM HHMMMMMMMMMM SWOOOSH..

I palm Irons sliding him on as I stand on one leg. The werecat composes himself and shakes like he's got fleas. Puffs of black purple ectoplasmic ichor oozes off him as he walks my way. In the seven or eight steps it takes him to walk to me he sheds the werecat like water dripping out a faucet towards the ceiling. Iisxiinii grabbing me by the throat and he power slams me into Fen.

"YELP!" Fen cries with my impact.

Thud Thud Thud Thud Thud Thud... THUD THUD THUD THUD

Holding me off the ground pressed against Fenrir's body he magically conjures a short spear in his free hand. With blur of pain he stepped away leaving me crucified to the side of Fenrir's shoulder. Four more spears get thrusted through me and into Fen. In my pain I thrashed tangling myself in the magic yarn. Putting a blade to my neck he smiles.

The island fog breaks, the sun had risen some time ago. Great big spotlights of sunshine melt away the clouds.

Sizzle crackle

The Skinwalker's skin burns from the light and he jumps away from me. Disappearing into the shadows of the forest as I passed out crucified to Fen.

BBBUUUURRRR..Bbbrr...BBBUUUURRRRR

Waking to brass horns legions of Red Capes surrounded me as I looked down at them. Lifting my eyes to see the sun low in the sky. The green glow of my magic has a silver blue glitter to it. Armies and armies of Red Capes and their familiars. Looking over the clearing Fenrir's had created by moving around. The battlefields of Middle Earth come to mind seeing the extreme numbers of Red Capes.

"Hey, FUCK FACE!" I yelled down to the nearest Red Cape as he inspected the magic yarn. His vulture looked up at, "They don't intend to cut me down, do they," I ask the bird.

He shakes his beak, "Screech SKREE SKREE!" and flies up to rest near me.

"My bones will eventually rot and fall away," letting that sink in. "FUCK!" I scream making the vulture's wings flutter.

Fenrir's tense with my outburst of magic, his silver blue magic turning green. The magical yarn cuts my skin with constricting force then burning me like a super-heated curling iron. We both slumped in pain.

Blinking the world back into focus a group of facken Red Capes were pointing up laughing at the considerable pain I was in. With one eye checking the horizon the sun was just a sliver now.

"Cut, Me DOWN!" I mumble loudly through my clenched jaw.

"HA, HA, HA, HO, HA, HA!" they all laughed.

My tattoos of the kids' names burn like a hot branding iron… Fen feels their fear with me. My tattoos glow bright silver and blue while Fenrir's magic is my bright neon green. The magical yarn hits like an anaconda.

"Last chance," I tilted my head back in pain and concentration.

They're laughter echoed, "**HA, HA, HA, HA, HA, HA, HA, HA, HA, HA, HA, HA, HA, HA, HA, HA, HA, HA, HA, HA, HA, HA, HA, HA, HA, HA, HA, HA, HA, HA, HA, HA, HA, HA, HA, HA, HA, HA, HA, HA, HA, HA, HA, HA, HA, HA, HA, HA, HA, HA, HA, HA!**"

Healing

Healing magic is magic devoted to improving the physical and mental condition. There are many different types of spells in this magic that have a variety of effects. There are also a vast group of potions and crystals that are dedicated to healing as well. Magical Beings who specialize in this area of magic are known as Healers.

Healing magic can be used for your own life or for others you know who need healing energy. If you are using it for someone else, always seek their permission beforehand and let them know you are casting a spell for their healing. Healing magic can be used for physical, emotional or spiritual healing, whenever you feel that you need a boost.

Using combined magic often add potency and power to the magical workings. Familiars have a built-in sort of healing magic.

Angus, Minotaur of Minoa

Chapter 36

So hot… My tattoos of the kids' names burn with pain this time. I know that something is really wrong a tear rolls down my face as I cried out for them…

"NNNNOOOOOOOOOOOOO!"

Like facken Dragon Ball Z, Fenrir and I go full on facken Super Saiyan. My tattoos glowing fluorescent green, my actual skin became bioluminescent, and silver green. My pain turned to determination with the combination of our magic. As the sun dies and the night eats the light. I watched as it slips below the horizon. With every muscle fiber I had straining I pull my arm off the end of a spear, as the yarn wraps tighter around me cutting my skin till I bled. I flexed my fingers in and out of a fist with every increase of strength I poured into my muscles pulling at the strings that entangle me. Watching the blood flow freely from me to drip down Fenrir's fur. My jaws clenched in hate. Irons' HUD highlights all 500,000 Red Capes and their familiars. One by one each Red Cape weapons and defensive gear are scanned. The animal familiar's species and other notable attributes are uploaded to my display.

"Sir, Sir's bonds cannot be cut," Irons started to say.

Slurp, Pop, SMACK

As soon as the short javelin is free from my arm it is pulled tightly against Fen by the magical yarn. Turning my head to the left I looked at the mini spear stabbing me through my bicep. The magical facken yarn tightens more, slashing deeper into my flesh, Hank powerless to stop the magical item. My blood flows down my forearm over Alex's, Nathan's, and Kara's names.

My ink glows an intense silver. Magic, emotional energy, surges through me of primal parental protection. Fenrir's fur bristles in magical power then his muscles tense. With great effort he pushes his paws under himself and begins to stand. The yarn cuts us both deeper as we both flex our combined magical strength.

"GGGGRRRRRRRRRRROOOOOOOOOOOOOOAARRRR!" we both scream. Our magic turning into a storm of emotions.

SNAP SNAP SNAP SNAP SNAP SNAP

Like high tension wire the yarn strands brake individually. The huge wolf shakes like he had just stepped out of the bath. With a quick snap I was dislodged from all the spears. Using that same momentum to my advantage I launched myself far into the ranks of the Red Capes. I tried to land all Superman like, but as my feet touched the ground the pain shoots through my tattoos. I grab my forearm in shock taking my attention away. Rolling to a stop, bowling over some Red Capes with my grace fullness. On my knees and hands my head bowing low the sound of Fenrir's yarn snapping fills my ears.

"Kill them all…" I whispered to Fenrir knowing he could hear me.

As I said this I released a wave magical energy 360 degrees around me intending to just give myself some room. The earth shattered underneath me like a comet had hit when I set off the magical grenade. The combined magic of Fenrir's and I exploded out of me sending the nearest Red Capes crashing down hundreds of yards away. Lifting my eyes to see my wave of magic spread over the fields of my enemies.

The shock wave burst towards the army of Red Capes and the animal slaves. Brilliant fireworks erupted as my magic struck the leashes of magic that held the animal to the Red Capes. The magical ribbons of runes that took me with great effort to break, erase, the last time disintegrate in a shower of sparkles. The bonds to their animal slaves broken, I stand to see the carnage throughout the battlefield. Animal familiar killing their former masters. Lou materializes in my hand as a huge broadsword. I focused my emotional volcano into raw magic and the silver green energy danced across my ink. I couldn't even feel all the injuries I had sustained. Music started to play in my helmet as I stepped out the crater. Screams echoing from my lips as I severed the first Red Cape from his mortal coil. I danced among the animals killing their masters. I slaughter the Red Capes cutting them down like wheat.

In the heat of battle, I scour the surrounding areas for a big enough stone. Seeing a clustering set of monolithic sized rocks out my peripheral vision on the other side of the battlefield.

“Fen!” pointing to the boulders as I called the massive sized wolf's name, “Fetch!”

“Whoofff!” Fen barks bounding over to pile of giant rocks. He ripped the biggest stone out of the ground and drops the 10 ft tall rock three yards in front of me with a thud.

“WHOOFFF woof woof ggggggrrrr whoof!” Fen calls to the freed animals.

The animal slaves create a defensive circle around me protecting me on all sides from attack. I walked towards it kicking a half dead Red Cape from in front of me. His ribs explode inward with the magical impact and is sent out of the protective circle. Now that my path was clear I made my way to the face of the huge boulder. I pull for the note in my back pocket. Unfolding it Irons' HUD highlights the spell and overlays it digitally on the surface of the stone. Using the blood that was dripping down my face I painted. My fingers covered in blood I continued to frantically draw the spell, willing more magic into it. Finishing the last rune, I took Lou and cutting my palm I coated my entire palm with wet blood. I made a fist letting the blood seep between my fingers to drip to the earth.

"With mine own blood and the blood of mine enemies," I don't scream these words I just speak them. Blood drips to the ground like a heartbeat. "The wrath of Thor," placing my palm directly in the center of the blood drawn hammer, "I summon."

SNAP Crack BOOM

A huge bolt of lightning lights up the sky. Thor's answer striking the Rune Stone with a cascading shower of sparks a burn of his great hammer left upon it. The force of the lightning strike blows me off my feet. I slump back... and a huge tongue licked my entire back and head drool dripping down Irons.

"WOOFF RRRuf Gggrrrrr!" Fen reminded me.

After all the dying was done and I look over the fields of the dead. Watching all the different creatures eat in the far distance the sound of a small brass horn rings. Then another and another turning into a sympathy. More Red Capes on the way, Fenrir's head turns with his ears tucked back from the sound of the horns.

"GGRRRR Whoofff!" he challenges the oncoming enemy.

I put my hand on his side rubbing his fur and projected my thoughts my feelings to him as I spoke it out loud, "Pack!"

He calmly sat down but never took his eyes off the direction of the oncoming Red Capes. I was still boiling over with magic, centering myself in a Kung Fu style breathing move. I looked like Ryu from Street Fighter, pulling a concentrated ball of magic to form from my core. Letting the glowing ball of raging storm clouds of magic grow I held my position.

KaBOOM WWWWWOOOOOOOOOOSH

I released the bursting ball of magic towards the brass horns. The magical glow of the spherical missile disappearing out of sight. Minutes passed then a small green and silver poof lights up the distant night sky.

"AAAAAAHHHHHHHHHHHHHH!" the Red Capes yell in surprise as their own animal familiar turn on them.

Gremlins

Although their origin are found in myths among airmen of the royal air force they are much older, in old English they are known has the Gremian "to vex".

These little creatures are wizard's at all mechanical machinery and have an uncontrollable compulsion to dismantle these things. They are resistant to all electrical current.

Gremlins are remarkable creatures and can fold space teleporting meters away. Their hairless skin color is always some version of green. The more they turn translucent the more they lose the green pigments by becoming gray.

Adult male Gremlins very in size smallest at 12 inches the largest at 29 inches, female Gremlins average 10 inches to 16 inches.

Gremlins can stick to any surface no matter the material of the surface or lubricant covering the surface. Each one of their three finger tips are covered in tiny spider web like hairs under their talons. The hairs are lined with microscopic suction cups.

From Angus's Library

Stolen Nazi Classified Documents

Written by SS Chief Heinrich Himmler

Chapter 37

Still listening to their screams, I relaxed my hold on the rest of the magic. With the magical release of power an unexpected thing happened, it begins healing me and Fen and repairs Hank and Irons as it departs. The sudden rush of all that magical energy leaving my body made my head spin. Grabbing Irons from my head I throw up just as the helmet passed my lips. After I recovered from the case of projectile vomit but stilling sweating profusely I stood knees weak. Hank pushes Alex's magical parchment up just enough out of his pocket for me to notice it. Unrolling the scroll the compass needle spinning to a stop. Rolling it back up, I tucked it in a pocket before I put my helmet back on. I look over to find Fen playing with one of the dead bodies of the Red Capes. As he played I gathered some of the longest pieces of the magical yarn as I could. Rolling it up like paracord I tucked the three rather large bundles inside Hank. You never know when you might actually need magical rope. Fenrir was actually eating the Red Cape when I was finished.

Crunch, Crack, crunch, crunch Gulp.

"You done?" I ask him.

His huge red eyes bare down on me like I was going to be next. He started to shake his fur, but his eyes never left mine. He shook all the blood from his fur. It fell from the sky like rain. The mountain sized wolf took a step forward lowering his head as his eyes locked on mine. His muscles ripple and tense under his coat. He shrinks smaller and smaller till he was only as big as a bus. I kept eye contact with him not backing off.

The monstrous proportions of the wolf aside, he was beautiful. His tail, legs and body where a deep midnight blue. Silver and gray fur traced over his amber eyes to flow down his jaws under his muzzle and down his chest. The outside of his ears are midnight blue but the insides of are lined silver and gray.

“RUURUFFFFFF GGRRRR!” Fen curling his lips back showing me his teeth. He inches forward, head down, ears back, teeth exposed and his tongue stretched out in challenge. His wet nose a frog's hair away from my face now. “Chuff chuffed chuff,” he growls softly.

I tilted my head a little, raising one eyebrow and grabbed his snout pulling him even closer so I could look at him at eye level. “Still not scared of you,” I told him and I shoved his head out of my way. Bumping his big muzzle into my chest because he was not finished. I turned and started to walk towards where the compass had pointed to. He let me get about sixty or seventy yards from him before he bounded after me.

“Whoof roo whoof bark!” Fen calls to me from behind.

“A magical feather,” I tell him answering his question. Looking up at the Earth and Moon high in the sky, “And it is a nice night for a run.” I slide Irons over my head and begin to jog while Fen keeping pace.

I didn't pour on the speed we just ran at a normal pace until we got to the beach. The beach was covered in deserted Viking long ships. Fen growing in size begins to play with ships like chew toys. I let him play making our way down to the beach. Walking to the water's edge I focused my magic and the water magic flowed into my ink effortlessly. Walking on top of the waves I made it about twenty yards or so. I turned back to call Fen as he was still wreaking havoc on the unoccupied vessels.

“Fen!” his ears popped up with his name. I smacked my leg, “With me!” snapping my fingers and pointed to my side.

“Roof!” he said with excited joy. Shrinking back down he bounded towards the surf. Like Yoda I reached out with the water magic swirling it up Fenrir's paws and farther up his legs. He didn't even realize until he was right next to me that he was not sinking.

“Whoofff roof!” leaping up and down on the water's surface he said in amazement. He headbutts me in the side still overjoyed with his freedom. I petted him knowing he had just exchanged one leash for a different kind of leash that he wasn't truly free. “Rowoof?” he asked.

“That direction,” I told him pointing northeastern. He took off at a dead sprint.

“BARK WHOOFFF!” he calls back to me.

“Oh, it's on!” I yell back to him and pour on the superspeed. We both made huge rooster tails of water in our wake. We reached the other side of the lake in only a few short minutes.

SMASH…

The shore line explodes when we hit the solid ground with the release of the water magic. Not even slowing, we raced to the tree line and through the dense forest. Irons’ HUD highlights the path with less resistance, the fastest way isn't always on the ground. Pushing and pulling the magic as I ran I bound from tree to branch to rock. Fenrir's seems to flow around the trees and rocks when he runs. The HUD displayed speedometer read a 112 MPH. We came out onto a huge grass covered meadow just as the sun peeks over the horizon.

“GGRRRR WHOOFFF WOOF GGGGGGRRRR!” Fenrir says when he skids to a stop and looks behind us. Turning to confirm what he had said. I see the rainbow bridge descending.

“FACKEN…Tyr!” spurts out my mouth before I could stop myself. I looked up at the massive wolf's head, he was petrified, I needed to strengthen his resolve. “Hey, Fathead!” I called to Fen. His big sad eyes looked at me. “PACK, you always remember that,” I reassured him.

I flared my magic, my tattoos glowing a florescent green with bright silver. Fenrir's own magic flared on my command causing his silver flame to dance with green highlights. I let the magic die down.

“And if one hand wants to lose his capability to masturbate on his facken own,” shrugging my shoulders as I finish, “so be it.”

“Chuff Chuff huff huff,” Fen smiles, “Chuff bark huff chuff.”

“Odin, really?” and I started to choke, then I coughed out a laugh getting myself back under control, “that's not...”

“Bark bark huff chuff,” Fen cuts me off.

With that image floating around in my brain now I joined him in the laughter.

SHIVER SWISHHH SHIVERS SWISHHH SPAT! SPAT! SPAT!

Hank shivering all over and the rolled up magical parchment is sent spinning into the sky. I yanked it from the air out of reflex.

Image of floating island but as 9 and 41 scratched over the beautiful picture. I watched as another image starts to be painted on the magical scroll. A gremlin, his long ears pulled back in a ponytail behind his gray scarred up face.

“Sir, that would be The Gremlin Market or as most know it as the goblin market,” Ironniesous say's in is Irish accent.

Nazi Secrets

Supernatural thinking was instrumental from the beginning of the Nazi regime. The Nazi fascination with the occult is legendary. The regime enlisted astrology and the paranormal, paganism, Indo-Aryan mythology, witchcraft, miracle weapons, supernatural creature and the lost kingdom of Atlantis in reimagining their own way to harness magic.

The Third Reich's relationship to the supernatural was far from straightforward. Even as popular occultism and superstition were intermittently rooted out, suppressed, and outlawed. The Nazis drew upon a wide variety of occult practices and esoteric sciences to gain power, shape propaganda and policy, and pursue their dreams of racial utopia and empire.

SS chief Heinrich Himmler also ordered research into finding the Holy Grail and other magical and biblical weapons from history. He was reportedly fascinated by any ancient use of magic.

This occult fixation with magic went so far that the SS experiment on witches and other magical creatures, included Gremlins. Eventually establishing divisions of elite magical soldiers.

Angus, Minotaur of Minoa

Chapter 38

"WHOOFFF!" Fen yanks me off the ground by my shield and leaps, the ground exploded where we had just been.

BOOM

A massive impact crater leaves nothing left of where I was. In the middle of the crater sat the rune-stone I painted in blood to summon Thor. Fenrir tosses his head back releasing me from his jaws, I tucked my right leg and extended my left. With my right hand I grabbed his fur around his neck and twisted. Fully mounted behind Fenrir's neck he pours on the speed. Getting bounced back and forth as I look back.

"So, do you think he was actually aiming at us?" I asked both Irons and Fen.

"If Tyr knew Sir's exact location. He would not just throw stones," Irons pointed out.

"Point!" I said turning around to face forward.

My ass already taking a beating from Fenrir's shoulder blades. I thought horseback riding was rough on the butt. It took me a minute or so to get the rhythm of his gallop down, timing it just right I popped up on my knees like I was on the inner tube being pulled behind my Dad's ski boat. So instead of riding him like a horse. I was up high between his shoulders, my left hand gripping his fur tight like the oh shit handle on the inner tube as my Pops would fling me around the lake, good times. With my knees tucked under me I could adjust my pitch as needed absorbing the impact of his movement.

"RUU RUFFFFFF!" he says tilting his head and with an evil glint in his eye.

Grabbing his fur with both hands I leaned into him as if I was on a jet ski. In that second his muscles flexed and he leaped from the ground, we were flying above the trees. Fenrir soared through the sky like he was weightless. I didn't even feel him land. His paws hit the ground without a sound and then we were up above the clouds this time. His magical energy ran from his fur down to my arms. My tattoos responds by pumping my magical energy into him. Feeding that magic into his muscles. With every leap we stayed in the air longer and jumped farther. Everyone knows that old saying when pigs fly, what about when wolves fly. Holding on with my shins and knees I pulled the magical parchment out to check the compass and sure enough Fen knew where he was going.

"Woof whoofff ruff bark!" he tells me.

"How was I supposed to know you knew," I told him as I put Alex's magical piece of paper back in my pocket. "In my defense you've been chained up for a while."

This time when we landed we hit the ground in a shower of dust and debris. Mass times velocity equals force. Fenrir paws smashed the ground in a crash then he hopped up coming down again with less force on the second hop digging his claws into the dirt. He makes a 30 ft deep and 100's of yards long dirt trench as we skid to stop. The dust settles slowly to the ground and I can see that Fen has made the peak of this mountain into a plateau.

"Grruff whoofff ruff," Fen say's as I slide off the side of his leg.

"Ratatoskr!" I said in surprise when I landed, "Really."

Glang chink glang

Whispered across the wind. Fenrir and I looked toward the ghostly sounds immediately. Not realizing that Fen had stopped yards from the edge of a cliff. I unconsciously took a step backwards.

“Sir is not far, those are chains, Sir is hearing. They hold the market to Asgard,” Liam Neeson tells me.

The debris clouds dissolving clearing the view. Off in the distance hovering in the middle of the snow peaked valley an upside-down mountain. Floating high in the sky, huge waterfalls cascaded off its edge's. Smaller upside-down hills orbit it like satellites.

The gravity defying island floats back and forth in the breeze. It was held by the biggest chain I had ever seen from floating away. Even from this distance it made an Aircraft carrier anchor chain look tiny in comparison. Figuring the only way up was either teleportation or we could climb up that big ass chain?

Climbing the bolts that mount the chains to Asgard.

Walking on the chain was like walking down a deserted three lane interstate freeway. Fen and I ran side by side up the moss-covered chain leaping the gaps. After scaling the rest of the chain straight up, we pulled ourselves up to the grass covered lawn.

Walking through the German countryside. Sheep and goat herds dot the breathtaking views. Walking through hedge separated groves of grass covered the fields. Fen leaps over the next well-groomed hedge.

“Huff bark!” he calls to me from the other side of the big ass bushes. “HUFF BARK!” he repeats with excitement.

Sure enough, when I land on the other side of the hedge I found myself on an old cobblestone and gravel road. As we followed the old road towards the entrance to the bombed-out town. Skeletons of tanks and other military vehicles litters the road way. The closer we get to the town, the older and wrecked military shit blocks the road. I tried to tell Fenrir to stay hidden behind the tanks because someone might recognize him, it doesn't go as I planned. The huge dog started to whine like I just kicked him in the balls.

“YYYYEEEEEELLLLPPPP Yelp yelp!” he proclaimed until I clamped his muzzle shut with both hands.

“Fine!” I tell him still holding his muzzle closed. Given his nose a kiss I let him go thinking to myself how the fucking hell I was going to disguise him.

“BARK WHOOFFF!” knocking me over with his head.

“Okay,” I tell him holding my hands up in surrender as I step backwards away from him.

Fen fur transformation is subtle but complex. The individual hairs of his fur started flattening with silver magic. Shaking his neck and head his hair gleaming like polished sword blades. Silver glowing magic shimmering as he shook, then he just vanished. I reached out to do the blind man check and I slammed my hand into him. Flexing my fingers trying to get feeling back into it.

“Whoof rawhoof!” he tells me.

“Yeah man,” petting my invisible friend.

“Sir,” Irons spoke up. I waited for him to continue but silence is all I received.

“What's up, Irons?” I finally gave up waiting and asked him.

“Sir is going to Market presumably to purchase something Sir,” he says in his heavy Irish accent. It only took me a second or two ta decipher what the hell he had just said.

“Hank!” calling my Kraken hoodie’s name out loud so I could focus on my voice. I rubbed my jacket lapel with my thumb while I spoke his name. Using that focus of magical energy I asked him in my mind to take Irons off my head. Hank’s hood pulls Irons off my head gently tucking him behind my back. The magical glow of my tattoos fades to normal.

Making our way towards the shell-shocked town it appears empty and deserted, a ghost town. We came to the outer wall of what looked like an old German town that hadn’t been rebuilt, still bombed from World War II. So a brand new brick and stone archway that elegantly sweeps over the road stands out. I paused before passing through it. I looked beyond the wall from empty building to half destroyed building, scanning for any movement. Nothing, nota I couldn't see a single person. Feeling kinda of uneasy Lou materializes in my left hand immediately morphing into a hiking staff. Okay it's time to put on my big boy panties thinking to myself. I'm not afraid of a spooky bombed out ghost town straight out of World War II. Shrugging my shoulders at my silliness I took a step.

"PheeRRRRUUMMMP!" the elephant boomed in surprise.

Empty facken ghost town, that's until I crossed under the stone arch and almost got stumped on by a Woolly Mammoth pulling a huge wooden cart, no scratch that, more like a wooden semitrailer. Dodging to the left in surprise, more like falling I hit the ground crab crawling on my ass. The huge hairy foot of the Mammoth inches from crushing me.

"GGGRRRRRrrrrr ruff!" Fenrir's invisible form smashes into the prehistoric elephant. The mammoth raised up off its front legs.

"Thanks," I whispered to Fen getting to my knees brushing myself off as I did so.

Fenrir body checks the Mammoth and the wooden semi-trailer over a foot to slam down next to me instead of on top of me.

"SKREEKKEEE NARK!" snapping is tongue down to emphasizing his profanity, the driver yells yet at me.

CLACKED clack

With a shudder of his carapace he guides the hairy beast past us.

Giving the insectoid driver the middle finger as I stand up watched him. As the walking wall of dirty shag carpet moved from blocking my view. I couldn't believe what I saw.

"Holy shit," came mumbling out my mouth in awe. "I feel like if Star Wars and Hellboy hooked up and nine months later. POOF! Out popped this place," dodging the other traffic on the road to get to the crowded sidewalk I tell Irons or maybe I was talking to Fenrir.

Who am I kidding? I was just saying out loud to hear myself say it so I wouldn't think I was hallucinating. Hell, I just walked into an empty, floating, bombed out World War II German town to almost get trampled by a facken elephant in need of a haircut.

The place was really crowded with different magical beings. Shops and restaurants line the cobblestone streets, glass tiles ascent the sidewalks. Small vendors are setting up their stands for lunch rush. Here and there along the extra wide sidewalk they hustled about.

My stomach rumbles, so I find a small cafe dinner with an outside patio. It was placed perfectly so I could see down two intersecting roads, one road had a clear view all the way to the fountain in the Town Square. Taking a seat on the patio an overweight dark forest green gremlin crawled up the chair opposite to me and stood on top of the table. He looks at me for a long moment then holds up three of his fat clawed fingers counting them down as he spoke with very heavy and thick German overtones.

"Burnt meat, stale bread and cold sweet tea," the 18" gremlin told me.

"Perfect," I told him, sliding a poker chip sized fragment of solid gold rainbow stone across the table towards him. He snatched it up and vanished, just faded away.

I pulled out my cigarettes. Putting one to my lips the tip with barley a second thought magically started to burn. Not half way through my smoke the fat bastard almost makes me shit my pants.

H-S-S-S-S-S-BAMF WOOSH

Looking down at the overweight gremlin, that just teleported, standing on my table. My asshole unpuckers as he places my food and drink in front of me. I scanned the Gremlin Market as I ate my food and chain smoke a pack of cigarettes. After eating I tried to explore more of the Market as I headed towards the Town Square.

Walking through the multi magical creature market I see a twinkle of light, crystal necklace out the corner of my eye hung in the window of a nearby shop. Pink, blue, gold, purple, orange crystals twinkle from the mid-morning sun. But most of the crystal where clear white. Walking in the little store I see it's not just necklaces but bracelets and canes mixed in with other random things. I picked up a rather large unmounted piece of clear crystal from the countertop in my right hand holding it up and inspecting it closer.

Every side of it had Samoan tribal tattoo like designs etched on it. I still hadn't put Ironniesous back on so when my tattoos slightly started to glow green it startled me. The entire right side of my torso is covered in Samoan and Polynesian style tattoos. A full sleeve envelopes my right arm from my wrist wrapping up around my shoulder and over my chest then proceeds down to cover my right rib cage flowing to dip below my hip. My Samoan ink flared fluorescent green, the illumination glowing brightly underneath Hank. Looking at the crystal in my right hand I could see the etched patterns start to turn green.

“May I…help,” a grandma voice with an almost Australian accent came from behind the counter but she stopped mid-sentence.

The crystal went from clear to glowing fluorescent green the etchings shimmered silver. The magic in my tattoos fades away and I am left with this huge glowing piece of kryptonite. Looking at the little Samoan Grandma for the first time her mouth hung wide open.

“I think I broke it,” holding the crystal out to her in my open palm.

Her tattooed face scrunched up as she looked at the crystal. She never touches it or try to take it from my open hand. She leaned over to me so I did the same, placing my forehead against hers we both inhaled through our noses deeply. She pulled away and smiled at me. She closes her hands around mine wrapping my fingers around the crystal. Then I noticed the iron shackles she has around her wrist.

“Keep it,” she tells me and shuffles off with the flapping of the curtain door behind the counter. Before the curtain stopped moving a huge 6’ 7”, honest to goodness, pirate stepped out.

SHIVER SWISHHH OOOF UUMPHH SHIVER SWISHHH OOOF UUMPHH

Hank freaking the fuck out wiggles and squirms fluffing air underneath my jacket.

This guy must have stolen his entire outfit from the set of "The Pirates of the Caribbean" down to his worn leather boots. The brim of his weathered Captain's hat was patched and tattered. His long bushy black beard had eight small braids with shells and beads tied into the braids. A huge bandolier crossed over his chest with five odd looking muskets holstered draped over his brown pea coat. His cutlass was tucked under the sash wrapped around his waist. He absently tossed in his right hand a leather pouch blackened with age a symbol of some kind I could barely see across the surface of the leather bag.

Pocketing the crystal inside Hank's sleeve. I ducked out of the shop and blended into the street traffic.

SHIVER SWISHHH SHIVERS SWISHHH SPAT!

Getting back on task Hank reading my thoughts I reached for the magical parchment refreshing the compass to check if the feather was near. The compass needle is pulsing a glowing orange color as it points to the center fountain in the Town Square. But then, does a 180 degree, pointing back towards the Crystal Shop. I shifted the parchment side to side like an Etch A Sketch, the compass needle settles pointing towards the center of town again. The orange glow pulsing faster. Assuming the orange glow means I'm close, I roll it back up and heading to the Town Square.

A letter to Hitler

We have finally found a solution to the identification and rank of SS paranormal division, Sabotage.

We will use the premises of a fighter pilot; a pilot must shoot down so many planes in single, air to air, combat to become an Ace fighter pilot. Division Sabotage will remain nameless and hold no rank until 500 enemy military vehicles that includes tanks, aircrafts, naval ships and have been verified disabled or completely destroyed.

The consecutive days since recruit is given their first mission to this goals completion will be the soldier's name and rank.

For example, the soldier takes nine months and three days from his first mission to immobilize 500 military vehicles, his rank and name would be 273."

I also believe I have finally found the perfect candidate for your personal SS Guard from Division Sabotage identification number 41.

From Angus's Library

Stolen Nazi Classified Documents

Written by SS Chief Heinrich Himmler

Chapter 39

Town Square is an open-air Farmers Market. Mostly vegetable stands surrounded the fountain with a few other farm related stands scattered amongst them. The market is bustling with all matters of magical beings and supernatural creatures. With the daunting task of finding a special feather inside a pillow of the exact same feathers started to weigh on me.

blink..blink VAROOOM HHMMMMMMMMMM SWOOOSH..

Rubbing my lapel with my thumb, Hank slides Irons over my head. The magic is instant, my tattoos glowing fluorescent green. The HUD blinked on and started to highlight everything. The magical wireframe appears overlaying each item just for a millisecond uploading the information then scanning another. I slowly made my way from table to table marveling at the different types of fresh food each farmer sold. I always stayed out of the way and not bring attention to myself. Irons continues to scan as I made my third lap around as the sun gets lower in the sky.

H-S-S-S-S-S-BAMF WOOSH Clank

Out of nowhere, this really tall Gremlin appears. Compared to the other Gremlins that I have seen in the market he was huge, he stood over 2 feet tall. The other Gremlins in the market that Irons's HUD had scanned were all between 18 to 19 inches tall. With his big ears pulled back it made him look even bigger. He has a metallic office trash can strapped to him like a backpack. It's wired to the stump of his left arm. Grabbing the trash with his good hand he'd move his stomp opening the trash can and tossed it in.

H-S-S-S-S-S-BAMF WOOSH Clank

He reappears fifteen feet way. His metal prosthetic leg making the metallic clank as he teleported. As he reappears, he is facing more my direction. I can see the number 41 branded into his chest, big and bold. The same number that was scratched into Alex's magical parchment hits me like a bolt of lightning.

Irons reading my thoughts HUD highlights the janitor and begins to compare the image from the magical parchment. I see the Gremlin clipping the feather to his tied back ears.

"He's got the feather," I whispered.

Approaching slowly and cautiously I grabbed some stray litter from the sidewalk as I came closer.

"Excuse me!" I called to the gray skinned Gremlin holding out the trash for him to see.

He flexed his stump opening the trash can backpack when he sees the garbage. I tossed it in the little waste basket and the lid slapped shut. Starting to ask him about the feather to see if he would trade me for it, the feather's magic spiked. Celtic knots of magic swirl from the feather supercharging the little Gremlin as he uses his teleportation magic. With an implosion of magic, he vanished but his mechanical leg stayed, and with a clank falls to the ground.

"That can't be good," as I watch the artificial limb collapse the rest of the way to the sidewalk.

H-S-S-S-S-S-BAMF WOOSH

He appears near the closet trash can some distance away. His war-torn body healed. Standing on two legs he rips off his backpack with his regrown arm and dumps it into the bigger receptacle. Lou materializes in my hand as the bone whip.

Sonic CRACK

Lou echoing as I flicked my wrist to snatch the feather from the now Super Gremlin.

H-S-S-S-S-S-BAMF WOOSH

Lou struck empty air and the Super Gremlin was running across the roof line across the street.

"Fenrir fetch!" I yelled pointing at the escaping Gremlin. The roof buckles with the invisible wolf's weight as Fen gives chase, it was like chasing Nightcrawler from the X-MEN.

Free running over and sometimes through the market in pursuit of the Gremlin. Using my own magical sight to track his magic teleportation. But he'd then turned translucent completely see through and jumped out an open window. He stopped teleporting so I couldn't track him that way any longer.

Irons' HUD blinked and then flickering through different light spectrums until I could see the Super Gremlin again. He was on the other side of the building already climbing down the side of it. I focused my magic pulling more magic to me, super jumping at the building. The water fountain in the center of town explodes emptying the water into the air.

SLPASH WHURL WHOOSH BLAM CRASH

Timing it just right leading my target as it arched through the sky. I draw the water magic to me and refocused its kinetic energy to punch a hole completely through the building except for the last outer wall.

SCKRATCH CREEK KaBoom snag H-S-S-S-S-S

I pull my legs up to my chest and draw my shield from my back. In one motion I flipped it under my feet and surfed the tunnel of wreckage. The outer wall underneath the Gremlin shattered as I crashed through it. My fist wrapping around his translucent neck. The little fucker really went ape shit then. He teleported with me still holding onto his neck.

H-S-S-S-S-S-BAMF WOOSH Smack

I came to a sudden stop as I hit the cobblestone road. I squeeze his neck harder as the Gremlin thrashes about like a cat that's about to get a bath. I try desperately to grab for the feather.

H-S-S-S-S-S-BAMF WOOSH Shatter

A glass display counter brakes into a million pieces as I wrestled the clawed Super Gremlin. Still holding him by his neck he digs his claws deep into my hand. I literally choke slam him repeatedly into the broken countertop. A mechanical hand grabs my arm from behind the destroyed counter. Holding the Gremlin out straight in front of me he finally starting to pass out from the lack of oxygen. I looked at the copper fingers gripping my upper arm in disdain.

Wheeze, click

"I must insist," a metallic voice said.

Wheeze whistle

"Leave you must," the long-lost brother of C-3PO made from brass and copper informs me politely.

CRASH CHOMP

"WHOOFFF!" Fen comes crashing through the shops bay window in pursuit of me becoming visible again as he bites the robotic man into chunks.

H-S-S-S-S-S-BAMF WOOSH

"Einundvierzig a mess you have made of mein Geschäft," a slight voice said with a very heavy German accent.

H-S-S-S-S-S-BAMF WOOSH

"Gutter puppy," something said as I turned just in time to make out an extra small green with gray Gremlin scratching my wolf behind his ear.

H-S-S-S-S-S-BAMF WOOSH

"Neun ist mein name...Einundvierzig ist his," the 16 inch tall Gremlin said from my shoulder.

H-S-S-S-S-S-BAMF WOOSH

"Spielen possum he is!" Neun tells me from the other side of the shop, his huge ears twitch. I was starting to get whiplash trying to keep up with the little Gremlin.

Click

Automaton and Golem

An Automaton is a moving mechanical device made in imitation of a human being that performs a function according to a predetermined set of coded instructions, especially one capable of a range of programmed responses to different circumstances.

A Golem is magically imbued with an elemental spirit. These are created entirely from inanimate matter or any sparkles material, sticks and mud or tubes and such. It's all in the applying of one's magic to the anatomy. It must flow and recirculate that flow on its own. The best way I have found magical runes carved, etched or tattooed around and in the creation itself.

My minions are very inept in both such crafts and if my theory is correct the combination with my own Necromantic magic will have spectacular results.

From Angus's Library

Personal Medical Journal

Dr. Victor Frankenstein, Necromancer

Victor's minions were actually Gremlins.

Angus, Minotaur of Minoa

Chapter 40

Turning back to my outstretched arm I find Einundvierzig, his eyes wide open. A little copper and brass gun held up to my face the hammer cocked back.

BANG

The hammer falls. My head rocks back with impact of the projectile. Stumbling around from spatial disorientation on instinct I let the Gremlin go. Putting both my hands on my helmet to get it stop vibrating.

H-S-S-S-S-S-BAMF WOOSH Smack

Einundvierzig teleported away but hit a magical barrier. Dust showers down from the cracks in the ceiling. The giant Gremlin dug his claws into the ceiling and started to dig through the now cracked ceiling.

H-S-S-S-S-S-BAMF WOOSH

"Warded mein Geschäft ist," Neun stands upside-down on the ceiling, his arms in parade rest. He looks at Einundvierzig like what the fuck, "Einundvierzig kennen this."

“Fenrir!” calling him but not taking my eyes off the Gremlins. I point with my thumb towards the gigantic hole he made during his perfectly time rescue of me. “No one leaves!”

“Bark huff chuff!” he skids to the hole, his paws not really able to get traction on the marble floor. He sticks his ass and tail out the huge exit and sits. The marble tiles cracked as he increased in size. The sound of the tiles breaking makes me take a glance over my shoulder.

“That's one way to plug up the problem,” smiling at the huge wolf knowing he couldn't see it but hoping he could feel it through our magic. “Good dog.”

H-S-S-S-S-S-BAMF WOOSH starches

“Zurückbekommen his regeneration abilities Einundvierzig has,” his heavy accent chirps from my back. Neun peaks around me while perched on the top of my shield, “Taken from him, bestrafung it was.”

Einundvierzig like a lunatic frantically breaks little chunks out the ceiling exposing the rafters. Lou materializes in my hand morphing into the bone whip.

Sonic CRACK Flopping flop flip flop…

The rafters Einundvierzig had occupied just exploded with Lou’s touch. Looking down to see Einundvierzig’s left arm twitching and spasming on the marble floor.

H-S-S-S-S-S-BAMF WOOSH

Einundvierzig materializes in the middle of the broken robotic man's remains of spare parts. His left arm regeneration was almost complete. With his other three limbs he grabbed seemingly random parts from automaton.

“See the Crow's feather,” nodding my helmet towards Einundvierzig. “It was stolen from the Morrigan by a really bad Indian Medicine Man Skinwalker guy,” I told Neun as I flexed my wrist.

Sonic CRACK

Automaton parts went everywhere as a good chunky piece of Einundvierzig's ear smacked wetly on the tile as Lou reached out as a whip.

"Näher to the feather at least you were," the 16 inch Gremlin said as he crawled onto my right shoulder.

"That's really not helping," scowling at the little dude through my helmet, "You know that."

The green fluorescent glow of my magic flares in warning kicking in my magical sight. An out of focus swirl of dust like magic smeared right in front of me. With the enhanced battle techniques I received during my military career combined with Irons' own version of battle magic. My arm moved before my brain told it to bring my shield to bare.

H-S-S-S-S-S-BAMF WOOSH Screeeettcchhh

Einundvierzig strikes appearing in the spot, my magical sight had seen the blur of magic. Both sides of the double-sided copper and brass energy dagger slash across my shield. My feet set in the legendary Bruce Lee one-inch punch stance. Pooling my magic into my hips as Einundvierzig made contact with my shield. Snapping my hip forward I sent that kinetic and magical energy up my body. Moving only an inch forward I put all my kinetic mass and magic behind the shield.

WOP… splat, SHATTERING CRASH tinkle crack plop

Einundvierzig hits the floor in a gelatinous mess every one of his bones broke. I sent him crashing into the shop's wall shelves and picture frames absorbing his impact. I watched it shatter as it hit the hard marble floor. Walking over to gooey mess Einundvierzig goes translucent. Expecting Irons' HUD to blink in some other light spectrum a message highlights the display on Gremlin abilities. The list opens like a file folder on my desktop and scrolls down the list stopping on adaptation.

Glang

I whirl around to face the sound. Catching movement out the corner of my eye I hurtled the last remaining countertop. Shield still in my left hand I bring the edge straight down into the marble floor behind the counter.

H-S-S-S-S-S-BAMF WOOSH

"Hilfe you I kann nicht," Neun says rubbing his bald head sitting on the unbroken counter. "Verboten it ist," he tells me while he turned translucent but pointed his finger up above my head right before vanishing, flexing my body into motion.

H-S-S-S-S-S-BAMF WOOSH CCRREEEKKKKK... KABOOM

The building shakes as the thick heavy oak workbench complete with tools rains from the ceiling. The workbench missing me by a frog's hair as I sprung backwards. Using the shield as an umbrella I deflect the random falling debris.

H-S-S-S-S-S-BAMF WOOSH

Neun appears hanging upside-down, his gecko like toe pads gripping the underside of my shield. Standing in perfect parade rest he looks at me as his tools ricocheted off the shield.

"Why was Einundvierzig punished?" I asked him as I flinched from something big hitting the shield umbrella.

"War kriminell he ist," he answered and began to pace back and forth upside-down. "Responsible for many grausamkeiten against Gremlins he was bestraft... punished for," Neun finished he was just gone, disappearing again.

Clank, rattle-rattle Clank, rattle-rattle rattle-rattle rattle-rattle.

Spinning like I was about to do a roundhouse backhanded punch I launched the shield at the sound. Einundvierzig waited till the last-minute to twist out of the impact and disappears. The air vent that he was desperately trying to free from the exposed ductwork crushed in like a tin can right above Fenrir's head.

"HUFF!" Fen glared at me as the ventilation ductwork bounced off him. The dust cloud settled to the floor. Right in front of Fenrir I saw the dirt cloud blur. "GGRRRRRR!" comes from deep inside Fen.

H-S-S-S-S-S-BAMF WOOSH BARK...

The crazy little fucken Nazi jumped into Fen's open mouth.

"Don't!" I began but it was already too late. Fenrir swallows the evil Nazi Gremlin, not even chewing. Now that Einundvierzig is physically passed the threshold of the shop.

"SHIT!" Instead of waiting for my huge wolf to unplug himself from the wall. I just walked out the door the doorbell chimed as I stepped out onto the sidewalk.

H-S-S-S-S-S-BAMF WOOSH clank

The gas lantern street lamp sways just enough to make the lamp vibrate. Einundvierzig upside down underneath the overhang of the streetlamp.

"Fuck this!" exactly at that moment Irons' HUD displayed a 3D holographic image of a typical Gremlin. A little red pulse of light showing where their heart is.

Click Clack BOOM

Loki

Loki is one of the great Trickster deities of the world's ancient pantheons. His power over magic and his extreme cunning are legendary. His sometimes fickle unpredictability, a trait shared by all divine Tricksters. He is known and sometimes rightfully feared as the god of mischief for this reason. Though he is eminently useful in the scheme of things due to his insuring the necessary level of instability in everyone's sphere of existence, he can cause disasters of various sorts.

The myths are filled with Loki getting his fellow deities into trouble with his antics, but then subsequently doing an equally good job of getting them out of it again. It was therefore clear that Loki was a god of many faces, using his shape-shifting ability to change into other individuals and animals of either gender.

Most interesting about Loki is that he is a member of neither of the two tribes of deities, the Aesir and the Vanir. However, the fact did stop, the king of the gods himself, the All-Father Odin, making Loki into his blood brother. Under circumstances never fully revealed in any of the surviving myths. He is not the son of Odin or the half-brother of Thor.

Loki fathered three of the progeny that he brought into the world as a result of his sexual dalliances with the female giant Angrboða who could apparently shapeshift just as Loki could.

Thus accounting for two of her three offspring with the god of mischief being born in animal form. The largest and most powerful dragon in all of history, Jörmungandr the Midgard Serpent. The enormous and uber-deadly lupine being known as the Fenrir Wolf. His daughter the goddess Hel, who was born with one side of her body living and healthy, the other side dead and decayed. She became the ruler of the Nordic underworld.

Each of these three offspring of Loki have a major role to play in the often-prophesied eventual downfall and destruction of all of the Nine Realms, the cataclysmic event known as Ragnarök.

The reason why Loki tricked the blind god Hodur into killing the beloved god of light, Balder, by striking him with an arrow composed of mistletoe wood is unknown.

Loki was said to be punished by being eternally bound to three huge stones inside a cave while an extremely venomous serpent was situated above his head, where it dripped a constant stream of its acidic poison down upon him from above. His loyal wife, the goddess Sigyn, did her best to stand at his side and catch the seething fluid in a large bowl, but during the moments she took to turn and dump the liquid onto the ground once the bowl was full, Loki would scream and writhe in agony as the flowing stream of poison stream hit and seared his skin.

In addition, it is said they transformed his son Narfi into a wolf, who then proceeded to turn upon Loki's other son, Vali, and ripped him to shreds.

This torturous punishment has enraged Loki and has affected his mental stability.

Angus, Minotaur of Minoa

Chapter 41

Darkness beginning to creep in as the crest of the sun winks passed the horizon. The bullet enters Einundvierzig's open mouth exploding out the base of his skull. His lifeless body hung there for a second before falling. I holster my Winchester.

H-S-S-S-S-S-BAMF WOOSH

A blur of green and gray scrambles over the tumbling dead body. Neun disappearing long before Einundvierzig hits the sidewalk.

"Chuff Huff," Fenrir's invisible head brushing against my right side. So, I found myself unconsciously scratching him behind the ear to let him know it was cool for eating the evil Gremlin.

H-S-S-S-S-S-BAMF WOOSH tug

Looking down at Neun clinging to my left bicep. The feather gripped in his toes wrapped tightly. He snags a small twine of the magical yarn that I didn't notice was tangled in one of my buckles. His hands move rapidly weaving an arm band around my upper bicep. As he does, Neun weaves the magical yarn around the three black feathers. He clasps it tightly around my arm the feather tied securely to the back of it. The beautiful crow's feathers dangling down my triceps. The magical glowing forest green Celtic knots of magic radiate like steam off Morrigan's feathers. One by one the gas street lamps illuminate.

Pisshh pisshh pisshh… Rip chew chew Gulp, Rip chew chew Gulp, Rip chew chew Gulp

I slowly pull my head up to see the Skinwalker. Leaning heavily on the street lamp the gas flames dances over his human form.

Rip chew chew Gulp

He takes another bite out of Einundvierzig.

"Cowboy!" the massive Medicine Man says staring dead at me as he spits out a bloody chunk of fleshy saliva.

His Mohawk draped loosely over to one side. The glow from the gas street lamps makes his skin look vampire pale. The red war paint on his face was so freshly painted it ran like wet mascara down his chalky pale skin. The blood red geometric patterns and designs continues down his neck to spread across his massively huge pectoral muscles. A huge bloody handprint covered his left shoulder on the other. A fingerprint dot with two rings encircling it. He still has the multi-necklace adorned with teeth around his neck.

Leather belts and fur straps wound around his waist with shrunken mythical creatures' skulls hanging from it. Extra leather and fur draped down creating a Tarzan style loincloth. Flexing his arms, I noticed braided hemp rope is tied tightly around both his upper biceps. His left arm has small but very toothy jaw bone with a purple lizard like skin woven around the jaw bone. His right bicep had mummified, Ogres fingers and ears looped through the hemp rope. As he drops Einundvierzig's corpse to the ground he leans away from the street lamp.

We both started unconsciously walking towards one another. My heart racing, I pull magic from everywhere, our walk turns to superspeed. My tattoo's fluorescent light turned a super intense bright green followed with my skin becoming bioluminescent silver as we both power leaped off the sidewalk. With the force, of the jump, we trail plumes of dust through the air. Already shield in hand because I had instinctively pulled it when we started towards each other. The

Skinwalker draws a knee up in anticipation of the collision with my shield. With Captain America grace I throw my shield.

SNAP

His collarbone breaks in his surprise. Lou materializes in my right-hand morphing to a Frost Giant sized Warhammer in mid-arch.

KABOOM

The Skinwalker does a 90 degree turn in midair as Lou hits with the force of a tractor-trailer.

WHACK

"WHHOOOFFF…!" Fenrir's invisible paw Hulk smacks the Indian straight up into orbit. I watched the Evil Medicine Man corkscrew through the night sky higher and higher.

"Fen!" I pointed up to the heavens with my index finger, "Jump!"

Fenrir's fur shimmers as he appears. He tilted his head up and with the smallest of movement leaped into the sky. Without a sound, just a small breeze brushed by me as he jumped. He disappears up into the night. Way up in the stratosphere a small but brilliant flash of light exploded creating a fallen star. With its rapid reentry it quickly became a shooting star. It lit up the dark night as its tail streaked across the sky.

KKKAAAABBBBOOOOOMMMMM

As if it was hit by a laser guided SCUD missile Neun's shop implodes upon itself. The clouds of debris from the vaporization of the building hovers thick in the air.

Creek SNAP

"RRRRRRRROAR!" The Skinwalker screamed from the destroyed building.

CCRREEKK CRASH

The saber tooth were-lion deadlifting the brick wall over his head. His cat eyes reflecting brightly with his hatred of me as dirt cascaded off the brick wall like mini-waterfalls. My vision still obscured by the dust cloud. I never even saw him throw the brick wall let alone see it descending out of the sky.

SMACK BOOM CRASH

The wall pimp slaps me to the sidewalk. Following the abrupt introduction to ground. The brick wall explodes on impact with my head. Facken buried alive is one of my biggest fears so a half ton of bricks pressing down on me caused me to lose my shit. Panic ran my veins cold, terror froze my muscles solid as ice. Fear crept over me in a wave and the magical glow from my tattoos faded away leaving me in the dark. Doubt in myself stole the rest of my magic and Irons' HUD displayed winked off.

"Daddy!" Kara's voice calls to me from the emptiness. Tears welled in my eyes in hopelessness.

"Pink Dragon," my wife's seductive breath whispers. I could feel her lips brush my ear as I heard her voice. Her touch sent tingles shooting down my backbone.

Clamping my eyes close and clenching my jaw so hard I was about to break my teeth. I opened my mind releasing the flood gate of every photographic memory I had of my wife and kids. Memories full of raw emotional power poured over me.

SSHHHUUUUCRACK

The brick wall turns to marble sized shrapnel as my magic erupted from me.

While I was buried alive Fen has been getting his ass kicked. He is no bigger than a regular wolf, his fur is matted with his blood. Because of my lack of faith in myself I not only affected my magic I affected Fenrir's magic also.

SNAP

Echoed from my fingers.

“With me!” I yell.

Fenrir's ears shot up angling towards my voice. In a zigzag pattern Fen bounded away from the saber tooth were-lion. Running past me he skids to a 180-degree U-turn, coming to a stop at my right side. Petting Fen’s blood-soaked fur the magic returns to him in a torrent of magical energy.

H-S-S-S-S-S-BAMF WOOSH

Appearing on my left shoulder Neun immediately springs to my other shoulder. In his hands he held mini energy blades.

The saber tooth were-lion leaps bounding over and over landing on all four paws I could feel the vibrations in the ground from his bulk. Side by side Fen and I charged. Fenrir grows to Greyhound bus size in seconds with the return of magic.

H-S-S-S-S-S-BAMF WOOSH

I fall out of the sky right above Fenrir's head. Sliding down the back of his head. I bounced to my feet pulling both 1911 twisting my body to land facing forward. I surfed on the huge wolf's back racing to intercept the Skinwalker. Turning my hips, I checked my peripheral vision to verify how much distance behind me I had. I stepped back to Fenrir's ass to get a running start. “Wait for it,” I tell myself. Seeing my moment, I kick in my super speed racing up Fenrir's back to springboard off his head. I flipped a roll, spinning my body keeping my 1911 sighted.

Bang, Bang, Bang, Bang, Bang, Bang, Bang, Bang, Bang

They sing to me. Landing behind the Skinwalker in a crouched slide still squeezing the triggers. Knowing my bullets meant nothing in the scheme of things. Physically hurting him was not the plan, chess is a game of maneuvering your opponent. He turned towards me, twisting in an awkward angle. Physics 101, what's in motion, likes to stay in motion and crashes trying to change directions. His momentum too great.

H-S-S-S-S-S-BAMF WOOSH slice slice RRRRRRRROAR slice slice

Neun is completely translucent, you can just see his bronze and copper energy blades as they cut. The werecat sinking all of his huge claws deep into the cobblestone road. The cobblestone in the road turns to gravel.

BLAM BLAM BLAM BLAM

All four VW Bug size paws steps on the werecat as Fenrir runs him over. Grabbing Fenrir's shaggy fur as he runs by me yanking me off the ground. Using Fen's inertia, I flipped to his back.

"Town Square," I whispered coming up with an idea as I said it. Fen jukes right, bounced off the side of a building flinging us left in a 90 degrees banking turn. He rebounds off another building and races to the Square.

H-S-S-S-S-S-BAMF WOOSH

Neun appears holding onto Fen's ear. "Following he does," Neun's heavy German accent informs me. Then says, "New at this you are not."

"No," I answer him, "Magic well let's just say I'm a fast learner." Leaning down to pet Fenrir between his ears, "Fen! Rip out the center statue in the middle of the fountain for me!" Looking up at Neun, "Can you get the fountain overflowing with water?" Without an answer he vanished.

I was standing in the middle of the overflowing swimming pool. The cool water splashing up to my knees. My shield in guard position Lou has morphed into a battle axe. Standing knee deep in the fountain I soak in as much water magic into my tattoos as I can.

Crash Crash SPLASH

With two massive leaps the werelion lands in the fountain with me.

H-S-S-S-S-S-BAMF WOOSH

Neun has teleported me right outside the fountain's edge the water cascading over the edge of the brick and stone retention wall. I slapped my open bioluminescent glowing hand on the top of the fountain's wall pushing magic from my tattoos into the water. Tendrils of water formed from the surface of the water. The entire surface of the fountain is now my weapon. Imagining huge octopus tentacles in my mind the water comes to life.

Splash splash splash

Water is sent every which way as the Skinwalker ran across the fountain totally oblivious. I closed my hand making a fist as the water pours over the edge of the fountain. In an instant, magical water tendrils wrapped around his arms and ankles. Pulling him into the air more tendrils snaked around his neck.

"RRRRROOOAARRRRRR!" he protested.

The Skinwalker trapped by the water fountain magic. With the water magic I pulled him, spread eagle. I held him about fifteen feet above the surface of the water. Opening my hand slowly stretching my fingers wide as I used the water to rip his arms and legs off.

"GRRRRooooaaannn!" his growl turns to a groan as his body is slowly torn apart. I flexed my magic opening my fingers quickly.

RRRIIIIPPP tttttaaaarrreee RRRIIIIIIIP... splish Splash, sploosh Splash, SPLASH, splish SPLOOSH

You could hear his muscle tissues stretch to its limits as his arms tear out of the sockets. Then his left leg is ripped out of his hips. The three body parts fell into the fountain with a splash. His right leg isn't torn completely off. From his thigh down, all the flesh is ripped from the bone.

Slither GURGLE drip..drop BURBLE SQUEEZE

More water tendrils emerge from the fountain's surface to wrap around the limbless torso. Black ichor oozes and bubbles out the monsters decapitations. Necromancer magical smoke rolled off it. Closing my fist as tight as I could the magical water tentacles crushes him like Mr. Miyagi said.

POP Splash

The black ichor sprays out like I had squished a grape. Little squirts of the ectoplasm seep between the tendrils of water. The ectoplasm was dripping up against the law of gravity. The Skinwalker lifts his werecat head. His eyes dripping black ichor up his fangs.

SSSSPPPPPLLLLLLOOOOOOOOOOOOSSSSSHHHHHH SSSSPPPPRRAAAYYYYY

Ichor sprays out like the facken Exorcist. Four torrents of gushing black ooze spews like an unman firehose. A fifth torrent explodes between his huge teeth ejaculating a jet stream of that shit right at me.

Reflexively I swooped my hand out of the water and all the tendrils vanished as the water flowed with my movement. Creating an arch of water in front me the black ooze hits, splashing off. Swinging my hand in a wide arch then I quickly made tornado circles with my wrist. The water wall turned to a cresting wave and encircled the circumference of the water fountain. The wave wall spun faster and faster keeping the black oozing ichor at bay.

“RaRuffffff whimper WHOOF!” his tail shaking behind him in anticipation as we waits for my answer. With the slightest of nods, he runs off.

GURGLE SSSQQUUUUUAAAAKKK BURBLE SSSKKKRRRREEEETTTCCHH

The black oozing snot reversed course with such force it echoes. The ooze becoming partially solid transforming and coalescing around the Skinwalker's torso. Oozing black fur ghostly materializing over the exposed bones of his right leg. The gushing wound of his left leg congeals morphing solid. Arms coagulate with ghostly fur of the Werecat. The Monstrous Skinwalker rolls his shoulders as he looks at me through the whirlpool wall.

“CCCCOOOOWWWWWBBBBBOOOOYYYYYY!” he bellowed and sucked in the rest of ooze growing bigger and bigger. Taking on Godzilla sized proportions his eyes burn with complete and utter hatred locked on to me. Ripping his arms and legs off wasn't such a good idea I thought to myself.

"Now!" I scream dropping the water magic.

BBBBBLLLLAAAAMMMMM

The impact shakes the entire floating island in the sky. The fountain water exploded like a depth charge went off.

H-S-S-S-S-S-BAMF WOOSH sssshhhhhhhhh

The air whips by me as I reappeared, skydiving over the rapidly descending Skinwalker without a parachute. Irons' HUD displayed the distance from the ground and distance from the Skinwalker to the relation of distance from Fenrir. His enhanced tactical information constantly refreshing new more critical data to the HUD, facken super Jarvis. I can see Neun out the corner of my eyes gripped tight to my left shoulder. His ears flapping from the wind. His smile was pure joy.

Falling in style as the great Woody said in the movie Toy's Story. More of my military training automatically took over. Hank extending his rubbery octopus skin. Morphing, flowing out becoming a living cape. My jacket popped the cape, opening like Batman gliding from the rooftops of Gotham City. Slowing my descent Irons' HUD displayed the angle and pitch to intersect with Fenrir. Folding my arms to my side, Hank folds in around me as I dive.

WHACK SMACK

Colliding like two 747, Fenrir attacks the *Godzilla* sized Skinwalker. The Skinwalker reacts with an oversized necromantic ectoplasm made claw, pimp slapping the massive wolf away.

Irons' HUD displayed the new interesting location and I flexed imaginary muscles. Hank flowed into motion morphing the fabric of the cape. I banked hard but also slowing my descent to correct my approach vector.

"Parachuting onto the flight deck of a moving Aircraft Carrier… piece of cake," my Master Chief says as we jumped.

The memory flashing up to surfaces of my mind. The HUD counts down the seconds. I correcting my trajectory. Milliseconds before I hit Fenrir, Hank extending out fully. Landing like Batman in a three-point stance. Hank draping over me to sweep down to drape across Fenrir's back.

The connection was instantaneous Fenrir's silver magic flaring fluorescent green and mine flares silver.

"Cannonball!" I tell Fen.

His magic tugging at mine as if he nodded. I opened the flood Gates of magic that bound us together overloading Fen's God like magic with mine, creating magical atomic bomb.

"YEAH MAN!" with adrenaline and magic rushing through my veins I yell.

BLAM TTTHHAAABBBOOOMMM

Our magical atomic cannon ball colliding with the Skinwalker right above the forest canopy. Pile driving him into the ground clearing hundreds of thousands of acres of forest with the shockwave. Tree trunks as big around as I am tall lay snapped in half. For the radius of a mile nothing lay in the impact zone just chard earth. Fen paces the perimeter.

"Ruff!" and flaps his ears.

Sliding off Fen's muzzle as he lowered his head to land on the ectoplasmic ichor saturated ground. I see the Skinwalker's saber tooth were-lion head and torso refocusing the necromantic ectoplasm laying ground zero of the impact zone. The *Trooper Overture* from *2Cellos* starts to play as the evil Indian, medicine man, gets up pulling the smoking ooze back into himself. His massive Godzilla sized head teeth, the size of a facken aircraft carrier focused down on me. Lou materializes in my left hand as a broken femur bone.

"**Cowboy**!" the sound pulses out his oozing black ectoplasm vibrating my teeth together.

"I'm your Huckleberry," tapping my right index finger as my hand rests on my 1911 doing my best impression of my childhood hero Doc Holliday. Old west showdown literally, with Neun on my left shoulder and Fen on my right side. My index finger kept tapping against the hilt of my gun. No one moved.

"HHHHHOOOOOWWWWWLLLLL!" a call to arms comes from the darkness of the tree line. Lana the gold and red dire wolf challenges as she leaps from the shadows of the dense forest. In three huge leaps she sinks her teeth into the Skinwalker's neck and back. Her claws tear at his back when she pounces from behind him.

H-S-S-S-S-S-BAMF WOOSH

Neun teleporting appearing on Lana's back. He rams his energy blade down to the hilt into the Skinwalker's back, stick and move, as he vanished. The hilt still in the Godzilla sized monster. The tiny blade must be doing something because the ectoplasmic ichor burned and fizzled.

Ruff CHOMP Yank Yank yank

Fen's bus sized ass clears the distance in one silent leap. Flirting with Lana right before his teeth sinks into the Skinwalker's right leg. He begins to thrash his head back and forth as he pulled.

Bang, Bang, Bang, Bang, Bang, Bang

The 1911 calls until empty. I dropped it as I started to walk towards the battle. Lou disappeared from my left hand as I pull my Winchester from my back with my right.

Click Clack BOOM, Click Clack BOOM, Click Clack BOOM

The Demon Indian's torso freckled from the bullet rounds. The ground slightly started to shake under my feet. I ignore it assuming the vibrations is from the two oversized supernatural creatures battling. The vibrations turn to a 7 on the Richter scale.

RUMBLED RUMBLE RRRUUUMMMMMBLE CLOMPING CLOMP CRASH RRRUUUMMMMMBLE

Then the tree line from all directions broke with the stampede. A tidal wave of animals washes over the battlefield. Thousands of freed Red Cape supernatural creatures emerge from the darkness of night. The animal stampede overtakes me. The battle-hardened animal warriors flowed around me. Feeling like facken Tarzan.

"OOHHHHHHHHHH...ohh...ohh...OOOOHHHHHHHHHHHH HHH...ohh...ohh!" echoing off the valley's walls, Irons must have amplified it. I could actually feel the vibrations of my voice resonate through my bones. My head tilted back, my chest out arching my lower back, my arms swung out in the traditional werewolf howl at the moon pose. As the last note ended with a concentrated vacuum bubble's force I back flipped off the ground onto an oncoming Asgardian War Elephant. The huge elephant was at least three times the size of a normal elephant. I surfed the top of the stampede towards my destiny.

SSSSMMMMAAASSSHHHH CRACK BLAM POW THUMP CHOMP WHACK

The stampede crashes. The tidal wave of supernatural animals flows up the dripping ectoplasm fur of monstrous Skinwalker from all directions. He looks like he's covered in army ants.

"YYYEEELLLPPP Whimper!" my wolf screams in pain when the saber tooth were-lion's oil dripping claws stabbed through his stomach. Fen cries softly has he is lifted off his paws as the Skinwalker's claws rip out his back.

"**NNNNOOOOOOOOOOOOO**!" screaming from the top of my lungs already mid-arch.

Lou materializes as a massive two-handed broadsword. I stabbed Lou into the top of the Skinwalker skull knowing it left me vulnerable. Taking the full force of the Skinwalker retaliation I sink Lou to the hilt. He pulls his claws from inside Fenrir's guts.

WWWWOOOPPP WWWWWOOOOSSSHHHHHHH BLAME tumble THUD tumble THUD tumble tumble

Crashing through every tree trunk in the woods then playing pinball with the last couple of trees. When everything stopped spinning I sat up, my everything hurt. Irons' didn't say anything. His HUD blinked, movement detected, then displayed a holographic outline of something making its way through the pitch-black forest.

A mystery man walks outs the shadows. From the looks of his acid torn, dirt covered cloak he must be the local Asgardian bum. His hood hung low over his face ripped and ragged pieces of the hood dangling from its edges. He touched the tree nearest him and it spontaneously combusted.

FaWoosh

Superheated fire engulfed the tree causing the trees next to it to burst into flames. The intensity of light from the flames casted him in eerie shadows.

Extracting myself from the forest floor. I grabbed my shield from my back and my right hand rested on my 1911 tucked in my belt of holding, now hidden behind my shield, as he came closer.

FFFFFaaaaaaaWWWWOOOOSSSSHHHHHHHHH

His fingers just brushed the next tree as he passed it. The forest fire…

SSNAP FaWOOSH CRACK SHATTER FLLOOOWWSSH FaWOOSH

The fire spread quickly and surrounded us in walls of flames turning night to day.

"Loki… SHIT...!" my stupid photographic memory only works when it wants to and all the legends of the Asgardian Gods flood my brain. ".....Freeing Fen, I freed you. Starting Ragnarok," I finished my statement with barely a pause.

Loki's voice sounds like he was drinking the snake's acidic venom not just getting it dripped on him, "Something like that."

SSNAP FaWOOSH CRACK SHATTER FLLOOOWWSSH FaWOOSH

Fight continues from afar as the forest fire rages all around us.

"Ask yourself why Odin didn't just execute me and my children instead of letting us live," Loki's eyes burning two different color fires. The only thing I can see through the shadows caused by the extreme backlight of the flames.

FLASH CRACKLE BURN FaWOOSH SSNAP FaWOOSH CRACK SHATTER FLLOOOWWSSH FaWOOSH FIZZLE Fizzle…

A hallway of flames clears me a direct path back to the battle like Noah parts the Red Sea flames reach the sky with a carpet of ash and soot.

"Burn him like the end of your cigarette," he tells me as he sidestepped just enough to let me by. "Burn him like the sun," Loki says to me after I walked passed him.

Running through the hall of fire. *You're Going Down* by *The Sick Puppies* starts to play. I pulled the amber magical energy into my tattoos like I did with the water magic. The fluorescent green glow of my tattoos turns amber with green highlights.

SONIC BOOOOOOM

The air clapped as I broke the sound barrier. The flames of the forest fire creating a tail of fire behind me as it is snagged in my magic. Focusing all the amber magic that was flowing through my tattoos pooling it, channeling it into my right fist. Irons' HUD displayed my jumping point the distance and the arch I needed.

KAPLOOM RRROOOAAARRRR GGGRRRRUUUGGGLLEEE FaWoosh

My fist of magical fire punched through his ribcage barring my arm deep into his chest. He roars as I released the amber magic. His ribcage glows with intense light. The comet's tail of fire catching up with me with dramatic results.

CCRRRACKLE crackle...KKKAAAABBBBOOOOOMMMMM

The Only Witness

The old crippled woman began, Hashaikeh had just celebrated his 38th birthday. Just a year prior he had earned the title of medicine man, after 18yrs of intense training and sacrifice. He was content and happy. With more good news he kisses his wife. She had just told him she was pregnant with his 3rd child. With great urgency, the elders called him into a closed tepee session.

As he entered the elders' tepee what he found angered him to his core. Two U.S. Cavalry Officers and three Cowboys were in aggressive negotiation with the elders. Finding out very quickly that we were being run off our land by the U.S. Cavalry.

The arrogant white Officer strolled out into the middle of our village and whistles. In the distance his whistle is returned as 500 mounted U.S. Cavalry men crest the far hill and halted.

We moved to a distant valley, far from the white man. Only one season had passed when the same white men came calling.

The U.S. Cavalry demands to see the Chief. Gathering the elders together, now sitting inside the tepee, they told the elders of our tribe that this valley had already been claimed. Without warning he shot the chief in the face. With that shot, the troops rode in and massacred our tribe.

Our tribe had 142 warriors plus the women and children. The 5th Cavalry had 500 soldiers on horseback, waiting in overwhelming numbers. We never had a chance.

The tepees were trampled first. They turned their horses around, taking full advantage of the surprise attack and shot all the men dead. The women and children were not so lucky, the U.S. Calvary didn't want to waste bullets, so our kids were trampled to death by the war horses. Some of the plain clothed Cowboy's made a game of it. Giving them a head start then chasing our children down at a full gallop. Most of them didn't die instantly, it took hours.

Hashaikeh was shot multiple times right away, but stubbornly wouldn't yield. They dragged him to the center of the village beating him with the butts of their rifles. Then they shot him in his left thigh over and over until one of Cowboys shouted that he won the bet. It took 12 shots to deflesh a man's leg.

They didn't kill him, he had to listen to ALL the women be rapped, multiple times by multiple men. When they were done they would discarded them in the village center, strangled to death or left to die from the abuse.

Crippled and bleeding out, he watches and watches. When finished they set everything up in flames. As they rode away our village burned and my people died and Hashaikeh was left for dead. As he laid there amongst the dying he watched his 3-year-old son, whom had both his legs crushed by horses. But the toddler still managed to crawl and drag himself to his dying father's side. Hashaikeh sat up and crossed his legs under him forcefully picking up his son. Cradling him in his arms tight to his chest, he cried.

Hashaikeh held his son tears running down his face. Pulled the knife he never even had a chance to use against the white man and plunged deep into his son. Screaming as he did so, then gritted his teeth knowing what he must do.

He carved out his sons still beating heart as quickly as he could.

Looking at the white men riding away he took the first bite of his son's heart. He choked it down, taking a second and third, he chewed all the while watching the men ride away.

Spitting blood on his hands he slapped his left shoulder leaving a perfect hand print. He started to sing to our gods from first world. He spit more blood on both hands still singing he traced war paint all over his body. Covered in his son's blood, he sat crossed legged, his son limp. All the goodness in his soul goes dark, his cheti becoming deformed. All the while singing to our gods to unleash the darkest of magic upon himself.

He swore to the darkest 1st World Spirits. Every cowboy and soldier that had taken part in this, he will eat their hearts, rape every one of their wives and sisters. He will crush their children under his feet. As Hashaikeh watches the troops ride off into the sunset.

From Angus's Library

Keeper of the Hidden, case file

Testimony from only Diné survivor, Hashaikeh wife....

Keeper Doc Holliday, Vampire

Chapter 42

"Screaming alpha as my Chief Petty Officer used to say in the Navy!" I said trying to recover from the back blast of the Skinwalker's chest exploding.

Smoke drifting across the battlefield from the out of control forest fire. Campfires of ectoplasmic ichor burn all throughout the clearing. The supernatural animals retreating trying to escape the blaze of the fire.

FaWoosh SSNAP FaWOOSH CRACK FLLOOOWWSSH FaWOOSH FaWOOSH ***AAAAAAHHHHHHHHHHHHHH*** *FaWoosh FaaaaWOOooOooSSSssSHHHH*

Flailing his arms about the Skinwalker screams as the flames consumed him.

"Ggrrrgggrrrrrr Ruff chuff Chuff!" Fen limps into view. Fenrir's guts pool out his stomach as the proud wolf walks to me and collapses. I wrapped my arms around his muzzle hugging him tight. Letting him go, he plops his head down on the ground, I start petting his cheek.

"Will he die?" whispering to Irons?

Irons' HUD scanned Fen's injuries showing me that his magic was trying to heal him but wouldn't be enough to save him.

Pooling my magic forcing it into Fen's body… imagining the green power mending the wolf's wounds. I started pouring sweat from the strain, my body covered in perspiration as the fire from the forest superheats the air.

SSNAP FaWOOSH CRACK SHATTER FLLOOOWWSSH FaWOOSH

Flames rage as the forest burns. Silver and green magical lights actually over shined the illumination of the fires. Willing more and more of my magic from my tattoos into Fenrir. My vision does that wonka wonka thing, you know that thing that happens right after you stand-up after one too many beers. The fluorescent glow of my ink fades to barely flickering. Feeling myself falling, I stumbled one way then the other way. Losing my balance with waves of dizziness I tripped wobbling then I stuttered stepped trying like hell not to land on my ass. Healing Fen used up all my magic.

"None left for you," my brain tells me drunkenly as I spoke it out loud unconsciously. Landing on my back looking at the night sky the earth, moon and the stars spinning wildly.

"Heimdall…," I whisper as the universe spins.

Drop sizzle Drop sizzle Drop DROP sizzle SIZZLE DROP DROP DROP DROP DROP fizzle DROP ttsss DROP DROP ttttssss…

It quickly turns to a monsoon. The wildfire dying out by the rain that fell as the rainbow bridge descends from a break in the clouds.

WHISSSHH WHISSST WHISSSSP… WHISSSHH WHISSST WHISSSSP

The world rapidly unfocused and refocusing as the rainbow bridge flows to the ground. Heimdall burst out the rainbow bridge in a full run before the bridge touched the forest floor as my eyes fluttered closed.

Waking up in my bed I stare at the bedroom wall. No clothes I realized as the blanket slid down me while trying to sit up. Fuck I feel like hammered dog shit. Dog, my brain clicked. *Where's Fenrir?* Naked Hank wrapping around my waist as I jumped out of bed and was walking out the master bedroom into the hallway. I walked passed Angus as he was coming out of the hall closet door. I step over Nathan laying in the middle of the living room.

“Sir’s animal companion cloaked himself with Heimdall's entrance,” Irons’ beautiful Irish accent eased my nerves.

“Neun,” I ask. Irons doesn't reply, my heart saddens. I walk through the living room with Hank like a towel. Without a word I opened the front door. Liz, Thor and Heimdall all on the couch. Liz gives me the stink eye as she watches me walk out the front door.

“Cindy, Dan's awake and he's not wearing pants,” my little sister tattling on me.

Angus, Thor, Heimdall, Nathan and Alex right behind their auntie pile out the front door. They all follow me out to the middle of the front yard. Kara appears from the house, her arms wrapping around her mother's leg as Cindy came out and watched from the porch.

SNAP

My fingers call out. “With me!” I demanded Fenrir to come to me.

“HUFF Chuff!” his fur coat shimmers becoming visible. His Miata Mazda sized head appears right in front of me. The wet steam from his nose puffs out like fog. Grabbing his neck in a bear hug we wrestled across the front yard.

“Everyone this is Fen,” Purposely not calling him by is full name. Thor's and Heimdall’s mouth dropped open, but recovered quickly. See even the all-seeing Heimdall didn't see that coming. Do to the fact that Irons’ is made of celestial metal known as Cold Iron that prevents magic from tracking or divining my presences. “Fen!” I grabbing his neck to turn him to look at me, “This is your Pack, your Family.”

"Puppy!" Kara running from the porch as fast as her legs would could go.

"Chuff," Fen lays down as Kara's arms go around his nose with laughter.

"How..." Thor's voice speaks up, "Did this happen?"

"Unavoidable circumstances," I replied. "Ended up bonding us together permanently."

H-S-S-S-S-S-BAMF WOOSH

Feeling the teleportation onto my shoulder I looked over at Neun in his hand was a wooden cube.

"Glad to see you Neun," saying with relief. He holds the 5 ¾ inch by 5 ¾ inch by 5 ¾ inch wooden cube out to me. Dropping it in my hand I was twirling it around in my hand taking a quick glance at it bringing to mind a Motherbox or Jedi Holocron.

"Unendlichkeit Würfel, carrying einfacher jetzt it ist," he says. "Geteilt das space I have," Neun pauses. "Wohnung I have made," looking away like he did something wrong.

"Holy monkeys, *Harry Potter's Magical Beast and Where to Find Them*!" Auntie Liz says excited that she was right from the beginning.

"Like Newt Scamander's suitcase," Alex's says.

For a second Liz just stood there her mouth open then she skews.

"Outstanding," with a sideways grin tossing her my infinity cube. "Welcome to the Pack Neun," holding my fist up to him Neun looks at me like I'm a moron... then fist bumps mine with a smile.

H-S-S-S-S-S-BAMF WOOSH EEEWWW

Liz completely loses her faculties for a second as Neun appears on her shoulder taking the infinity cube from her.

H-S-S-S-S-S-BAMF WOOSH

He teleported standing next to Liz's leg. He taps the cube with his index claw, "Regenbogenbrücke goldsteine and das pure silver mondsteine in das Unendlichkeit Würfel already stored they are." I nod as he finished, "Show you I will."

Flap flap flap

"CaaWww CAW!" Huginn and Muninn… land on the railing next to my wife by the porch.

"Where the hell you two been?" I ask them.

"Caw... aawww," Muninn answers me.

"Figures…," I tell them as I crossed my arms over my chest.

"GGGRRRRRRRR RaRuffffff chuff!" Fen stands quickly as his fur broiling.

"Yes they are and No, you can't facken eat them," I tell Fenrir pushing magical will power into my words.

"Bark whoof?" Fen asked.

"Caw CAW ccaaawww!" Huginn chimes in.

"Swear to me!" I reinforced my words with a little more magic to ensure that they would play nice.

"BARK!" Fen swears.

"CAW CAW!" Huginn and Muninn both give their words.

Waving my hand like yeah go ahead. My kids also saw and joined in the game of catch a crow.

CLIP CLOP CLIP CLOP CLIP CLOP CLIP CLOP NNaaee CLIP CLOP CLIP CLOP

Turning to look down my rather long driveway to see Lady Rain on her beautiful winged horse. Her huge horse bird stopping at the edge of the Viking Rune-stones that warded my yard.

"GGGGRRRRRRRUUFFFF WHOOF!" Fen says swiveling at the Valkyrie.

"I know who she is... she's a friend," turning from Fen to look at Lady Rain. The Valkyrie smiles with a hint of a bow to her head in acknowledgment but that she was here for other matters.

"Odin, the Allfather demands your company," she says robotically. And holds her hand out to me to get on the winged horse.

I grabbed her hand and she flings up behind her. Angus nods to me and throws me my boots that Thor had given me.

"Fen stay with Cindy till I come home. I mean it. Stay!" looking the wolf up and down.

SWOOSH flap flap flap

I could barely hear Fen over the flapping of the huge wings of the horse as we took off.

Flying on a facken horse with nothing on but Hank as bath towel wrapped around my waist and a pair of boots. Irons' started to play Johnny Cash, *Hurt*.

We flew for what seemed forever till all you could see was trees below our feet. Until we finally started to circle a little patch of grass in the middle of the thick pine tree forest. As soon as I slid from the horse Lady Rain lifts off and flies away. He just sits on an ancient Rune-stone waiting. I take a deep breaths getting ready to confronted Odin in protection of Fenrir.

I freeze in my tracks when he holds up his hand then slowly closes his fingers to hold up just his index finger.

"Tell me if three crazy bitches started talking shit about your best friend's kids," Odin began.

As soon has he said best friend I immediately thought about Tasi as he continues.

"Saying they seen it in a bowl of soup that they are evil spawn and must be destroyed," Odin looking up at me as he finished talking.

"For the ones I cherish, I will do great and TERRIBLE things," Loki steps from behind the shadows. "That is what that says," pointing to the tattoo that covers my entire right rib cage and swoops around my back and down my right side. A huge crow, her wings extended, the feathers have a Polynesian tribal pattern hidden in the realistic shading. She is holding a scroll with Viking runes written on it, that floats open down my side that ends at my hip bone.

Loki reveals himself like a Sith Lord as he approaches pulling back his ripped and torn up hooded cloak. He walked up to stand behind Odin's right shoulder. Smaller than most Aesìr at 6' 8" the older man had a lumberjack frame. His clothes old and worn. A sword sheathed at his left hip, a battle staff and shield on his back. Black leather gauntlets were tied around both his forearms, from elbow to the back of his hand. He crossed his thick bulging arms over the leather straps that crisscross his naked and battle-scarred chest. His eyes were empty dark sockets and scarred from the acidic venom. Moving his head to dislodge his dark black beard from under his arms. To his waist long black hair with streaks of gray cascaded down his back.

"Yeah man," I answered him while looking down at my tattoo. My brain putting some more of the pieces together.

It was Odin's and Loki's plan from the very beginning to prevent Ragnarok. The ultimate Con convincing the world that Loki was the villain. Knowing how to use and harness the word of your enemies, they plotted, waited. I am the unknown variable. Something that no prophecy has foretold.

"Tyr!" I blurted.

"That is your problem," Odin says as he stands up and placing his hand on my shoulder. I feel a rush of Asgardian magic and my tattoos glow fluorescent blue.

KABAMF WWWOOOOSSHH

Opening my eyes, I'm standing in my front yard again I puked immediately from the abrupt teleportation. I'm 42 and the biggest overgrown man child you've ever met and very prone to motion sickness. Walking in the bathroom to drain the main vein, head still spinning. Paused in front of the mirror checking out the ink, my tattoos still glowing fluorescent blue with Asgardian magic.

"Sir does know that Sir's tattoos have always been magical," Irons inform me.

"Tasi!" I said turning around like a puppy chasing his tail trying to look at the blue glowing magic of my tattoos that cover seventy percent of entire body.

I stood 5'11" and 174 pounds and have stayed in shape do to mix martial arts. My muscles rippled as I flexed, my six-pack, is more like an eight-pack, now. I rubbed my head, pulling at my braids and stroked my graying foot long goatee, that's new. Walking to the toilet I reached into the shower turning it on to preheat and finally make it to the porcelain goddess. Shaking off the drain I climb into the now hot shower. I hear somebody walk into the bathroom I peek out of the shower and my wife is getting undressed. I feel the cold draft as the shower curtains is pulled back and my 5-foot one Thai wife climbs in the shower with me. Cindy runs her fingers crossed my back.

"The color is amazingly vivid," Cindy whispers.

I shiver and turnaround and look down at her, "You like it by the fact that it gives off a romantic glow," pointing down to her legs and look at the tattoo that wraps from her calf all the way up her leg to her hips.

"Pink dragon," she smiles at me and I grin ear to ear.

"Yeah pink dragons," sliding my hand between her legs. The door burst open the youngest one runs in the bathroom.

"I have ta potty…" as she reaches for her potty seat clumsily places it on the toilet.

"Hi monster," I peek out the shower.

"Daddy!" Kara replies with surprise to see me home! She climbs on the toilet rubbing her eyes as she potties, "Going, going, gone."

I closed the shower curtain and looked at Cindy, "Somebody wants chocolate milk." Mommy peaks her head out of the shower Kara still on the toilet looks at her mommy.

"Mommy," Kara mumbles while she's tries to wipe. Cindy nods then turned as she looked up at me.

"No pink dragon for you," winks and smiles. She washes her hair with a quickness and jumps out the shower stealing my towel as she went.

"Hey, I'm going to want that back!" I call to Cindy as she swoops Kara up in arms.

"Let's get some going, going, gone," Kara smiles at her mommy.

"What about daddy's towel?" Kara asks, Cindy turns and peaks through the half-opened shower curtain and looks at my junk and says to Kara.

"Daddy's a big boy, he can manage." And strolls out the bathroom.

Before I can rinse the soap off, my cell phone rings, someone else opens the bathroom door.

"Dad!" Nathan calls into the bathroom, "Uncle Tasi's called!"

Wrapping the towel around my waist. I don't even look at my phone on the counter as Kara runs by me pulling on my towel she explains.

"Tell Nay-Nay to stop…" She tells me as I grabbed my towel and look down at her.

"Stop what?" I asked.

Nathan came bounding around the corner into the bathroom with my werewolf mask on growling, runs smack dab into me bouncing off me… I smile, "Don't make me get the silver bullets." Nathan whines like a puppy and sulks off.

Kara follows him yelling, "Bad puppy!"

"WOOF!" Nathan replies.

Kara comes running back in the bathroom. "I want to play with Fen," I take Kara in my arms and nod sure.

Later at dinner Alex hands me two things. The first one was some ridiculously expensive field trip to Smithsonian Institute of Museums in Washington DC without a thought I signed it and handed it back to her. The second was her Davinci magical sketchbook.

A picture of the tree, Yggdrasil. Then proceeds to tell me that deep down for some reason she thought I should get it as my next tattoo.

Cindy saves me by interrupting Alex, "Some garage called saying that the Van was ready."

Angus hands me my backpack as I put a pair of old tennis shoes on. Planning to come right home I didn't change out of my super old, used to be grey but are so faded they are almost white, torn up Echo jeans. I just slung my bag over my shoulder in a, gun metal grey, wife beater style tank-top.

My little sister volunteered and dropped me off at the garage to pick up Honey bear and I tell Fen to protect the Pack while I'm away.

The garage owner beamed with delight as he walked me into the back lot to reveal Honey Bear. When I saw it, I squeed and the owner miss took my involuntary noise as disappointment.

"Well, you asked for an updated military style A-TEAM van," he declared.

"It's perfect!" I finally managed to say as he handed me the keys.

After he finally left me alone in the back parking lot, Fen steps out of thin air. I just looked at him knowing he must have just chased after Liz's car. He starts shrinking to dire wolf size and crawls into the open backdoors of Honey Bear.

“CAW Caaaw caw!” Huginn lands on the roof rack of Honey Bear. He flaps his wing in encouragement.

“CAAWWW!” Muninn lands on my shoulder.

I drove 2 hours outside of Atlanta to a tiny Town of Royston. I pull Honey Bear into the parking lot and parked under the glowing neon sign that read, TATTOO SHOP, as it turned off. I had called my wife on the way to let her know I was going to Tasi's instead of going home. Too bad I didn't tell Tasi.

“Surprise Fucker!” I announce to Tasi as I open the door to his tattoo shop.

Putting my white and gray backpack, with dark grey almost black leather straps, down on the counter. Floating back and forth three black feathers attached to the backpack by golden string. I pull out Alex's magical parchment and zipping it back up.

“You got time for one more,” I ask him as we grasped for arms and touched our foreheads together.

Getting a new tattoo on the inside part of my right calf of Alex's vision of the tree, Yggdrasil. By the time Tasi completed it I had told him almost everything... skipping the boring stuff even though I was explicitly told not to tell anyone.

8 hours later...

He pulled the black surgical gloves off... “And you think it's all because I gifted you with magically blessed tattoos. You know I love you like a brother but...” Tasi said to me.

Walking over with just one sock on and my right foot sockless I ignored him. Grabbing my backpack as the shops speakers start to play *AC/DC Highway to Hell*. My bag was already unzipped I reached in and took out the 5 ¾ inch by 5 ¾ inch box. I flipped my backpack over my shoulder pulling the Samoan tribal crystal out the ornately carved oak box. Holding the infinity cube in my left I handed the crystal to him with my right.

He looks at me in utter shock. The green light of the crystal magical tribal designs illuminates the air around Tasi's hand. My green magic jumps out the crystal in arcs of green lightning. My best friend's tattoos started to glow, like mine, up his arm. The glow goes from green to magenta. His tattoos swirl around his body glowing fluorescent magenta to be redrawn.

In pain Tasi hits one knee, the concrete floor of the tattoo shop cracks by the sheer force. Puffs of magenta fairy dust covers his entire body as he started to expand.

The crystal glowing magenta cast, Samoan, Polynesian tribal designs over the entire tattoo shop as it spun on the tattoo shop's floor. The glow pulses in rhythmic tones of the ancient Polynesian warrior chant. The chant grew louder and heavier as the fluorescent magenta glow increased. The crystal started to crack with intense energy.

K-RAK! K-POW! K-POW! K-RAK! K-POW! K-RAK!

Ka-BAMF WWWWOOOOSSSHHHHHHH

EPILOGUE

Dreaming to the sounds of ocean waves, with my head spinning from another forced teleportation, the mist off the ocean waves feels wonderful. With great effort I open one eye to find myself lying flat on my face on old wood planks, which smell of sea water and gunpowder. I'm aboard some type of French sailing Vessel from the early 1700's.

Already suffering with motion sickness, the gentle rocking of the ship combined with the rustle of the sails makes vomit explode out my mouth, nose and my eyes flutter shut again.

Standing in small meadow with soft green grass. Small animals hops and skitters around as I watch them I see the meadow is surrounded by sheer cliffs of solid ice and the Aurora borealis lights the sky.

A single gigantic glowing tree made from the combination of many tubular tentacles sits in the very center of the meadow in the middle of a glacier. It reminds me of a super-sized bonsai trees, perfectly manicured and sculpted.

Mystical magic forces of all colors and patterns float through the air and weaves together as it gathers into the living tentacles of fiber optic cable. I can see how it flows through the ground and from the spark that lies inside all living things. The grass, trees, insects and birds all life on the planet creates and fuels magic.

Like the great Jedi Master, Yoda, in his speech about the force and how it flows through the universe. The spark of life radiates magic, if you will.

The dog, the cat, bird or fish, the trees or snake, a person or magical creature, it does not matter they all have a spark of raw magical energy inside them, their souls. Hate to say, size does matters, for you are born with that spark and that spark never grows or changes over time. You're created with your soul that sparks life. With that magical spark all life exists.

Closer you are to a root the stronger the magic is. Where these fiber optic cable merge and cross the magic is extremely high. This magical spark can be unlocked and harness not created. That's why throughout history Temples and other magical places were built over these major intersection of ley lines. All this flashes in my mind as I touched one of the many roots that grew forming the trunk of the tree.

Pulling my hand from the living embodiment of magic. A massive black Crow, bigger than Huginn or Muninn with eyes glowing bright red flew from the tree branches.

FLAP FLAP FLAP FLAP FLAP SSWWOOOSH-SH-SH-SH-SH Step..

Hitting my knee before one of my Gods, in the way a Kryptonian would kneel before General Zod. I watched the most majestic and beautiful bird I have ever witness fly at me then her feathers began to malt and trail fog, thick purple puffs rolling from each wing. The massive crow's feet extending to land before me but as the tips of her razor-sharp bird talons touched the moist green grass the purple fog of her feathers cloaked her for just a fraction of a heartbeat.

Her feathers becoming more and more like smoke. Then the fog fell away like a prom dress as her bare human feet touched the earth.

The Morrigan had transformed from crow to woman, right before my eyes. She walked towards me with purpose, my eyes traced up from her feet following the Celtic knots of her tattoos up her legs and to her very naked hips that swayed like a grandfather clock.

She wasn't very tall, maybe 5’5”, but her magical energies rolled off her like the fog did. The Celtic knots of her ink is intricately designed and flawlessly placed pronouncing every curved surface of her beautiful body. Her muscles flexed as she walked making her skin move with cat like grace.

She didn't look like any of the art I have seen her depicted as. She had long straight black hair that shimmered like it was made more of feathers then hair. Her skin was light golden mocha and when sun hit it just right it created golden halos of light that danced around her. She stood a hair's breaths away from me now.

“Druid warrior, one of the Faé’s greats, you will be. Through blood passed down to you by generations forgotten. You are directly connected to the Tuatha De` Danann. The old magic of the Faé resides in you,” her slightly raspy voice tells me.

Inside my brain, replayed, the past event of the exact moment the magical reverse lighting struck me while we were upside down in the van. Then through me… to the fuel, no supercharge, my wife's and children's magical spark.

My spark isn't just supercharged, it’s growing, now generating a gigantic amount of magic. Looking at my bare feet on the ground I can see the lines of magic flow like spider-webs, weaving into the roots of the great tree.

“You have prayed to me for many years, when many thought you mad. Pledging your very destiny to the Carrion Crow,” leaning down to make me stand.

Looking into the magical stars of flames dancing in the pupils of her almond shaped eyes as I stood.

“Now, I pledge my destiny to you,” she whispered as she ran her fingers across her three feathers tied around my upper bicep.

She pulls me to her and kisses me. My tattoos glow with her dark forest green Faé magic.

“Open your eyes, your dreaming,” she whispered as her lips slowly left mine… I looked at her puzzled.

“Sir, open Sir’s eyes,” Liam Neeson's voice came out Morrigan’s mouth.

The ship tilted starboard sliding me across the wood deck smacking me against the ships rail. Jarring me wide awake with the impact. My eyelids wide open.

Bonk

Continued in

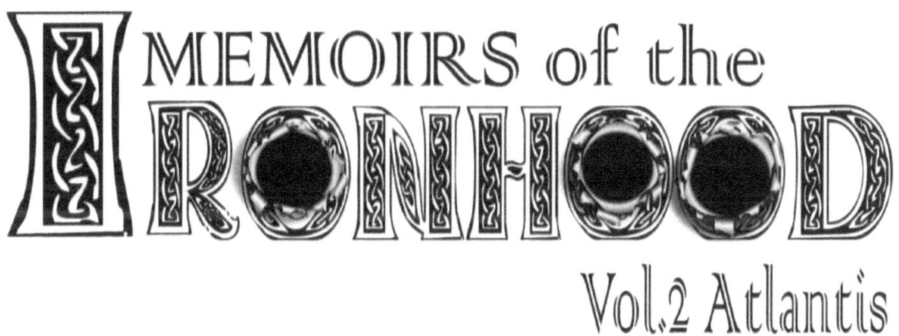

ABOUT THE AUTHOR

A veteran of the U.S. Navy who put himself through college as a bouncer at different Night Clubs and Strip Clubs. **D.L. CROWSON** grew up traveling the United States with his Grandparent's carnival, The Great American Carnival. He now resides on the Southside of Atlanta with his wife, three children and his dog Ace. He is an avid comic book geek, a hardcore cosplayer and absolutely addicted to getting tattoos.

www.ingramcontent.com/pod-product-compliance
Lightning Source LLC
Chambersburg PA
CBHW031439240626
47154CB00001B/326

* 9 7 8 0 6 9 2 1 0 5 1 2 2 *